I0595941

Carol L. Craig

A Thousand Bits of Wonderful

Library of Congress Cataloging-in-Publication Data

Craig, Carol, 1957-
    A Thousand Bits of Wonderful / Carol Craig.
        p.   Cm. -- Historical women's fiction
    ISBN 978-163625231-5

Edited by Sara Rolat.
Cover design by Darrin Brenner: D. Brenner Art & Design.

For Les, Sara, and Kaylee, my thousand bits of wonderful!
And for my father, two mothers,
my sisters and brother.

When I despair, I remember that all through history, the way of truth and love has always won... always.

~ Mahatma Gandhi

One

Kate Roberts paced the concourse of the Jackson Hole Airport, rolling her luggage behind her.

"Where is he?" she mumbled, the odor of diesel trucks and the sound of idling taxis jarring her already frayed nerves. She peered at her watch. Almost an hour late.

Behind her stood the Tetons dipped like chocolate cupcakes in a frosting of white snow. She set her luggage down and patted her hands together to stay warm. She hadn't thought to bring gloves... or a stocking hat. She tugged at her wavy auburn hair that fell well past her shoulders. This cold was sure to make her hair frizz, but she couldn't help that now. She shoved her hands deep into the pocket of her coat. With a pang of regret, she felt the ring that her boyfriend, Palmer, had given her--a promise ring. To marry once he made partner at his law firm.

Before she could dwell on that further, a man dressed in blue jeans and a cowboy hat jostled her as he walked past. For a brief moment, she thought that perhaps she had found her contact, but instead the man apologized then jumped into a waiting taxi. She tamped down her rising anxiety as she wondered what to do next. Here she was, from Manhattan, untethered in Wyoming, of all places, where she knew no one.

Fearing she'd missed the man she'd come here to meet, she stood on her tiptoes, canvassing the area. Wyatt Madison would be her first client at this far-off outpost, *if* she could locate him. Her new boss, Ian, had sent her here. It was his way of getting rid of her--of getting rid of *all* the former workers after he'd purchased the marketing firm in a hostile takeover. It had broken her former boss, Jack Cummings. He had loved his business, thought of his workers as family, which is why he had added the clause that Ian keep all former employees.

Kate bounced on her toes, trying to keep warm, as she scanned the concourse once more. Jack was everything Ian was not... loyal, trustworthy, kind. The first thing Ian had done, once the ink was signed, was to rent out places in the middle of nowhere and send each of Jack's former employees to distant outposts. Then he'd hired his own people to replace them.

"Take it or quit," he'd said.

Those were the only options. And it had worked. Most had quit, but Kate had made the decision to at least give it a try. After all, she really had nothing for her in New York. She once again palmed the ring in her pocket. A Cartier. At least Palmer had thought enough of her to give her the best, and yet...

Just then a mom with a dog and baby in a stroller ran past, the dog going one way, the mom and baby the other. Within moments Kate had been lassoed by the dog's leash and was laying on the ground in a heap, nursing her wounds. The mother quickly stopped and reeled her dog in.

"I'm so sorry," she said, bending down and hauling Kate to her feet. She appeared as harried as Kate felt. "He's a puppy. I never know what he's going to do. Are you okay?"

Kate looked down at her pants as the puppy danced around her, nipping at her pant legs. Except for a bit of dirt, her pants were fine, but her high heel was shot. She picked it up off the ground and hobbled to a bench, the woman apologizing the entire way while reining in the dog with one hand and steering the stroller with the other.

Great! Had Kate even thought to bring another pair of shoes? She unzipped her suitcase, but she had packed it so tight that all of her unmentionables spilled out and began blowing in the wind down the concourse. Kate closed her eyes and forced herself to breathe. She opened her eyes slowly in time to see people walking past, ogling her. She quickly gathered her things together with the help of the young woman, who was only making it worse between the dog snagging her black bra and walking around with it as though he had just been handed a prize, and the woman holding her underwear out for all to see. After what felt like a lifetime, Kate finally had it all stuffed back into the suitcase, at the bottom this time. That's when she recalled that she had another pair of shoes in the side pocket of her rolling luggage. Finally, she put the new ones on, a pair of black pumps. She took a look at herself in the airport window. If Wyatt ever did arrive, he would think he'd picked up a homeless woman. She quickly put herself back together as best she could and then assured the woman she would be okay.

"I would be happy to pay for the shoes," the woman said, but Kate politely declined.

Finally, the threesome was off, and Kate once again returned to scouting the concourse for Wyatt. She wasn't even sure what he looked like. All she knew was that he was somewhat tall, dark haired, and owned a ranch for veterans. As she listened to the sound of the jets taking off and landing, the wind buffeting her hair and clothes, she fought to remain calm. What if he didn't come? Where would she go? She walked out a ways to get a better view of her surroundings. The pictures in the brochures hadn't done this part of the world justice. The high jagged peaks of the Tetons made her feel as though she'd just landed in Tibet. All she needed now was a Sherpa.

As she stood there, the wind howling a warning, all sorts of scenarios went through her head. Should she book a flight back to New York, return hat in hand? Oh, right, she had no hat. That was an irony if ever there was one. She could ask Palmer to take her back. Then she could go on living in the high-rise loft with its tall ceilings and chrome fixtures. Palmer had gone for contemporary furniture, sleek lines, metal and glass. It had all felt so... so sterile. She'd felt like she was in a doctor's office. A weight pressed down on her as she thought about him and their home together. She had always been happiest at her grandmother's farm in upstate New York where she'd snap beans with her nana on the back porch. At night, they would take chairs out and stare up at the thousands of stars that dotted the night sky. Her favorite time was in August, when the meteor showers would take place.

"See those stars?" her grandmother would say. "They're like a man and woman. There may be a thousand bits of wonderful out there, but when you find the right one, you'll see only each other. Remember that."

Then Kate had seen a shooting star and said, "Is that my thousand bits of wonderful, Grandma?"

And her grandmother had smiled, as though she knew a secret that Kate didn't. Kate wondered about that now as she thought about Palmer. His thousand bits of wonderful were his job, his friends, not her. Her throat tightened at the realization that he could never be that one shining star in the night sky. But if not him, then who?

No, she couldn't go back home. Not until she had proved herself. Made it up to Jack, to all of her coworkers for letting that conniver, Ian, through the door. How was she to know what he was up to? All she needed was a second chance to make things right, but how? She stared down the road, toward the Tetons capped in a sea of white snow.

"Where are you, Wyatt Madison?" she murmured.

Two

Exhausted from searching high and low for Wyatt, Kate reentered the Jackson Hole Airport lobby and went in search of a cup of coffee. As she waited for her order to be filled, she once again removed her ring from her pocket and inspected it. But no matter how many times she looked at it, she could never imagine walking down the aisle with Palmer. Frustrated, she sighed. That's when she saw an elderly woman staring at her with a kind smile. Just then, the elderly woman put a wrinkled hand covered in age spots on her shoulder, her skin crepey, nearly transparent. There was something familiar, comforting in the gesture.

"I couldn't help but notice you staring at that ring, honey," she said, her voice jittery with age. "My husband Simon and I were married for seventy-two heavenly years. He was my soulmate, as you young people like to say."

"What's your secret?" Kate asked, hoping that it was something simple like "love conquers all" or something equally schmaltzy.

The old woman paused, her expression growing distant as her mind traced back the years. Her eyes brimmed with tears, her voice soft, almost tender as she recounted a past that must surely have been painful.

"We were neighbors in Poland when Hitler came to power. My family was sent to Auschwitz. My mother was sentenced to the gas chambers and my father was sent to work on the railroads. He was shot trying to steal a loaf of bread because he was starving to death in freezing temperatures. Before my parents died, Simon promised my parents he would take care of me."

Kate worked down the lump in her throat.

"He kept his promise," the old woman said with a watery smile. "But more than that, he knew the value of love... and the cost. And I knew it, too. We paid a high price for that love, but

I wouldn't change a moment of it." The woman patted Kate's shoulder. "Find someone who understands your value, honey. Do that, and you'll be happy forever, no matter how crazy the world seems at times." With that, she walked away. Kate blinked and the woman was gone. An apparition.

Frowning, Kate heard her number called. She paid for her coffee then walked back to the lobby and took a seat on one of the brown-and-white cowhide sofas, waiting. The hub was a sleek mixture of state-of-the-art architecture with huge wooden beams and a floor-to-ceiling firepit with a decorative wooden partition, a giant circle with an H branded into it.

As Kate took a sip of her coffee, she straightened her jacket, recalling the day she had entered Ian's office and had done the same. One wall of his office had been lined floor to ceiling with glass shelves showcasing pictures of Ian with celebrities, Ian with titans of industry, Ian with politicians. He came from money. Big money. And he liked to flaunt that fact. She had taken a moment to inspect the pictures. In almost all of them Ian had his red hair slicked back, his skin pasty white. She'd heard it rumored that he actually owned a Stuart Hughes Diamond Edition suit and, looking at the pictures, she could believe it. One of those suits cost more than she would ever make in a lifetime.

"Take a seat," he had said as he stood behind the wide teak desk, something he had imported from Korea.

"Here are the details." Ian handed Kate a photograph of a ranch. "Your first project is in Wyoming. It's a rehabilitation facility for vets with PTSD."

Her eyes shot up. "PTSD?"

She thought of her brother and everything he had been through since his return from Iraq. He had never been able to hold a job, had never been able to form relationships other than very brief encounters with former vets. Even then, that usually involved evenings at the bar or a trip to the medical marijuana dispensary to ease the physical pain of shrapnel to his leg he'd received from an exploding IED.

"I bought a ticket for you," Ian said, placing it on top of the photograph. "You can stay at the ranch while work is finished on the new office. The office will be small, but you'll adjust."

Kate tightened her fist around the ticket as she sat across the massive desk with its dark red meranti inlay from Malaysia. She hadn't even *agreed* to the position.

"When you get there, take a look around the place, then I'll send out a photographer to take pictures once you have your marketing angle. It's a promo for the military. To show that they're looking out for the vets' best interests. Or at least that's the angle we're going for."

Best interests. She wondered who had been looking out for *her* brother's best interest when he was sent home without any debriefing, any long-term counseling to help him heal emotionally.

Ian tapped the photograph and handed her a printout with the address. "That's it. It will be a perfect way for you to get your feet wet."

Ian had an odd habit of penciling in his lips with his thumbnail whenever he was trying to be persuasive. For a moment, Kate merely stared at the photo of the log cabin with its wide expanse of corrals, a barn out back and behind it a small copse of trees that led to a mountain with a snow-capped peak. She had to admit, it *did* look amazing. She was tired of being surrounded by skyscrapers and glass. Yet the idea of going into the unknown, alone, was worse.

"A guy named Wyatt Madison will meet you, take you around to meet the vets, go for a ride around the ranch so you can spot the best sites for the photo shoots. Hopefully, the new office will be done by then."

"And by then you mean...?"

"One week."

She looked down at the ticket in her hand. Now she had to decide. Stay, and try to find a new job, or go and try to maintain a long distance relationship with someone who may or may not love her. Either way, she had a lot to figure out and very little time.

Now, as Kate peered down at the remainder of the ticket, she wondered if she had made a mistake in coming to Wyoming, in believing that she could start a new life. But then she thought of her friend Sara who had encouraged her to go that day Kate had visited her at her high-rise apartment.

"How can you not be thrilled!" Sara had said, stuffing as much laundry into the washer as it would hold... and then some.

"Thrilled? I don't know anybody in Wyoming. And this isn't a vacation. It's permanent." Kate walked over to the sixth-story window of Sara's high-rise apartment that looked out onto another dreary skyscraper. Looking back at her from the window opposite Sara's was an older gentleman who wore a tank top that reminded Kate of Sara's washer. Overstuffed.

"And what did Palmer say about you going?"

"Hmm?"

"The guy you're living with." Sara snapped her fingers. "Focus, Kate."

At the sound of the dryer buzzer, Kate had turned away from the man who she could have sworn was making lewd gestures at her.

"He uh... umm..."

Sara snorted. "Just as I thought. He wouldn't commit."

"Oh, he committed, all right," Kate said as she pulled out the laundry detergent and set it on the washer. "We keep living together until I find another job here, then we go back to everything like it is. He's gone all the time and, on the rare occasions he's at the apartment, he's thinking about work or on his phone. Basically, I'm alone, with or without him."

"So?"

"So?

"What's stopping you, chica?" Sara said. "What do you have to lose?"

What *did* she have to lose, Kate wondered as she warmed next to the fire in the airport? But then again, Wyatt *was* running over an hour late. She had tried calling him, but no one had answered. What if he never showed? Kate stood, needing to pace. Maybe she had just missed him. Maybe he was out on the concourse.

And maybe you're tilting at windmills.

Three

Steam rose from beneath the hood of Wyatt's truck as it lumbered down the highway.

"Damn truck," he muttered, smacking the steering wheel. His old blue Ford Ranger always broke down when he needed it most. The old girl had been cantankerous for years now, but had put her rumbling into overdrive the last few months. Everyone told him he should get a new model with a shiny coat of paint, and with all the bells and whistles. But this one brought back memories. Good memories. Painful ones too, but he loved her, right down to the old coat of paint and the busted mirror. And dumb as it might sound to most, he kinda thought she felt the same about him, looked past the newly forming lines around his eyes, the scar that ran across his chin after his ex had chucked a plate at him during one of their heated arguments. He didn't like to argue, never had. Life was too tough as it was to add *that* to the mix.

Wyatt picked up his phone and tapped in the number given to him for Kate, the woman he was supposed to pick up from the airport, but he quickly realized he was out of range from the cell towers. With a huff, he dropped it onto the bench seat. Then he exited the truck and walked over to pop the hood open. The radiator sizzled, steam rising in hot bursts. He would have to sit it out, wait for the radiator to cool, then add water. Fortunately, a fallen snag lay close to the road. He could stop and have his sandwich there while he waited for his truck to cool. In one swift motion, he reached into the truck bed and grabbed his cooler, then walked it over to the snag and sat.

As he ate his lunch, he peered up at the sky. It reminded him of Fallujah. How glad he'd been to come home following his tour of duty. After Iraq, he thought he had wanted a relationship with no strings attached. And his girlfriend had too, only she apparently wanted it a little more than he had. Wanted the sex, the romance, the vacations, but none of the hard work of loving someone in the good times and bad.

Wyatt wolfed down most of his sandwich in a few large bites, followed by a long drink of water. He held no illusions anymore about how things would have gone, had he ever come down sick or needed someone to be there for him. She would have run for the nearest exit sign. Hell, she *had* run for the nearest exit sign. And she'd kept on running. Sure she'd cried, said she loved him and that she'd never stop loving him, but not enough to want him full time. Too much baggage, she'd said. He knew if he wanted, he could have had her back in his arms johnny-on-the-spot, if he called her and begged her to see him. But she would never want him full time. If there were a name like Disneyland Dad for women who wanted only the good times and none of the work, she would be it. Loving her was an addiction, not a relationship. It had been hard, but he had ended it only to marry on the rebound.

He welcomed the warmth of the sun as he took the final bite of his sandwich. The sunshine acted as a balm to his tattered nerves. From the very beginning, he knew his marriage had been a mistake, but he had wanted it to work. He just didn't have what it took. Then came a daughter, the light of his life. But he had been too busy wallowing in darkness to be a real dad or husband. God knows, he'd tried. But in the end, his wife had walked away. Now... well, now he was ready to be all those things, but he hadn't found the right woman.

He wiped his mouth, closed up his cooler then trudged back to the truck to add water to "the old girl." In one quick motion, he jumped into the truck and tried the key in the ignition. To his relief, it turned over. Then he checked his watch and winced. One more hour to the airport in Jackson Hole, and he was already an hour late to meet the woman who would write the ad copy for the ranch. The woman who would save his ass. If he was lucky--and he prayed he was--the woman who would rescue the rehab center from foreclosure.

* * *

The truth will set you free.

That's what Sara had said after she delivered the shattering blow that had set the wheels in motion for the move to Wyoming. Kate bent down to pull off her shoes. Her feet were sore from traipsing up and down the concourse, searching for Wyatt.

Palmer never loved you.

Even now, she felt the wind leave her lungs as though she'd just been sucked through the exterior door of the plane and sent hurtling into space.

He's been seeing other women the whole time he's been with you.

She closed her eyes as she replayed the scenario in her head. The glass filled with Chianti Sara had given her to soften the blow, suddenly tumbling to the floor, spilling red liquid onto the pale berber carpet. Then why had he asked her to marry him?

It was a career move. A high-powered couple looks good to a company searching for people to promote into top management positions. You had all the right qualifications, Kate.

Except...

Except for chemistry. He just didn't feel anything for you.

"But he said he loved me. He was so affectionate and warm. Sure, he was never there, but how can a relationship be so intimate and it all be a lie? Tell me that?"

Afterward, Kate had asked around but received so many varying opinions that she didn't know what to believe. *I know he loved you and he still loves you.* She'd heard that several times, but who was right? Finally, she decided to ask Palmer himself.

I do love you. I've always loved you, he said. *And there were no other women.*

But then he apologized and said he felt guilty, but guilty for what? Now, as she sat in the airport waiting for Wyatt, she rubbed at the blisters forming on her feet. All she knew was that she had needed to get away, to think, to breathe. Figure out who she was without her career. Figure out who she was without Palmer. They had planned to wait until his career was firmly established before they actually held the wedding, but the time had never come. The day before she was set to leave, he had knelt and said, "I suppose it's time."

"Time?"

"Yeah." He shrugged. "To make it official. This is just a promise ring, a Cartier. I'll give you the engagement ring when I make partner." He handed her a ring with a simple band and a small diamond. "So we're good?" He stood and returned to what he had been doing, as though that had settled everything.

She had spent a sleepless night, unsure what to do. In the end, she had to listen to her gut. Her relationship with Palmer had been a business deal, nothing more.

As she packed her bags the next morning, she handed him back the ring. "I think we need to take some time... to think about what we want," she said, her voice thick with unshed tears.

For one brief moment, he palmed the ring in his hand. Then he handed it back to her and said, "Hang onto it. Until you decide for sure."

Now, as she sat in one of the black leather chairs, nursing the pain in her feet, she looked down at the ring, at this link to her former life, and wondered what the future held in store for her. She wasn't sure. She only knew she needed to figure out what she wanted for her life. And what she wanted was to love and be loved.

Heaving a loud sigh, she put on her shoes to try the concourse one more time.

* * *

Wyatt scanned the people exiting the debarkation area, searching for a woman fitting the description he'd been given-- brown hair, blue eyes, five foot eight. That could be anybody. He wondered how an editor from New York might look. He envisioned someone with hawkish features, wiry hair, thinning. Or worse, one of those women who yakked a mile a minute and would never shut up. A month of that and he would be running for the hills.

The women he seemed to attract were all pretty little things without a brain in their heads that seemed to think cowboy was synonymous with sexy. Forgetting the fact that he was hardworking, loved horses and could build just about anything. If one more of them giggled and batted her eyelashes at him while spouting inane rhetoric about hair, nails, and clothing, he would bugle like an elk.

Finally, after ten minutes with no luck, he stopped a portly steward with a goatee and said, "Excuse me, is this the 357 flight from New York?"

"That one came in nearly two hours ago. Try luggage handling or the information desk. They can page your party."

Wyatt winced. Two hours late. He wasn't exactly making the best impression. "Thanks!" he told the steward.

After a couple of tries Wyatt found the baggage area. *Damn!* No one there matched Kate Roberts' description. Next, he rushed to the info center and asked that she be paged, but still no one. Sweat dripped down his sides as he pushed past a mother with a stroller topped with luggage on his way out the sliding glass doors.

Once outside, he looked left at a bank of taxis, quickly scanning each one for occupants. He turned and ran the other direction, colliding into a thirty-something year old woman and nearly knocking her down, luggage and all. Fortunately, he was able to catch her as she fell backward.

"I'm so sorry--"

But before he could finish, the young woman said, "What a day. I was supposed to meet a client nearly two hours ago. The airline lost part of my luggage. I'm moving to the back of beyond, and now this."

Wyatt suddenly felt cold.

She threw up her hands, then added with disdain, "I'm supposed to meet some guy who owns a *dude* ranch, if you can believe that."

As their eyes met, he saw the newfound awareness brimming in those blue-green eyes, first narrowing, then widening into two perfect orbs.

"The dude at your service," he said, tipping his hat.

Four

"I'm so sorry." Kate stood on the airport concourse and dipped her head so Wyatt wouldn't see her flaming cheeks.

She had expected some backwoods guy from *Deliverance*, a stereotype for sure, but one she hadn't been able to shake since going into catastrophe mode after hearing she was being sent to Wyoming. It was an unfortunate quirk of hers that she saw disaster around every corner. Maybe it's because her life had been such a disaster, she decided as she watched Wyatt pick up her heavy luggage as though he were carrying a bag of groceries and walk off with it, her in tow.

"My name is Kate," she said, nearly skipping alongside him.

"Wyatt," he said, pulling up next to a blue Ford Ranger and opening the door.

"And this here is Bessie." He motioned to the truck. "Better than any woman," he added with a chuckle, "*when* she runs."

Bessie ran fine after a brief hiccup and cough. Ten minutes later, they were driving down a long stretch of road surrounded by jagged peaks and dry landscape with little human activity. For some reason, Kate had expected to see tall pine trees and a lush green landscape. Instead, it felt as if she was starring in an old western, the landscape dry and unyielding.

"So how did you end up running a rehabilitation center for vets?" she asked, taking in the firm set of his jaw, the lines beginning at the corner of his gray-blue eyes.

He paused and stared off into the distance. Normally, silence bothered her, but for some reason, she felt comfortable despite the rocky start. He had an easy way about him, an "aw shucks" sort of humility that seemed endearing.

"Let's just say I saw a need," he said, making it clear to her that he didn't want to open up about his past.

By his age and mannerisms, Kate guessed he had been an Iraqi war veteran. He had an ease that welcomed people in, but only to a point. She had a feeling that he kept things light in order to keep people at bay... so they wouldn't see the real man behind the mask. It made her that much more curious to get to know him. Besides, she would need to learn at least some of his background if she were to put together a decent marketing campaign. If she were to sell the U.S. government on the idea of a rehabilitation center for vets, then she needed a hook, something to reel them in.

She'd been so lost in her thoughts that she hadn't realized he had just spoken until he said, "Like I was sayin', the government wants to warehouse these young men in sterile, hospital-like conditions. Feed 'em a truckload full of drugs to mask the pain. Good for the hospitals, not so good for the guys. They come in wounded, physically and mentally. The world just wants 'em to shut up and be men." He shook his head and, for a second, Kate was sure she'd seen his eyes glisten. He obviously cared for these young men, which made him a real man in her book.

Still, she couldn't help but wonder how successful he would be with men who were that wounded. Her brother, Craig, had returned from Iraq a basket case after he had accidentally killed an Iraqi woman, a mother of three. He had never been the same afterward. Nothing had helped.

"And what do *you* think they need?"

"Nature. Lots of it. And unconditional love. A lot of these boys come from troubled backgrounds to begin with. Or poverty. They escape it by going into the military. It's a way out. A leg up. And sometimes it is, and sometimes it's not. Depends on the person and where they land, ya know?"

She frowned, even though she was glad to see the terrain change, the dry chaparral turning to a lovely mixture of meadow and white pines. "I'm not sure I'm following you."

"It's like this," he said, ticking off each of his points with a thumb tap on his steering wheel. "Some kids know how to keep their noses clean, do what's expected. They're tough, street smart. But some are college smart. Or maybe too independent. Or maybe they're just not fast on the draw. Those kind get their clocks cleaned. And god forbid if they're too soft..."

"Or too kind?" Kate offered.

"I was going to say humane, but close enough." He let out a slow sigh, which told her he fit into the latter group and it hadn't been easy. And if the pain etched in his brow and the lines around his eyes were any indicator, he had seen plenty of ridicule. More than a man... more than *anyone* should have to bear.

"By the time I get these boys, they're in crisis. They're to the breaking point. Either one of three things will happen: They'll kill themselves, kill someone else, or die by cop. That's if they don't drink or drug themselves to death in any number of ways, sex addiction included. Problem is, not all of them are out of the military before they reach a breaking point. And some of them are but don't know where to turn. My job is to find them before that happens."

They had been driving for several hours and had passed the Tetons when he motioned to a turnout high above a canyon that overlooked the Yellowstone river.

"Those are the Bighorns," he said, pointing to a broad sea of grass and a cascade of forest beyond. "Don't know about you, but I need to stretch and work off the wiggles, as I like to call them. Get a little antsy talkin' about this stuff."

They parked at a turnout higher up, then climbed out of the truck, the air smelling fresh, clean. The mountain grasses in the hot summer sun filled Kate with anticipation.

"There's a trail." Wyatt pointed to a drop-off that looked like it would take them straight off the cliff.

As they neared, and then began the descent, Kate could see that the trail merely hugged the precipice and led to a mountain meadow below.

Wyatt pointed to flowers that shot up like little red fountains amidst the lush sage green foliage. "Indian paintbrush. And that there is a kind of lily," he added with a nod of his head.

"The orange flower?"

"Hmm," he said in confirmation.

Off in the distance, a deer lifted its head and its ears twitched like two satellite dishes searching for the correct station. Just then a baby deer, which had been hidden in the thicket of tall grasses below, craned to see what its mother had been sensing.

Without thinking, Kate grabbed Wyatt's arm, an intimate gesture that she hadn't yet earned. She saw that it took him by surprise, that it took them *both* by surprise, and she quickly released his arm, apologizing with a brusque sorry.

"A deer," she said by way of explanation.

"They have 'em here," he said, unable to stifle a chuckle.

Sweat instantly formed on her brow, not as much from the exertion, she felt sure, as from the embarrassment. She must really look out of place in the wilderness, but before she could ponder too deeply, his cell phone rang using the song *"Momma don't let your baby grow up to be cowboys."* It was her turn to stifle a grin.

None of the perfunctory hellos, how are yous, just "What? Where? I'll be right there. Wait!" But before he could ask anything more the phone went dead and he swore.

"Run!"

"Why?" she tried to ask.

But he just grabbed her hand and yelled, "Let's go!"

Five

Kate's heart went into overdrive, as Wyatt punched the gas pedal with his foot, sending his tires spinning in gravel as the Ford Ranger accelerated onto the pavement. She wanted to ask Wyatt about the phone call he'd just received, but it was clear by the set of his jaw that he wasn't ready to talk.

As the miles whirred by, the pines replaced by a yawning valley of green, Kate once again noticed the early worry lines that creviced Wyatt's cheeks and jawbone, making him appear older than his years. To her, that didn't matter. It meant he had lived a life, a full life, and was somehow still standing after all these years.

For the next fifteen minutes, she watched the scenery go by in a blur. She wished her brother, Craig, could get past his years of service. He had come back from the Iraqi war so shattered that he had never been the same. He still lived in the basement of their childhood home, only coming up for the occasional meal. Otherwise, he played video games and watched TV, eschewing sunlight and nature. She winced, recalling. It pained her to see him that way. She prayed that someday he would get the help he needed, but that day might be a long way off, she knew, because a stigma prevailed that said, "Real men don't cry. Real men don't ask for help." She squeezed her hands together. The idea that men shouldn't show emotion was a bunch of hogwash as far as she was concerned. The fact that these servicemen and women couldn't ask for help and couldn't get the help they needed was the real tragedy.

Following another few minutes of silence, Kate turned to inspect Wyatt as he stretched his neck muscles to ease the tension. He must have noticed her watching him because he glanced her way.

"I didn't mean to shut you out," he said, studying the road as he pressed harder on the gas pedal. "It's just that we've got a guy in crisis. One of our boys is threatening to commit suicide. He's in the bunk house and he's got a gun."

"I'm so sorry," she said, leaning in.

He drummed the steering wheel. "We don't allow guns at the ranch as a policy, except for me and one other person. For protection. But these boys know their way around guns and they can find one, if they want one badly enough."

Kate felt a tightness in her throat. How many times had she been called out by her mother to come look after her brother because he'd had one of his "episodes" as her mother called them? Each and every time she had driven the turnpike to upstate New York, she had breathed a silent prayer that he would be okay until she got there, and each and every time the fist that was lodged firmly in her stomach didn't go away until she had seen him safe and sound. Until she had talked him off the ledge.

She hadn't expected to be dealing with similar situations when she had agreed to put together a marketing campaign for a dude ranch. Sara had assured Kate there would be strapping young men, late nights under the stars, and singing by campfire. It was Sara's way of urging Kate to move on with her life, to keep her from wallowing in self-pity. And it had worked, for the time it had taken Kate to board a plane and arrive in Wyoming.

But now...

"What happened to set the guy off, did your friend say?"

"Family trouble. We have a no socializing clause while they're there, except for scheduled family activities. They need time to heal, and they can't do that if there's drama in their lives, and there usually is, if they're referred to us. The ones that do the best are the ones who have a supportive environment to go home to. A lot of these kids come from troubled backgrounds to begin with. That's why they go into the military... to get away from problems back home."

For the next twenty minutes, they lapsed into silence, each caught up in their thoughts. Finally, they pulled up to a gravel driveway with a ranch head gate that read *Strangers Welcome Here*. They drove the nearly half mile of graveled drive to come upon a large white farmhouse, not the rustic log cabin Ian had shown her à la Brad Pitt in *Legends of the Fall*. There was an almost feminine touch to this place, Kate realized as they took the potholes a bit too fast for her liking, despite the urgency. Maybe it was the gingham curtains blowing in the breeze through the open, screenless windows, or the three hanging flower baskets, but it maintained a certain charm that bespoke of a feminine touch, of a wife. Kate dipped her head in disappointment. Of course Wyatt had a wife... and kids, most probably.

And I have a job to do. Nothing else.

Fortunately, she had no time to dwell on Wyatt as the truck came to a screeching halt.

"You stay here," he ordered, "while I go help Ryan."

She grabbed his arm. "I have experience with veterans in crisis. My brother's a vet. Maybe I can talk to your guy."

"It's too dangerous."

Kate squeezed his arm. "Please. Let me try. My brother has been through this and I was able to help him. *Please!*" she pleaded, her eyes never wavering from his.

He hesitated, then finally nodded.

They jumped out and Kate trailed Wyatt as they ran toward the barn. Already, she could hear shouts and a tussle as though a fight were underway.

Her eyes had trouble adjusting to the interior of the barn, the smell of hay and horses overshadowed by the metallic odor of sweat and... what, she couldn't say. Fear, perhaps? Anger? Whatever it was, it left her with the same fist to the stomach she'd had when her brother had lost control on more occasions than she cared to count.

"Out of the way!" Wyatt yelled, pushing his way through the throng of men who had gathered around to witness the fight. "Les! Get off Ryan. Give us some air."

Then, in a move so swift that if Kate had blinked she would have missed it, Wyatt slammed a foot on the man's arm and kicked at the gun, sending it skittering in circles to a stop in front of a horse's stall with the ironic name "Annie" posted on the outside, as in "Annie Get Your Gun." Under different circumstances, Kate might have laughed, but until things were settled with the man on the ground, there would be no laughing... not from her, not from anyone.

"Okay, Ryan," Wyatt said, bending down beside the young man... only a boy, really. He talked to him like he would one of his horses, no doubt... calmly, softly, as if the only two in the world were him and Ryan. "Tell me what happened."

From where Kate was standing, she could smell alcohol on the boy's breath and it was clear that he was drunk, but strong nonetheless.

"My mother said she needed me to come home, to help out. Said she was done doin' drugs and that she could find me a job. Then her dealer calls and it's like we never talked. I'm gonna kill her, I swear."

Wyatt squeezed Ryan's shoulder blade and said, "You're going to do no such thing. You're going to sober up and stay right here."

With lightning speed, Ryan threw Wyatt on his back and crab walked toward the gun, his hand touching the grip. Before anyone could do anything, Wyatt grabbed the boy by his ankles and flipped him.

The gun skittered into the stall where the horse reared up and began stamping at it. Wyatt jumped to his feet and undid the stall door. In a flash, he stood coaxing the horse to settle down as the thrashing hooves pummeled the ground in front of him.

Remembering all the times she'd had to come to the rescue of her brother, Kate rushed to where Ryan was readying to strike from behind.

"Stop!" Kate said, shaking Ryan's arm.

The surprise of seeing an unknown woman shaking him gave her the time she needed to begin talking to him, really talking to him, about her brother and all the things he had been through. How she had cried herself to sleep night after night, worried that he might end up in prison or worse, dead.

"Think of the people who love you, Ryan. I know it feels like life will never get better. But think of your family of veterans, your friends. They would be devastated if something happened to you. I know the pain of everything you've been through doesn't go away in a day or even a month. It takes a long time, but the more you can help other people, the more you can help yourself."

At first, Ryan seemed ready to strike, but gradually his eyes glistened and he poured himself into her arms--let himself be held like a child. For a brief moment, it was as if everyone in the barn breathed a collective sigh. Soon, the silence turned to titters of laughter and relief, but only for a moment. Because at that precise second, Annie, the black mare, reared up on her hind legs and stamped the floor of her stall. The gun sounded along with a flash of light. With a loud groan, Wyatt crumpled to the floor and a rivulet of blood flowed through the open stall amidst the fresh hay.

<h1 style="text-align:center">Six</h1>

"Wyatt!" Kate screamed as she ran to where Wyatt lay bleeding in the stall, the horse still stamping and snorting, the whites of his eyes registering fear. One of the braver vets grabbed the reins of the horse and pulled him out of the stall, asking those around him to give him a wide berth.

Once the horse was outside the barn, everyone forgot about Ryan as they rushed to help Wyatt. A tall, thin man with sandy brown hair, introduced himself as Les, the ranch manager. Then he bent down next to Wyatt.

"It's just a flesh wound!" Les told her. "Corey, get the first aid kit," he called.

Kate tried to press herself between the crush of men, each offering help in his own way, all except for one young man with tattoos, who stood near the entrance of the stall, arms crossed, malevolence written into the set of his expression.

"That's Toby," Les said, under his breath. "You'll want to give him a wide berth."

But she had no time to ponder why as she moved toward Wyatt. From where she now stood, Kate could see that the bullet had gone through Wyatt's calf and out the other side, but he would live. Kate couldn't say why, but she felt a relief that was out of proportion to what little she knew of the man. Not that she would want to see *anyone* hurt. Maybe it was because he was her only tie to her new surroundings or because he was the first man who had been kind to her after the callous way her boss and Palmer had treated her, but she cringed at the thought that something might happen to him.

Corey returned on a run with an opened black medical bag. Within minutes, they had the wound cleansed and bandaged to much wincing and groaning. Once the moaning had lessened, Buck, dressed in Levis and a brown tee shirt, attempted to help Wyatt stand. He draped Wyatt's arm over his shoulder and anchored him on one side while Kate asked one of the men nearest her to watch over Ryan as she leapt to do the same. Fortunately, Wyatt was able to limp his way out of the stall.

At that moment, a tall, wiry woman who looked to be in her seventies appeared at the door to the barn. Her skin was tough as shoe leather and brown as the wheat fields Kate had seen in the field out back.

"Out of the way!" she yelled, her words punctuated, ending in a clip, English clearly not her first language. She pushed her way through the throng of testosterone-filled men. "I said out of the way, you yahoos."

With begrudging respect, the men stepped aside.

"Let go, Les," she said, reaching under Wyatt's other arm and taking over as though he were just another hay bale to be lifted and moved. "Name's Emajean," she told Kate. "You?"

"Kate."

"Well, Miss Kate, you sure know a thing or two about timing, I see." She gave Kate a once over and then snorted as if to say, "You are in way over your head." And Kate had to give her that. She *was* in way over her head, but she would never give Emajean the satisfaction of letting her know it.

Then, as if to prove Emajean right, Kate said, "Have you called 911?"

Emajean threw her head back and laughed as she tugged on Wyatt, maneuvering him toward the barn door and out into the sunlight, dust and hay filtering in off the light in a vee. "Honey, that's not how we do things around here. Watch and learn."

Slowly, they made their way across the field and up the old wooden steps, each one creaking as they worked their way toward the screen door.

"Hold tight there, Slim," she told Wyatt, then tugged at the screen door, which screeched like a banty rooster.

In moments, they had Wyatt tucked into the covers of a big old four-poster bed that looked as if it had belonged to somebody's grandmother. It swallowed him up in the downy quilt.

"Keep an eye on him," Emajean ordered. "Don't let him

out of that bed."

No sooner had she left than Wyatt attempted to do just that. "I've got work to do," he protested as he pushed up onto his forearm.

"Work can wait," Kate said. "We need to get you fixed up first."

Moments later, Emajean returned with sutures and a pair of surgical scissors, as well as a tray of various antiseptic liquids and gels.

To Kate's lifted brow, Emajean said, "Hospitals are for sick people." Then she laughed and added, "If you have a blood phobia, you'll probably want to skedaddle because I won't pick you up off this floor."

She wielded the words like a threat. And Kate had to admit that since the adrenaline had passed, she *was* starting to feel light-headed. With a wan smile, she excused herself, but not before giving Wyatt's hand a gentle squeeze.

Reluctantly, Kate left the room, shutting the door behind her. Stitching a man up seemed like a private affair.

Normally, she would have felt like an intruder in someone else's house, especially since she hadn't received a proper introduction. However, for some odd reason, she felt like she was coming home, as though she had lived in this house her entire life. The house spoke to her, from the dusty gray and pink rug on the floor to the sagging couch with its white chenille bedspread embroidered in roses. Even the pictures above the mantelpiece felt familiar somehow, as though she had been here at some other time in her life, or maybe another lifetime, if she were to believe in reincarnation. She wanted to hug the house, give it a great big squeeze of gratitude for being just what it was, old and plain, a wink and a nod to another era, a simpler era, if there was such a thing. A time before cell phones and internet. Before browsers followed your every move and cookies were the thing you ate, not the thing that facilitated the browsers. She felt nostalgia for something she had never had but longed for, nonetheless.

Her thoughts turned back to what Les had said about Toby. Though she'd never met the guy, something about him had her hackles up, even now. Hopefully, she had seen the last of him, and she would heed Les's words. She would give Toby a *very* wide berth.

Putting those thoughts aside, she looked out the front window across the wide expanse of lawn and saw that someone had a green thumb. A row of dahlias straddled the lawn, and closer to the house were roses and lavender. In a rototilled section of the yard off to the right, a rectangular area was filled with every kind of flower imaginable: faded peonies, malva, delphinium and sweet william, penstemon and bee balm. She could almost imagine the sweet smell from where she stood.

Just then she heard a loud shout that made her jump and she turned to stare nervously at the closed door. Moments passed before she realized her cell phone was ringing from her jacket pocket. Thinking it might be Jack, she scrambled for it before he could hang up. However, when she heard the feminine voice, it took her several moments to figure out who was calling.

"This is Jack's wife, Nora."

"Nora? How is Jack?" Kate frowned, remembering the last time she'd seen the former owner of the company. He had looked haggard beyond belief, his normally well-kempt gray hair appearing limp and lifeless like his blue-gray eyes, which had lost their luster. He had always been a tease. She could count on him to keep things light. The few times he had shown anger were well deserved. He was a good man and she missed him. Nora was his rock, a well-heeled woman who dressed impeccably, wore a year-round tan, and a perfect A-line hairdo that framed her oval face.

A long pause told Kate all she needed to know. Jack wasn't doing well.

"I've got a favor to ask you," Nora said with a hesitance not normal for the very forthright older woman.

"Go for it."

"Jack doesn't get out of bed these days. I'm worried about him. Marketing was his life." She paused as if afraid to go on. Kate waited, not wanting to risk upsetting the woman by asking too many questions. "Ian stole the company from him and I'm

afraid if we don't do something now, Jack's going to... I don't
know. I'm just worried. I need your help."

Seven

Kate heard a moan from the farmhouse bedroom and pictured Emajean suturing Wyatt's wound. Emajean had assured Kate that Wyatt had just been grazed by the bullet and that his wound would soon heal. Still, she'd never seen a man shot before and she had to admit it had rattled her. And now she had Jack to worry about. Advertising had been his life. He'd loved it only second to Nora. She plopped down on the farmhouse sofa and felt it give. To gather her thoughts, she closed her eyes and pinched her brows. Right now, she needed to focus on Jack and Nora. She would deal with Wyatt later, once Emajean was through cleaning and suturing his wound.

"How can I help?" she asked Nora, who had waited patiently on the phone as she thought through what her friend had told her about Jack. Kate had known he was depressed. Who wouldn't be? To have someone as underhanded and unscrupulous as Ian steal his company out from under him.

"Problem is," Nora said, "Ian is taking the best and brightest from the company. He's splitting them up and sending them to locations where marketing doesn't stand a chance of survival. I mean, Cody, Wyoming?"

Nora echoed Kate's thoughts exactly. There wasn't nearly enough work here to keep them busy. And when what little was finished, what then? Ian would have divided and conquered. Depending on their circumstances, those sent away would either go job hunting or return home, hat in hand, probably to live with family until they could stand on their own two feet again. Unfortunately, she would fall into the latter category, not a happy prospect for someone so independent... and proud.

"So I took matters into my own hands," Nora continued.

"Oh?" Frowning, Kate walked to the window and peered across to the cowhands who were just exiting the barn. They came in all shapes and sizes, from big bruisers with tattoos to lithe young men who seemed ill-equipped for shaving, much less war.

"Yes." A long pause ensued. Kate peered at the phone, wondering if she'd lost cell phone connection. Finally, Nora said, "So I bought them up."

"Hmm?" Kate squinted at the blaze of sunshine and decided she needed some fresh air, so she walked out onto the porch. The sunshine bathed her in warmth, the sweet smell of roses scenting the air.

"I mortgaged our penthouse and bought the rural part of the company from Ian. He was only too happy to dump that portion of the business."

Kate stepped off the porch and nearly lost her balance. She quickly sat down on the top step before she risked falling down them.

"Why?" she hissed. "Why would you do that? You'll lose everything."

Kate hadn't meant to blurt out those words, albeit the truth. For a moment, she felt physically sick.

"No, Kate, I won't," Nora said, her voice calm and filled with confidence. "And you're going to help ensure that I won't."

The woman was crazy. Plumb, out-of-her-head nuts. Kate needed to walk, to think. Before she realized where she was headed, she found herself out by the horse pen. As if waiting for her, knowing she would come, a Palomino stood patiently by the wooden railing, its head resting over the fence.

"Kate, you're smart; I'm smart. We both have a head on our shoulders. You know as well as I do that we can market anything from anywhere. This is the age of the internet, Kate. If we can prove that location is no longer an obstacle, we win."

"Yeah, but how are we going to get people to even consider us when they learn we're in Smalltown, USA?" Kate asked, stroking the Palomino's mane.

Nora snorted, or maybe it was the horse. It was like suddenly they'd developed the same brain. "You're in marketing, for God's sake. Market!"

"So, do you have a strategy?" Kate laid her head against the white diamond of the horse's forehead. It's as if she heard a male voice say *"You'll find a way."*

"So you talk now?" she whispered to the horse.

"What?"

"Oh, sorry, Nora, I was talking to a horse."

Now that sounds perfectly sane.

"Uh... okay. At any rate, that's for you to work out, Kate. I want you to be my partner. I'll put up the cash, you do the legwork. You'll be our ideas person. In lieu of cash, we'll offer you forty percent of the shares of the company. You won't earn it back until it sells, but what have you got to lose?"

Kate shook her head at the audacity of what Nora was saying. And yet, it would be a chance to show what she was made of...

"We're going to turn this ship around. You and me. And Jack. What do you say?"

"Make Jack proud," the male voice inside her head said.

"Alright, Mr. Ed, quit pushing." She climbed up onto the fence and scratched behind the horse's ear.

"Are you okay, Kate?" Nora said, with a note of concern.

Kate would either return home to her mother's "I told you so" about everything she'd done so far in her life, or she got on with it. Tried. That's all she could do, right? Mr. Ed stayed silent this time.

"Let's do it."

A huge sigh of relief wafted through the phone line. "Great. I'll be down in a few weeks. In the meantime, I want you to meet with Stanford and Gladys. I set them up on Main Street. I'll text you the address. They'll fill you in until I can get there. You have until then to come up with a strategy to save the company. That should be enough time, right?"

Nora laughed and the Palomino snorted, spraying Kate. Then he whinnied, as though he too were laughing at her.

Yuck it up, flyboy!

"One question," Kate asked, "does Jack know about any of this?"

"Not yet. Fortunately, I came to this marriage with a pretty hefty dowry and a prenup so most of our money is in my name." She paused, her voice suddenly more sullen. "But I

can't lose this for him. I want to give him back his company as
a gift. He deserves that after all he has put into it. It's the son
he never had."

Kate, more than anyone, knew that about Jack. His
company was his family. It's what drove him, made him happy.
She had seen what happened when he'd had to tell everyone
he'd lost his company. It had changed him. He had always had
a quick wit, and even under pressure he stayed calm and
thought things through. Everyone loved him. Everyone except
Ian and his ilk.

Now, Jack was a shell of his former self. Nora had often
called Kate in Manhattan to keep her updated on his
condition. Mostly, he just stayed in bed, forgot to dress or
shave. It was so unlike the driven man she had known, who
always wore dress shirts and slacks while at work, Hawaiian
shirt and shorts everywhere else, and yet even at work, he never
seemed stuffy or pretentious. He came across as one of the
boys, but treated the women just as well. Easygoing and
lighthearted. She loved him like a father. Whether saving the
business was a lost cause or not, she had to try. She had to give
it one-hundred-and-twenty percent.

"I'm all in."

"Good, see you in a few weeks? I'll get the papers drawn up
and you can sign them then."

"You've got it." Before Kate could say more, she saw
Emajean come hauling out onto the porch, hand over her eyes
as she scanned the area until she saw Kate. With a hurried
gesture, she waved Kate to come quickly.

"Gotta go," Kate said as she jumped down off the fence.
"And Nora..."

"Yes?"

"Tell Jack I'm thinking of him."

"Will do," Nora said. The horse stamped and snorted as if
reminding her to include him in the goodbyes.

"Mr. Ed says goodbye, too."

"Huh?"

"It's a running joke. I'll explain it when you get here. In the
meantime, take care of Jack."

She pressed the screen and the screen went blank. Seeing the urgency on Emajean's face, Kate hustled across the yard and up the steps, taking them two by two.

"What's up?"

"Wyatt needs you. He's got something to tell you." Emajean seemed reluctant to say more. Then, with a shrug of her shoulders, she said, "There's something he should have told you before bringing you all the way out here. I told him he should have said something before you made the trek."

"Oh?"

"I'll let him tell you, but you're not going to be happy. In fact, I'll rustle you up some stiff coffee. You're gonna need it, girl."

Kate could almost hear Mr. Ed laughing from here.

Eight

Kate downed her first sip of coffee and nearly gagged as she sat on a wooden chair across from Wyatt, who lay in bed, his face ashen after his ordeal with Nurse Nightingale.

"What's in this stuff," Kate asked Emajean, "pure grain alcohol?"

"That, and I like my coffee strong."

"A spoon could stand up straight in this stuff and never fall over."

Somewhere between the time Kate had last seen Emajean and now, the woman had braided her hair. She threw her heavy black braid over her shoulder and lifted a brow. "You city slickers could learn a thing or two about that dessert you call coffee. This here's the real stuff. None of that French froufrous and sweetener."

"God forbid," Kate said, making a face.

"Would you two *ladies*," Wyatt said through gritted teeth, "shut your traps long enough for me to say something?"

Although Kate knew she should be peeved, she couldn't help but giggle, while Emajean just shot him a look that could curdle milk. Of course, the coffee could do *that* on its own.

"Did Emajean tell you I had something to say to you?" he asked.

Kate and Emajean exchanged glances and Kate nodded. Then she turned to Wyatt, who appeared dwarfed against the immense down comforter and huge four poster bed. Off to the side was a large antique dresser with an old-fashioned mirror that appeared wavy and made her head look big and her body small, which was partly why she was avoiding it now.

"Did she also tell you that you're not going to like what I'm about to tell you?"

Again they exchanged glances.

What on earth have I gotten myself into?

"You know how I said I had a government contract and I

33

wanted to put together a marketing campaign for them?"

Kate could feel the sharks circling the water and the music playing. This is where he told her the truth, where there was no marketing campaign. Where basically she had come thousands of miles to this outpost to learn she had no job whatsoever. As if just catching up, her heart began stuttering in her chest.

"Well, that wasn't exactly the truth." He held up his hands to keep her from butting in. "I mean I *want* it to be the truth and with your help maybe it will be someday, but see I've been running the show on my own. I've been providing services for these vets, but I'm not endorsed by the government. I'm just one of those do-gooders who want to help. I saw a need and I tried to fill it."

Holy...

"Hear me out." He grabbed her hand as though expecting her to bolt for the exit and keep on running all the way to New York. "These guys are important. What I *do* is important. Men are alive because of what we've done on this ranch. I know it."

Kate could read the sincerity in his gray-blue eyes and suddenly felt warm.

As though he sensed it too, Wyatt released his hold and said, "Just promise me you'll listen until the end, and then you can make your decision about whether or not you want to return to the city, okay?"

She nodded, her throat suddenly dry.

"Tell her about the ranch, Wyatt," Emajean said with a dip of her head. "She's gonna find out soon enough."

Kate's eyes widened, but again she chose to say nothing.

"You're scaring her now, Emajean. Could you just zip it for a minute. I'm getting there."

"Sure are slow." Emajean raised a brow. Then, as if figuring that she had worn out her welcome, she turned and said, "I'll let you two be." She walked out, shutting the door behind her.

The room suddenly felt as though all the oxygen had gone with the woman, leaving the room stuffy and thick with tension.

Finally, Wyatt broke the silence. "I'm two months away

from foreclosure."

Kate shook her head, hoping she had heard wrong. "Then why did you bring me here?"

"Because I was hoping that you could help me with funding."

Feeling faint, Kate pulled the wooden chair closer to him. "How could I possibly help you with funding? You understand that even if you did get a government contract for these young men it would take months if not years. This isn't something you can fix overnight."

Gingerly, he shifted his weight in the bed and winced. "I understand that, but if I can get the word out about these men's needs, maybe we can find enough sponsors to keep the cause alive while we work on getting government funding."

Kate leaned back in her chair, feeling exhausted from all the hairpin twists and turns since she had landed in Wyoming. Her head was still spinning and she felt parched. Then, like one of those cartoon characters with a light bulb above its head, an idea began to form.

"GoFundMe."

"Huh?" Wyatt lifted himself up onto the pillow.

"They have accounts for people with immediate need. You just need a good marketing campaign."

And suddenly she had her angle. *Do good, live right.* That would be her marketing slogan for her company. That would be her core mission. What made this even better, she could work from home with once-a-week office visits. And she could do it anywhere. She became more and more excited as she thought about it, because all their employees could work from home, if they chose, giving them more time for their families. Better yet, the admin for their company could split office space with other companies who shared similar goals so the overhead would be far less: shared lighting, shared heating, shared costs for furnishings. Employees could earn a percentage of sales with a minimum earning potential, so they could earn as little or as much as they wanted. They could even be independent contractors. Kate jumped to her feet and clapped her hands. Then she gave Wyatt a huge hug. He groaned, peering down at his leg.

"Oh!" she said, releasing him. "Sorry. But I think I can help you."

"How?" he said, wincing again and closing his eyes as he struggled with the pain.

"Don't worry about it. I'll tell you later. In the meantime, rest up. I need to get to the office. Is there anyone who can take me?"

"Use Bessie," he said, nodding to the keys resting on his nightstand. "Just be sure to take good care of her. I don't want my girl hurt."

Kate thought of the little blue Ranger. Must be a guy thing. "I will." She tried not to dance her way out of the room, she was so excited. In fact, she didn't let out a whoop until she was in the living room. She could have sworn she heard male laughter from the adjoining bedroom.

From the big ranch kitchen, Emajean appeared with a white dish towel looking sheepish. "Sooo...?"

"So, I think we have a plan to save the ranch, *and* my job!"

Emajean clasped her hands around the dish towel and dropped her head to her chest as though thanking God for this new turn of events. Then she lifted her head and said, "Thank you."

"Don't thank me yet," Kate said, giving the woman's heavily wrinkled hand a squeeze. "But I plan to give it the old college try." Kate winked. She was about to turn to leave, but upon second thought she said, "By law, don't you have to turn in a gunshot victim to the police?"

Emajean smiled for the first time since the accident. "You really *are* new to town, aren't you?" She laughed. "This is Wyoming, honey. The Wild Wild West. Besides, it's only a superficial wound. He'll heal soon enough. He'll be sore for a bit, but we all are at one time or another. It comes with age. You'll find out soon enough," she said and smiled.

* * *

Twenty minutes later, and after numerous missed turns, Kate

pulled up alongside a building that looked like something truly out of the Old West, complete with wood railing to tie a horse. And what made it especially funny, she actually saw a horse tied to one end of the railing, a beautiful pinto.

She walked up onto the wooden boardwalk and listened to the hollow sound beneath her feet. All that was missing were the spurs. Across a large window, in silver letters outlined in burgundy, were the words J and R Marketing--J, for Jack and R for... She snapped her fingers. Roberts, her last name. The company name thrilled her.

Today was Monday and the boardwalk seemed busy, despite the size of the town. Tourists no doubt, if the cameras and selfies were any indicator.

"Please let this work out," she whispered and heard a responding whinny from the pinto down the block. "Do you *all* have ESP?" she muttered.

As if the horse had indeed read her mind, it nodded.

"Oh dear God!" She took a deep breath and then entered the office, but stopped short upon entry.

"You can close your mouth now. I'm Gladys," the heavyset woman seated at the front desk said, "and this is Stanford. And yes, he's gay and I'm black... and this is Wyoming. That's what you call irony," she said with a laugh.

Nine

"Quick," Wyatt called to Emajean, who he could hear rattling around in the kitchen with her pots and pans from where he lay in the bedroom of the old farmhouse. "I need help getting dressed." He groused when he heard no response. Scooting the chair aside, he pulled his leg out from under the covers. Unfortunately, he knocked the chair over in the process and nearly fell out of bed onto the pinewood floor. He used the nightstand to try to pull himself upright, breathing hard from the exertion despite his usual fitness.

"Hold your horses!" Emajean called. Moments later, she brusquely entered the room, elbows out while giving him the onceover. "I swear you are *the* most impatient man I've ever known, and I've known a few in my time."

Although Emajean always sounded gruff, she, like Wyatt himself, had a soft heart. And like him, she could intimidate people with her rough exterior, but there wasn't a mean bone in her body. He'd seen her go up against the toughest men, ex-Marines with tattoos of skulls and crossbones, criminals and congressmen alike. He gave her a sideways smile. That woman could hold her own. Whether the problem involved something as simple as an injured sparrow, or as difficult as a wife being taken down by her old man... or almost as bad, the destruction of the environment... That woman could be downright scary then. But when she was done with her cause, she could just as easily sit down and comfort the victimizer as the victim, because they were all victims in some form or other. After all, wasn't the victimizer just someone who felt powerless in his or her own life? Like him, she had learned this early on and he respected her for it.

"Help me with my jeans, would ya, Jeanie?"

She just laughed and walked to the dresser. Opening it, she pulled out a pair of gray sweatpants.

"Oh, hell no. I'm not wearing those in public." He tried to

stand and fell back onto the bed.

"Oh, yes you are, buster. Your leg will get infected if you wear those tight jeans of yours. And you're never gonna make it out of here without crutches. Besides," she said, squinting up at him through those nearly transparent blue eyes of hers, so at odds with her heritage, "why are you in such an all-fire hurry? The fight is busted up. The boys are talking to Ryan and taking him under their wings for now. And so far, no one's the wiser about this little... *mishap* of yours."

The attempt to stand made Wyatt feel like a deflated balloon, suddenly. He hadn't realized how much energy he'd lost from the gunshot to his calf. He closed his eyes and sank back onto the bed. He didn't like feeling helpless. Besides, he had work to do if he planned to save his ranch. He peered out the window at the huge expanse, at the oak tree where his father had carved his and his mother's initials nearly half a century prior, and before that his grandfather and grandmother. This had been a pioneer homestead. He felt the weight of history on his shoulders to keep it in the family, pass it on to his daughter, and his wife, if the right woman came along. For some reason the image of Kate popped into his mind unbidden, but he quickly pushed it away. She was different from him. A New Yorker. She would never understand his connection to the land, to the people, to the town. He loved everything about the wide open expanses. The thought of city life gave him the willies. He could never be happy in a concrete jungle.

He moaned as Emajean started to lift his legs and tuck him back under the huge down comforter. "Hey, I've got to mow the back forty if we're going to have a photographer here soon. If it gets too high, it's hard to get looking nice again."

"Okay, Gunga Din," she said, ignoring him completely. "You drink this." She handed him a pill and a half filled glass of water.

"What's this?"

"Something for the pain. It'll help you sleep."

He shook his head, nearly spilling the water. "Haven't you been listening to a word I've said? I have to mow, woman."

"Woman, is it? I'll have you know," she said, rolling up the sleeves of her gingham shirt, "I've mowed a yard or two in my time, and I know how to run your riding lawn mower, if you haven't forgotten. I rope cows, shod horses, and I'll spit in your food if you're not careful," she added with a laugh.

"They don't make 'em like you anymore, Jeanie," he said, feeling tired already.

"They sure don't. I'd like to see that prissy Miss Kate keep up with me. I could outwork her any day."

Wyatt laughed and immediately winced from the pain. "A little *friendly* female rivalry, eh?"

"A woman like her won't last long in a place like this. One winter here, and she'll be searching for the next flight out of here. Mark my words."

Wyatt pushed himself up on the bed. "I wouldn't be so sure. Something tells me she has more grit than we give her credit for."

Emajean raised a wary brow. "Buck says Kate *did* calm Ryan down."

"And she helped me when I was shot. Has she met the pair running her business here in Cody, yet?" He smiled, despite the pain. *Stanford and Gladys.* He couldn't think of a more unlikely pair. He'd first approached them about marketing his ranch when he'd seen them talking to the realtor about their new business. But they had told him that they had to wait for the arrival of the marketing manager. Then they had handed him their company card and suggested he contact Ian. That's how he had come to hear about Kate.

"I don't think so, but she should be finding out..." Emajean peered down at her watch. "...right about now, if I'm not mistaken."

Wyatt slapped the bed with his hand and laughed, then immediately howled at the pain.

"Serves ya right, ya old coot."

"I'm thirty years younger than you," he said through tears of pain mixed with laughter.

"Only by age, boy, only by age. Now if we were going by maturity..."

The overhead light was starting to hurt Wyatt's eyes, so he covered his face with his arm. He didn't know if it was the drug or the simple fact that the throbbing in his leg made him tired, but he started to drift off. The last words he heard were, "Do you think she'll stay once she finds out what's going on there?"

Ten

Kate sat outside on the wooden boardwalk eating an oversized waffle cone filled with rocky road ice cream. After what she'd learned at the office, it's as if all the events of the past few months had come crashing down like an avalanche off the snowy slopes of the Sawtooth Mountains at once. She pulled the very expensive Cartier diamond ring out of her pocket, the one Palmer had given her right before she left with the promise that he would be there waiting for her once she came to her senses and realized he was the best thing that had ever happened to her. Well, now might be that time, whether she agreed or not. She looked at the diamond. It sparkled in the sun, a glistening rainbow smattering colors onto every object in its path. The woman at the table next to hers turned around, eyes wide.

"Oh my," she said, inspecting the diamond carefully.

She was one of those people you could see a dozen times and never remember, she was so plain. Her face was round with thinning gray hair, and she wore a seersucker pantsuit. Her lips were small, like her nose, but her eyes were kind, grandmotherly almost, which is what Kate needed most right now--someone who would tell her that her life wasn't a disaster after all. That she hadn't made mistake after mistake, that someday, somewhere, there would be someone who loved her completely and truly. That life wouldn't keep handing her surprise after horrible surprise. And the latest surprise hadn't been her two new partners in the business. They had been wonderful, actually. The surprise had been what Ian had done to insure J & R Marketing's demise as a company. That's what had turned her to drowning her sorrows with this rocky road ice cream cone, which pretty much summed up her life, currently. A rocky road.

"Fiancé?" the woman asked, nodding toward the ring.

Kate frowned, confused, then looked down at the diamond.

"Oh!" How to explain? All she could come up with was "sort of."

"Hmm."

"We're taking a little time apart, to figure out what we want."

"You'll know if it's right," the woman said, dabbing at the condensation on her large Dixie cup filled with soda.

"Did you?" Kate asked, embarrassed that she was talking to a complete stranger about something so intimate.

"Oh, honey, I was blessed. My Harvey was a wonderful man." She fingered the cup, her eyes centered on a memory long ago. "He was part of the second wave off Normandy on D-Day. Later, he was captured behind enemy lines and spent three months in a German hospital. His parents and I were sick with worry."

"But he survived," Kate offered.

"That he did, but he'd been shot in the hip and arm. He was handicapped the rest of his life, but he never felt sorry for himself. He just got on with life and was one of the happiest men I knew."

Kate looked at the ice cream cone that was now running down her arm in the afternoon heat and felt guilty. By comparison, her problems were small.

"I know this may sound odd," the woman continued, "but that was one of the best things that ever happened to him, because he learned to appreciate the small things in life. He never took anything for granted, including me. We had a wonderful marriage and three amazing kids." Her eyes filled with tears. "Well, I've taken enough of your time, honey," she said, rising to her feet and depositing her disposable cup into the trash can. "Just remember that *bling* isn't what's important. It's the man and what's inside." She picked up her cane, tapped her heart then winked at Kate.

Kate could have sworn her eyes sparkled nearly as bright as the diamond, if not brighter. She shook her head and laughed. When she looked up, the woman was gone. With a quick dart of her head, Kate scanned the boardwalk then peered inside the ice cream shop.

Nothing.

Kate felt the same shiver she had with the old lady at the airport coffee shop. It was as if she had been visited by a ghost. Reluctantly, she rose and deposited the now melted ice cream into the garbage can. She had damage control to attend to, if her new joint venture with Nora and Jack was to survive. No time for resting on her laurels. She had to stop Ian, and fast.

* * *

Ian cackled as he stared out over the rainy Manhattan skyline. It had taken him days, but he'd had his new secretary go through every single file of every rural client and had wooed them back to his company instead of going with the new company. He and Nora had agreed to let any and all clients decide which firm they would go with and they had all decided on him. All except that one creep from Wyoming. Well, Ian would take care of him. He had it on good authority that the man was just two payments away from losing his ranch, a ranch that had been in his family for generations. Ian planned to be personally on hand when he bought it for next to nothing at auction. And he would make sure that this Wyatt character knew just who had purchased his land and why.

The satisfaction of his plan made him smile as he gazed out over the watery landscape. He loved Manhattan in the rain, the way it smelled of wet asphalt and smoking chimneys. He had been made for this type of environment. It suited him to a tee. Each of the buildings below looked like giant pieces on a chessboard to be moved around until voila! Checkmate. His father had taught him to be ruthless and cunning. And he had learned the lesson well, some would say even better than the old man. He chuckled as he peered down at a photo on his desk of the large man who had grit and determination written all over his square jaw and in his nearly jet black eyes.

To win the clients, he had used a play straight out of his father's toolkit. Trips, tickets to see favorite teams, and not just any tickets, box seats. And if none of that worked, he would call in a favor that they needed. That, too, he'd taken out of his father's playbook. Know your client better than they know themselves, then use it to your advantage. He had taken the old man's words to heart and it was paying off. In dividends.

A knock on the door pulled him from his reverie. His secretary, Sally, a petite little brunette, opened the door and leaned in. "A client is here to see you."

He lifted an angry brow. As far as he knew, he had scheduled no client appointments for this hour. He was about to berate her when she added, "It's Mr. Majors."

"Oh!" he backtracked. One of his biggest and most respected clients. "Bring him in! Bring him in!"

Mr. Majors never came by without an appointment. Fear set Ian's teeth grinding, but he straightened his tie to give himself time to think. Nothing to worry about. Nothing at all, right? But when he saw the man, he knew his worries were well founded. The thin, elderly man was red-faced and livid. Despite his name, he was small and squat, with a year-round tan, silver hair, and just the slightest paunch. He could be polite and even fun, with a few whiskey sours in him. But you didn't cross the man, and Ian had a feeling that he'd somehow crossed him without his knowing and that didn't settle well.

Before he could attempt to soothe the man by welcoming him in, Arnold Majors said, "To think, I went with you instead of Jack. You will pay for this. By god, no one messes with me the way you have. No one."

Eleven

Wyatt awoke from a deep slumber, his phone ringing. He fumbled for it, flipped it open, his eyes still closed. But within seconds, he was wide awake. By the time he was finished with the call, his hand was shaking as he closed his phone. The nerve of Ian Phelps to get some guy named Ewing to try to bribe him into staying with Ian's outfit. And why hadn't Kate told Wyatt the company was splitting before he'd signed the contract with Ian Phelps Marketing? This meant he'd have to wait at least a month for them to send someone new. By then it would be too late. He was hanging by a thread as it was. And here he was laid up in bed. He had to get up, wound or no wound.

"Emajean!" he barked.

The woman had been a fixture in his father's household and when his father had died she had come with the place, a comfortable, if sometimes cranky, addition. She belonged here as surely as that oak tree out front or the weeping willow on the back lawn.

"Emajean!" he yelled again.

Emajean appeared in the doorway. "If you don't shut that yap of yours, I'm going to shut it for you."

"Where is Kate?" he demanded, ignoring her outburst.

"She went to town," she said. "Why?"

"I need to talk to her. Now!"

Emajean put her hands in the air and stood her ground. "Hold your horses, Wyatt. She'll be back soon."

"Not soon enough. Get me my trousers."

"Now, Wyatt..."

"Just get 'em." He knew he was being unreasonable, but he couldn't help himself. Everything he, his father, and his grandfather had worked a lifetime for was about to go up in smoke. He couldn't let that happen, and that's what *would* happen if he stayed in bed all day.

As he struggled to put on his pants, Emajean whistled. "I think you've just had your prayers answered," she said. "Here she comes now."

Wyatt heard the sound of tires on gravel and peered out in time to see his beloved Ranger flying up the driveway. It was bad enough that she'd screwed him, but now she was getting Bessie dirty. He flew to his feet and nearly stumbled to the floor before he grabbed ahold of the nightstand.

"Use your father's old cane," Emajean said, fishing it out of the closet and handing it to him.

He hobbled around the bed to where Emajean stood. The pair watched as Kate pulled up to the house, got out, and began running up the steps with a pair of crutches in her hands.

"Well, at least she was thinking of you," Emajean said with a chuckle.

* * *

Despite Kate's need to speak to Wyatt, when it came right down to it she couldn't go inside. She needed a moment to compose herself after what she had learned from Nora. It seemed like every time she turned around, she was experiencing either a new high or a new low. Her thoughts were swimming as she laid the crutches onto the porch and sat down on the porch swing, trying not to cry. First she'd lost her home, then her fiancé, and now she might lose her job and her client if things didn't pan out. How could she possibly explain what had happened in the course of twenty-four hours, and would Wyatt even believe her?

As she gazed out over the pastureland, the mockingbirds calling in the distance, she thought about her talk with Nora. Ian had pulled the rug out from under all of them. Nora had assured Kate that the fledgling company would be okay, that she had a plan in place and not to worry, but how could Kate *not* worry with her entire life in flux?

She was nursing a headache when the door opened and Wyatt appeared. By the look in his eyes, he'd obviously heard

47

the bad news and was set to pounce. She bent her head, hoping he wouldn't see the tears brimming in her eyes, which were about to run down her cheeks at any moment. Too late. One lone tear fell, then another. She looked up in time to see him appear first angry, then confused. Finally, he hobbled over to her and sat down gingerly onto the swing. It swayed back and forth, an intimate gesture that made her feel better somehow.

"I received a call," he said, handing her a handkerchief from his pocket.

"I was sure you would." She felt like a child as she blew softly into the pale linen, then laughed at the absurdity of crying, in front of her client no less.

"So you didn't know?"

She shook her head vehemently. "Not until I went to the office today."

"Why don't you start at the beginning. What's going on?"

His blue eyes seemed bluer somehow, more penetrating as he gazed at her with a kindness she didn't deserve after all that had happened, even though she had no control over any of it.

"The company I work for was the product of an amazing man... Jack. He grew the company into a multi-million dollar business and treated his workers like family. We loved him."

"And then?"

"And then there was a hostile takeover. Jack was bought out, but more like forced out. Fortunately, he was able to add a stipulation to the contract stating that the workers could keep their jobs, which sounds good on paper, but anyone loyal to Jack was sent to..."

"The sticks," Wyatt offered to which Kate simply nodded.

"Most people wanted to stay put, so they quit."

"And the others decided to try to make a go of it in rural USA."

She nodded.

"And most likely those areas will fail, so the few remaining workers will be on their own and safely out of the way. That way this new boss is in the clear," he said in conclusion.

Again, Kate nodded. "Jack's wife decided to buy back the rural portion of the business."

"What the hell for?" Wyatt rested his arm over her shoulder in an easy gesture that felt familiar, as if he'd done this a thousand times before.

"To try to save our jobs."

Wyatt whistled. A sandy colored Shetland sheepdog came from the side yard and ran up the steps.

"Meet Henry," he said.

Seeing her, the Sheltie ran to her and put his head in her lap as though he understood and had come to her rescue. She had to laugh. She petted his moist muzzle and scratched behind his ears feeling instantly relieved, as though the day's struggle was suddenly behind her.

"Now let me get this straight. A bright woman invests money in a company she knows will fail. Does that make sense to you?"

Kate frowned. Put that way, it didn't make sense, but Nora had assured her that with the internet they could get this business up and running. And Kate had felt positive that she could help make that happen. Now, in the light of day, she wondered if she could, and if so, how long that would take. Had she been overly optimistic?

"And she didn't put *anything* in the contract to protect the clientele she had?"

Kate had to admit a woman as smart as Nora would have never overlooked such a thing. Even if she had, Jack would have made sure that she had taken care of a detail as important as that. But then again, Nora had yet to tell him about the deal.

"Look, I don't mean to tell you how to run your business, but something's not quite right about all this. You don't get to be a multimillionaire by making these kinds of mistakes."

The headache she had been sporting suddenly felt like a freight train coming at her at full speed. She rubbed her temples.

"Let's go get you some aspirin and a glass of water. Then I want you to start putting together your marketing angle. I've got a foreclosure on the horizon, if you don't get that pretty little rear of yours in gear."

She attempted to stand and stopped, nearly tripping over

him in the process. Had he just called her pretty? Warmth rushed to her face. He grasped her hand to steady her, his grip strong, his hand rough from years of hard labor, so different from Palmer's soft hands.

She peered at him sideways. "So you're keeping me on?"

He simply laughed and looked down at his calf. "As you can see, I love a good fight."

Twelve

"Jack, get out of that bed," Nora Ingram said, glancing at the clock on the side of the French Provincial nightstand. 9:00 am. Jack had never slept a wink past 5:30 in his life. He was a workaholic who equated work with family.

He moaned, then turned over, still asleep.

Nora peered around the room searching for something to motivate him but found nothing. The entire room had been done in what Jack termed her "frou-frou" style, but he had eventually come to love it as much as he loved her. She peered down at the mountain of covers. Tucked beneath the white bedspread with brown accents, against the tufted brown headboard, lay her husband. When had he aged? He had always been so meticulous about his appearance, but without a place to be each day he had sunk into depression and she needed to pull him out of it as soon as possible.

"Jack!" she repeated, shaking him.

"What?" He sat up and rubbed his eyes.

"We have work to do."

"What's going on?" He squinted over to the clock and rushed to his feet until he remembered he didn't have anywhere to go.

"I bought a company."

"What?" he said, suddenly alert.

"And I've lost most of the accounts."

Now he seemed fully awake. "Start at the beginning," he said. "I'm going to take a shower while you tell me all about it."

For the next twenty minutes, she explained amid the steam and humidity. Like the old days, he dried his hair rapidly, his thoughts focused as she told him every gritty detail. It was worth every single penny to see her husband so alive and well. A half hour later, he was dressed in suit and tie and looked every bit the handsome man he had always been. Better yet, they had a plan. A good plan.

Two days had passed before Wyatt finally felt well enough to move around again for any length of time. Still, it came as a surprise to Kate when he told her he wanted to take her riding. He wouldn't tell her where, simply saying, "Be patient. You'll see." Patience had never been one of her strong suits, and nothing was different today, she realized as they stood in the corral, the day turning out warm and sunny.

"Put your feet in the stirrups," Wyatt said, giving Kate's backside a gentle shove to get her onto the Appaloosa pony. It was a spirited mare that lifted its head and blew air in protest as it backed away.

Twice she missed until at last she found purchase and pushed herself onto the largest saddle he had available so that the two could ride together. Despite his leg, Wyatt easily pulled himself up after her. He put his arms around her and picked up the reins.

"Hold on to the pommel," he said.

"The what?"

He guided her hand to the saddle's knob, then he kicked the Appaloosa's sides. Ten minutes into the ride, he handed her the reins. "Your turn," he said, placing his hands around her waist.

"I've never ridden a horse before."

"No time like the present to learn." He laughed at her expense.

"Where are we headed?" she asked, flicking the reins. As though sensing an inexperienced rider, the horse stopped and refused to budge, even when she copied Wyatt's earlier movements.

"It's a surprise. And here," he said, cupping his hands around hers and helping her with the reins. "First, relax. The horse knows when you're tense and senses danger. That's why it stops. Could be a rattlesnake or a mountain lion. Spot here doesn't know."

"Spot? You call your horse Spot? You couldn't come up

with a more imaginative name than that?"

"Okay, Miss Know It All, what would you call her?"

Kate thought about it carefully then snapped her fingers. Her name was no more original, but at least it had a better ring to it. "How about Spirit."

She turned toward him and saw a devilish twinkle in his eye. "Like that's never been done before."

Although she felt herself flush, she followed up with a forced confidence. "Okay, Spirit." She clicked her tongue to spur the horse on. "Let's go."

At that point, he out and out laughed at her. "No city girl here."

With an attempt at false anger, she scowled, but Wyatt merely hugged her tighter to him. The warmth and proximity reminded her how much she missed the touch and the feel of a man. And yet, he smelled so different from Palmer--Palmer, who was always in suit and tie and who wore expensive cologne that she had never grown accustomed to. Wyatt smelled like a man should smell. He smelled of sweat and the outdoors. Of soap and hard work. She liked the smell of a man who worked with his hands, who wasn't afraid to get dirty. A man who could wrangle a horse or a cow, then bend down and pet a dog. A man who was strong and virile, but who also had a soft side, soft enough to care about men he hadn't even known, men who had suffered as he had in the never-ending wars. A man with a heart.

For the next fifteen minutes, they rode in silence except when Wyatt pointed out the occasional Indian Tobacco, a tall narrow-leaved plant with brick-colored plumes. Or the big boulder where he and his brother James would hide out as children to play army, or cowboys and Indians. Or to a spot where a cougar had ambushed one of their cattle many years ago. Each time he pointed something out, his eyes would light up with excitement and she could read the enthusiasm in his voice. These were memories. Good memories.

His mood suddenly changed, however, as they came upon an old makeshift cemetery. Around it was a faded white fence. The soil was sandy, filled with potholes and mounds, as though the ground had been shoveled and shoveled again. Kate remained in the saddle as he halted Spirit and glided to the ground with no more than a brief moan. He had steadfastly refused to use crutches and had given up the cane by the third day.

Next, he helped her down with not quite the same grace that he had exhibited moments earlier. When she was at last on solid ground, he dipped his head to point out a weathered gravestone.

"That's my mama over there. Great lady. There was nothin' she couldn't do. Never complained, not even when she found out she had cancer."

"Sounds like a bit of hero worship there," she said softly.

"Got that right. Couldn't have found a better human being on this planet. She was tough, mind you," he said with a small chuckle as he pulled off his white felt hat and wiped his forehead with the bandana that lined it. "But she was fair. Never said I love you. Not until she knew she had only days left. But I knew it."

Kate caught the glint of tears in his eyes, however he quickly bowed his head then looked away for the time it took to recover his emotions.

"What about your dad?" she asked.

Wyatt laughed, breaking the earlier mood. "That man was a cuss if ever there was one. God almighty, he was a character. But mama, she knew how to handle him. They loved each other, in their own way. Later in life, before he died, he got to see what a tower of strength that woman was and I think... no I *know* he appreciated her for it."

It was her turn to laugh. "Did you like your dad?"

He paused, then looked up at her in a way that stilled her breath, a penetrating look that held no punches. "I *loved* that man. Sure, he was a cuss, but the older you get the more you learn about life and what it takes to live it. No one is simply good or bad. Maybe there are a few out there who are all bad, I don't know. But what I have learned in life is that you never really *get* a person until you've walked in their shoes, and sometimes those shoes are mighty uncomfortable."

She took his hand and gave it a squeeze. Then, feeling awkward, she let go and watched it fall to his side as though he didn't have any energy left after the release of pent-up sorrow.

"We probably better get going," he said, his voice husky with emotion. "We're almost there."

"Where?" she asked.

"To the old homestead. We turned it into a cabin... for the men."

* * *

The horse pulled up into a clearing and halted, whinnying as though it too understood the utter magnificence of this place. In front of them stood a towering log cabin, immense in size with a wide front porch and flowers in amazing shades and colors: blue delphinium, pink and white lupine, and Russian sage in the back with a border of lavender, salvia, and white alyssum. The walkway leading to it was paved in gray, orange, and sage green flagstone. Beside the walkway, more low-lying flowers met a swirling gravel path that led to a birdbath on one side and a pond on the other. Flashes of orange koi glinted even at this distance. Over the pond sat a wooden bridge with scrolled ironwork handrails, hummingbirds and lilies woven into the design.

"It's breathtaking," Kate said, leaning back to gauge Wyatt's reaction. What she read in those pale blue eyes was a humble pride.

"Thanks."

"This cabin is yours?"

"Me and the guys added on to the existing homestead," he said, bending his head as though suddenly shy.

"And you're not living in it?"

"I built it for the men." He cocked his head as if surprised that she would imagine he would keep something so magnificent for himself.

"I don't understand," she said, holding onto the pommel as she strove to get a better look at him.

"When I returned from the war, I was pretty angry. I didn't

55

trust anyone and I didn't like myself very much." He took off his hat and tapped it on his knee to remove any dust or sweat. "At first, I drank a lot, and I slept around too much. I pushed people away. It's how I dealt with the anger."

He paused, his eyes searching the horizon, but Kate knew he had gone back in time, to a darker place when the world and everything in it seemed hostile. "I knew I was going to die if I didn't find a way to deal with the anger, so I set to work building this log cabin, one log at a time."

"But this is *massive*... How...?"

"How did I do it?" He shrugged. "I started out on my own, but as buddies returned from the war just as wounded as I was, they started to help me. Then it got so other vets heard about it and started offering donations of time, money, or materials. From there, it sort of snowballed," he said with another shrug of his shoulders. "I wasn't sure what I was building it for, just that I was building it to work off my frustrations. But the longer I worked on it, the more obvious it became that I wasn't doing it for myself. I was doing it for these guys."

"But it's so beautiful. So beyond--"

"Anything they could expect? I know. That's why I did it. They've seen ugly. Real ugly. They deserve some beauty in their lives. They think they can find it in a bottle or a one night stand. Or even an affair. But once the novelty wears off, they're right back where they were before, having to look at themselves in the mirror. Most times they don't like what they see. This place," he said with a sweep of his hand, "gives them time to relearn who they were before the war. To do something good. We grow fresh veggies for the food bank. We go out as a group and help build houses for returning vets. When one of us gets knocked down we help support and pick each other up. Each vet is assigned an animal to care for. That's their responsibility for as long as they stay here. It teaches them how to care for something long term, and in turn they learn what it is to be loved unconditionally by that animal so that maybe they can take what they learned and give it back to another human being."

Kate thought about this for a moment. Just then a

swallowtail butterfly fluttered past, eventually landing on a purple butterfly bush. The smell of it was sweet and made her think of younger days on her grandmother's farm when life had seemed simpler somehow, though looking back on it there were no simpler times. She had just viewed life through the eyes of a child, with wonder and innocence. Now, like the vets, she felt jaded, hurt once too often and uncertain of herself and the world around her.

Kate surprised herself by saying, "Did you learn how to give back?" To his questioning look she added, "Unconditional love, I mean." The instant she spoke the words heat rose to her cheeks. "I didn't mean..."

"No, it's a fair question." He ran fingers through his prematurely graying hair. "Let's just put it this way, I'm trying. I'm still a little gun shy. When I marry, I want it to be to the right woman for the right reasons, but until I'm happy with myself, I can't be happy with anyone else."

She understood, more than he would ever know.

"How about you?"

"Hmm?" she said, taken off guard.

"Have you found the right person?"

For a moment, her heart stammered in her chest. Palmer... the right person? The right person would be someone who loved her unconditionally, not because she looked good on a resume. She wanted someone who wasn't always searching for greener pastures. Someone who could see her worth, her value. Someone who respected her. *Was* that Palmer? She knew the answer was no, and yet, despite the fact that she had at least twenty messages on her cell phone pleading with her to call him back, she couldn't do it. Like the vets, she needed time and space to figure out what she wanted for her life. To learn to love herself again. Her confidence had been shattered almost beyond repair when she had unwittingly introduced Ian to Jack. She had met him through one of Palmer's parties, put on by his work. Ian had seemed charming, at the time. If only she'd known his true nature, she would never have allowed such a man into any of their lives. Now she lived with that guilt every day. Until she learned to rebuild her confidence, to forgive herself for her mistake, she was no good to anyone. What scared her most, though, was the single question: what if she could never rebuild her life or find a way to make it up to Jack and Nora? That was a question she hadn't yet wanted to face.

Had she found the right person in Palmer? He had offered to marry her before she left, and told her she wouldn't need to work ever again--that his company encouraged career wives to wine and dine the execs when they were in town. The women were expected to fall in line, and the men were expected to drink scotch and water and to have discreet affairs. Although Palmer had tried to make light of it, the very thought of it had made her cringe. It's as though they'd taken a step back into the Dark Ages. Could she marry a man who could accept such medieval practices in this day and age? She shook her head no to Wyatt's earlier question, and for a brief moment she thought she'd read a flash of relief in his eyes. She attributed it to the sun glinting off his irises.

"Well, Kate, do you want to take a look at the inside of the log house or are we just going to stand here gawking?"

She laughed and flicked the reins. This time Spirit responded.

Thirteen

Kate twirled around the inside of the log cabin, her eyes traveling to the ceiling, which was at least thirty feet high, maybe higher. Large wooden beams straddled the vee-shaped roof, while a huge freestanding stone fireplace ran floor to ceiling. A bank of windows ran along the side of the cabin providing a view of a winding path outside with three poplars and a variety of ferns and undergrowth.

Around the back of the fireplace was a kitchen done in knotty pine and granite countertops. But what surprised Kate most was the sheer artistry of every piece of furniture in the place. It was as if each item had been handcrafted especially for this home.

When Wyatt saw her looking at the furniture, he said, "The men and I made those. You take more pride in somethin' when you do it yourself. These guys never get tired of hearing how nice things look."

Wyatt took her on a brief inspection of the upstairs bedrooms, nine in total. Then they sought out the gym-sized bathroom with lines of shower stalls and lockers for the men's clothes, before heading downstairs to view the two remaining bathrooms. When they were done looking around, they returned to the kitchen.

"Where *are* the guys?"

Wyatt walked over to a calendar tacked onto the refrigerator and scanned it briefly. "I'd say they're in the back forty haying right about now. Do you want to go meet some of the men, maybe hear some of their stories? Then you'll see why they need this place and why I need them."

They were about to walk away when Kate caught sight of an amazing piece of photography on the wall next to the refrigerator. It was a picture of thousands of stars swirling in the night sky as if in perpetual motion.

"Who photographed that?"

He shrugged. "I'm not sure. One of the vets, I think. I'll have to ask Emajean. She might know."

When they were finished surveying the cabin, they found Spirit and mounted for the third time that day. This time around, Kate felt more comfortable in the saddle, but she still couldn't get used to Wyatt's close proximity. It felt too intimate for only a second meeting, and yet it felt right somehow, as if a glove made just for her. She prodded the horse, not wanting to dwell on the thoughts and emotions stirring inside her.

Ten minutes later, after crossing first one hill and then another, they came to a clearing where men with pitchforks were throwing bales of hay to other men atop two flatbed trucks. Still another man was driving a tractor and rototilling the stubble back into the soil. As she came upon the man on the tractor, she could see he had no arm and was driving the tractor one-handed. He simply yelled a hearty hello and kept driving. One of the other men helped a man with a silver-and-blue prosthetic leg down from a flatbed so he could come say howdy to Wyatt.

"He was one of the lucky ones," Wyatt said softly into her ear. "Some of these men have to wait years to get a prosthetic. I've worked every angle I could to get these vets help, but I'm running out of prospects. And, well, I must say I'm getting tired of trying. I've been at this a long time."

"That's why you called me?"

"Yep." He removed his hat and wiped the sweat from his brow. Just talking about these things seemed to tire him out. That, and the lingering effects of the bullet wound.

"Well, then, we'd better get busy."

For the next two hours, she took turns interviewing the different vets and listening to their stories in gory detail. For some reason, they opened up with her. Maybe it was because she explained that her brother had been in the army, so she understood the aftermath of the pain they were going through and the consequences to the family.

At first, when her brother had returned, he had gone through the motions of preparing to marry his long-time fiancée, Julia. But it soon became apparent that the demons

following him home had come to roost. He had turned to
booze, sex, and video games as a way to numb the fears that
trailed him into his dreams, *when* he could sleep that is, which
was sporadic at best. His fiancée had tried--God knows she had
tried--but the affairs and the abuse, had proved too much. She
had left him, sad and broken, a shell of his former self. She
wondered if Wyatt had followed the same pattern, and if he
had found a way out of the cycle of anger, fear, and self-
loathing. If so, maybe his foundation could be a model for
recovering vets.

Foundation.

For the first time since Kate had heard the bad news about
the company, she felt truly excited. Of course this place should
become a nonprofit. The money could be funneled into the
many projects for these men, and women, too, now that
females were allowed in combat and suffered many of the same
difficulties as the men. Maybe even take it nationwide. But they
would need good men and women, strong men and women
who really cared about these young people who had served
their country.

Well, Wyatt might be tired but she wasn't. She had energy.
She could almost hear the ticking clock telling her time was
running out.

"This has been wonderful, Wyatt," she said upon his return
from a stint on the tractor. His face appeared ashen and his
eyes so tired that he looked as if he could fall asleep standing
up, but he seemed genuinely happy to be "back in the saddle,"
so to speak.

"I think it's time for both of us to get some rest," he said.
"So, any ideas?"

"I've got some calls to make and you should take some
down time, because I'm going to need you tomorrow. I'll call
Nora and see how quickly we can get someone over here for a
photoshoot. In the meantime, I'll work up an ad campaign
starting with that amazing log cabin. Then I want to put
together some human interest stories in most of the major
newspapers. We need coverage and we need it now."

"Wait," Wyatt said, rubbing his temples. "You're going so

fast you're giving me a headache."

"I have to move quickly," she said. "These men need us."

* * *

Later that evening, after Emajean and Wyatt had assured Kate numerous times that she needn't stay at a motel in town when they had plenty of space at the ranch, Kate walked the perimeter of the place, talking to Nora on her cell phone. As she hung up, she looked out over the wide expanse of meadow and at the Sawtooth Mountains that acted as backdrop. A swing hung in one of the great pin oaks. She sat on it, feeling the gentle creak as it bore her weight. The sun edged the mountains, rays of light shimmering through the oak leaves, appearing almost heavenly. It filled a hole in her just knowing that there was still beauty in the world.

She mulled over her conversation with Nora. She could have the photographer out by Friday and the print copy could be ready to go by Wednesday at the latest. In the meantime, Kate had work to do. She would stay up all night, if necessary.

What stuck with her, however, as she listened to the crickets chirping and the sound of frogs ribbiting in the cool grass around her was what Nora had said at the end of their conversation.

"Be careful," Nora had warned. "I mean about bringing too much media attention to these men."

"What do you mean?" Kate had asked, unable to fathom what her former boss's wife could be getting at.

"These young men are fragile. Media can be good, but it can also serve to exploit these men and women. They've already been through so much, Kate. Just be sure you do this for the right reasons and really *think* before you act. Every step forward is going to have a consequence, for either good or bad. Jack and I know because we've been through this so often over the years. You're still young, not jaded. Just be careful, okay?"

And now, swinging gently against the breeze and smelling the pungent odor of grassland at dusk, Kate was still pondering Nora's words. So it surprised her when she realized that Wyatt was standing beside her, waiting for her to notice him.

"May I sit?" he asked. "There's something I think you should know."

Fourteen

Wyatt sat down gingerly beside Kate. Even before he had called Ian Phelps Marketing, he had worried about his past coming to light. If Kate knew who she was really dealing with, would she be putting this much effort into helping him? Would she be here at all? That question had weighed heavily on him and he'd had trouble sleeping the last few nights because of it. He still didn't know how much he could or should tell her, but she needed to know at least some of it, because there could be a maelstrom coming if anyone dug too deeply into his past. In the end, he decided not to lie to her, but to tell a partial truth. Enough to help her decide whether she could stand the heat, if it came to that. And it *would* come to that, eventually. Secrets could never be kept secret forever. That much he knew.

"What did you want to tell me?" Kate twisted in her seat to get a better look at him, which only made him squirm.

"I think there's something you should know about me."

Why did it suddenly seem like the breeze had stopped blowing and the crickets had fallen silent in the field? For some reason, it now felt muggy and he mopped at his brow with his handkerchief.

"I got into some trouble a while back."

"Oh?"

He could see he had her undivided attention now. "Six months after I came home from Iraq I found my girlfriend livin' with another guy and I came undone." Somewhere in the distance a coyote howled. "He ended up in the hospital and I ended up in jail for eight months."

She whistled, but more than that, even in the moonlight he could see that he had scared her.

"Is the guy okay?"

Unable to face those eyes that seemed to read more in him than he was willing to offer, he peered out over the field, the grasses that shushed in the daytime now silent for the night.

"Yep. The two married and now they have a passel of kids."

"And you're okay with that?"

He stared down at his boots a while before answering. "At first, I wasn't. I had a devil of a time getting over it. But now that I've got some distance from it, I realize we were never right for each other, and if it hadn't ended then it would have ended later. Sometimes things happen for a reason, you know?"

It was her turn to stare at her very impractical pumps, for this neck of the woods. Despite everything, he smiled at how unprepared she was for ranch life. Who wore pumps on a ranch? He would need to take her into town tomorrow and buy her some proper clothes.

"So who *would* be the right person for you?"

Wyatt tugged at the collar of his shirt. He could swear the temperature had climbed a good twenty degrees despite the setting sun.

"Someone I can trust," he blurted out without thinking. "Someone who can look past the scars and the weather, and time, and..."

His voice trailed off. He'd said *way* more than he'd ever intended. Normally, he was a man of few words, but tonight he seemed to be running off at the mouth. And he hadn't even told her the half of it.

For some inexplicable reason, her eyes misted over and in a husky voice, she said, "I've got to go... work." Moments later, she was gone.

He sat in the dark for at least a half an hour taking in everything he had said. Maybe she had realized the mistake she'd made in coming. Her career was already nearly up in smoke. Perhaps this had been the final straw. His announcement had no doubt doomed any chance of her putting together a good marketing campaign. She had backed the wrong pony. At that moment, he heard Spot... no, *Spirit*, whinny.

"Okay, girl, I get the point," he said, jumping to his feet with slumped shoulders. He would get up early tomorrow and take her to a motel until she could book a flight home. Then he would accept the fact that he had done all he could and lost. He'd fought the good fight.

As he was turning to head back to the ranch house, he heard Spirit snort and give a disgusted stamp that he knew only too well. It was her version of a temper tantrum when things weren't going as she saw fit. He decided to stop in on the old girl and see what she wanted.

To Wyatt's surprise, when he entered the dusty barn, moonlight glowing through the opening to the hayloft, he saw that Spirit had somehow freed herself from the stall and was standing in the warm halo of light. She dipped her head as if to say they needed to talk and they needed to talk now. He walked over to her and gave her mane a thorough rubdown.

"So what did you need to talk to me about, girl?"

The horse whinnied and stamped again.

"You think I'm giving up too soon?"

The horse shook its head, and he could almost swear the old girl laughed, teeth glistening in the moonlight.

"Okay, girl. I'll keep trying, I promise. Kate or no Kate."

That settled, Spirit lay her head on his shoulder and made soft snuffling noises, happy at last. They stayed like that for several minutes. Then Wyatt led her to her stall.

"And stay in this time," he admonished playfully, giving her one last slap on the rear.

As he walked out of the barn and headed toward the house, he saw a light in Kate's window. From the silhouette of the oak tree, he looked up in time to see her outlined against the window pane in a lacy, cream-colored negligee. It had been a while since he had seen a woman in this state of undress and for a moment his heart stammered in his chest. Then he could almost swear she had turned and was looking directly at him, though he was sure he was well hidden beneath the canopy of the oak tree. She was probably just looking to see if he was still seated on the swing, haloed by the moonlight.

Well, if she was going to look, he was going to give her something to look at. Taking in a deep breath, he walked out from under the oak and peered up at the window. To his amusement, she scrambled to shut the curtains, but with the windows open the breeze merely picked up the curtains and blew them outward so that she was still visible.

Maybe Spirit was right. Maybe he shouldn't give up on the ranch. And maybe he shouldn't give up on Kate, either.

* * *

Yesterday had been such an emotional day for Kate that she struggled to get out of bed. The room was cool, but quickly warming, and the down comforter was soft and inviting, like the bed itself. She had stayed up way too late putting together ideas for her campaign and writing op-ed pieces and human interest stories for magazines and newspapers. She hadn't fallen asleep until nearly four in the morning, so it was a surprise to her when she looked at the old-fashioned alarm clock on the table and discovered it was only ten am. Six hours of sleep. She was one of those people that needed a minimum of eight to feel decent.

Groggy, she rubbed her eyes, then stretched. She had just jumped out of bed and was getting ready to take a shower when she heard a knock. Kate padded over to the door and opened it a crack. There stood Emajean, hands on hips, looking at Kate as though she were a slacker.

"Wyatt asked me to come get you. Just so you know, he was going to tell you to go home, but he changed his mind. He wants to take you into town for some new duds. You're going to need them if you're going to live in this neck of the woods." She looked pointedly at Kate's negligee.

Kate flushed and stepped away from the door so that only her head was visible. "I need a shower first."

Emajean lifted a wary brow. "We ate nearly three hours ago."

"I'll hurry." Hoping to dismiss Emajean without further ado, she shut the door.

But Emajean called through the door, "We'll be waiting. Don't take too long!"

"Hang on!" Kate yelled, opening the door before the

woman could get too far.

"Yes?"

"In the cabin, there's a photograph of stars swirling in the night sky. Do you know the one I'm talking about?"

"Sure. That's one of Ryan's."

"Ryan?"

"The boy who shot Wyatt, now hurry up!" she said in exasperation.

A half hour later, feeling as though she'd run a marathon and lost, Kate stood at the table trying to guzzle down enough of Emajean's stout coffee to get her through the day without falling asleep. Kate wanted to ask "what's the rush," but she knew it would be impolite, so she merely hurried, managing to wolf down a dry piece of toast to keep her going.

Ten minutes later, the Ranger was bumping along the dirt road headed toward town. When they arrived, the main street was already bustling with activity. It would do Kate good to spend a little time at the office and get caught up on everything that was going on. Plus, she wanted to be sure to have Gladys and Stanford look over her copy before submitting it to any and all major newspapers and magazines.

She laughed when she thought of the unlikely pair, Stanford with his GQ looks: tall, tanned, with brown hair that had been dyed at the ends. No man could be more handsome, which seemed a little unfair in her book. How many times had her friends lamented the fact that all good looking men were gay, a stereotype for sure. But this time, a valid one.

On the other hand, Gladys looked like a Brooklyn cop: chubby, personable, and a straight shooter all the way. The woman couldn't be more affable. Kate had adored her instantly. She was the real deal--what you see is what you get-- and with so many pretentious people clamoring for attention, it was as refreshing as Cody itself. Still, Kate couldn't get over the feeling that Gladys and Stanford looked like they'd been picked up from an alien universe and transported to Cody--small, beautiful Cody with its wide boardwalks and feel of the Old West. From the looks of the place, she kept expecting a gunslinger to exit the tavern and draw.

She'd been so lost in thought that she didn't realize they had pulled up in front of the Five and Dime until she heard Wyatt whistle under his breath and say "Incoming."

"Who is it?" Emajean started to say. Then her voice turned bitter as she said, "Oh."

Kate craned her neck to get a good look at the person of interest, which turned out to be a very well-heeled elderly gentleman, tall, in a Levi shirt and blue jeans, and decidedly handsome. Although she wasn't certain why, he seemed familiar. What had Emajean and Wyatt found so wrong with him?

"There's your fellow," Wyatt said to Kate, nodding at the man as they all gawked while he seemed to take no note of them.

"*My* fellow?"

"The one your boss asked to contact me... to let me know what was going on with the business and to advise me to stay put or else."

"Or else what?"

Wyatt turned and smiled at Kate, but it was a smile that harbored an undertone of menace that unnerved her.

"What are you going to do, Wyatt?" Emajean said, taking his arm and holding him there by sheer determination.

"I'm just gonna talk to the man," he said, eying Emajean's hand until she reluctantly dropped it to her side.

"Don't do anything stupid," she said, to which Kate inwardly agreed.

For a moment, Wyatt paused to look at them both, then he turned and let himself out of the truck. Kate rushed to stop him but couldn't get the truck door open on the first try. Before she could reach him, he had leapt like a cat and, within seconds, had maneuvered his way around to face the man so that the elderly gentleman had no choice but to halt.

"Hey, buddy, looks like we have some business to go over."

"Oh?" the man said, frowning. "Do I know you?"

"Name's Wyatt. Ring any bells?"

"Like Wyatt Earp?" he said with a chuckle. "That joke must get old."

"You have no idea," Wyatt countered.

"How did you know who I was?" the older man asked, reaching out to shake Wyatt's hand.

Wyatt merely looked at the man's hand until he finally dropped it.

Kate frowned, still perplexed by the man's seeming familiarity.

Suddenly, with a snap of her fingers, it came to her. He was the man Ian had hired to do his dirty work, to get the ball rolling by purchasing or renting these out-of-the-way places to maneuver people along. Kate had seen him only once. He and Ian had held a heated session behind closed doors. She had been eavesdropping. The entire staff had been trying to get the skivvy on what was happening, especially with all their jobs on the line. She'd wondered then what such a decent looking man like him was doing with someone like Ian. And she still wondered.

Kevin was it? No, Kaden Ewing. That wasn't quite right, either. Hmm. She had it! Karl D. Ewing III. She couldn't recall his title, but she knew from the scuttlebutt that this man was called in to either close businesses or to expand them.

"I looked you up online after the call," Wyatt said. "I wanted to know who was telling me how to run my business."

Mr. Ewing threw his hands up in protest and backed up a step. "Hey, I would never tell you how to run your business."

"Good!" Wyatt said with a sudden gleam in his eye as he nodded toward Kate and used his best Wyoming drawl. "Because I've decided to back this little filly." He winked at Kate and chuckled at her reaction.

The older man paused, hand to his mouth as though thinking, then said, "Fair enough. But if you change your mind and it doesn't work out--" He glanced over at Kate, his eyes now icy blue and aimed at her. "Well, you know how to get in touch with me." He handed Wyatt a business card to which Wyatt promptly deposited it into the trash.

"No thanks," he said. "I believe I've found my winning horse. C'mon, Kate, Emajean."

For the next hour, Emajean and Kate shopped while Wyatt

left to take care of some unknown business. Emajean kept steering Kate toward Wranglers and cowboy boots, and even the prerequisite checkered gingham shirt. Reluctantly, Kate acquiesced, but in the end was surprised and inwardly pleased at her new look. Her friend, Sara, would have laughed her out of the store. But on the other hand, with *her* romantic streak, she probably would have encouraged Kate. It was Palmer who would have cowed her for wearing such a "get-up." As if the very thought of him had telegraphed its way to him, the phone rang.

Palmer.

Emajean was busy with one of the clerks, haggling over the price of a blouse that had a missing button. Kate knew she couldn't avoid Palmer forever. She closed her eyes for a brief moment, then picked up the call.

"Kate, please don't hang up," he pleaded.

Kate turned her back to Emajean and drifted further into the clothing section so she wouldn't be overheard. "I won't."

Her heart beat wildly. Who was he with tonight? Was he all alone, missing her, or did he just feel guilty for leaving things the way they had?

"Kate, I know I've made some mistakes, but, well, I miss you. I mean, I was kind of used to having you here and now, after being alone for a while... Well, don't you think it's time to come home?"

For a moment, she couldn't speak. She felt as though a weight had fallen on her chest and she couldn't breathe. She didn't know how she felt. The wound of Sara's revelation was still too fresh, too raw. Everything she thought she knew about him had come into question. Now she just knew she needed time and space to figure things out, to try to fit the puzzle pieces of her life into some sort of meaning.

"I'm not ready," she said, feeling the tears well in her eyes.

"But I am," he countered, followed by a protracted silence that brought the rawness of her emotions to the surface.

Emajean had just finished haggling. Kate didn't want such a strong woman to see her cry, not here, not in the store, and especially not with Wyatt due to meet them any minute.

"I've got to go," Kate whispered into the phone.

"Wait, Kate, I love you. I mean it this time."

Kate felt a wave of nausea. *This time?* Had he been lying to her before when he told her he loved her? She didn't know. She wanted to believe that he had just made a mistake. Yet, nothing about her life made sense anymore, no matter how much she wanted it to.

"I'll call you later." She hung up and turned quickly, running straight into Wyatt's arms.

*   *   *

By the time Ian's lawyer arrived at the Carlton By The Bay, Ian was sweating. He ordered a martini from one of the waiters who wore a duck-tailed uniform and hovered. Normally, he would have appreciated the service, but today he wanted privacy and was kicking himself for having chosen this restaurant.

"There you are," Dave Jenkins said, shaking Ian's hand and then taking a seat across from him. Bald, with owlish glasses, Dave looked more like an accountant than a lawyer. Fortunately, he was good at what he did... until *this* fiasco. Oddly, he didn't seem the least bit flustered about what he had learned.

After the preliminary formalities, Dave buttered a crusty piece of sourdough bread and took a bite while the waiter delivered Ian's martini. He gulped down enough to relax him, then said, "How could this have happened, Dave?"

"I've looked over the contract you signed. I agree, we left a big hole. But who would have guessed they'd make an end run? We *both* dropped the ball on this one," he said, making sure Ian understood that he wasn't taking the fall.

Ian sagged in his chair. "They went after my big accounts."

"You were the one who asked me to remove the no compete clause."

"Because I thought I could go after their accounts, not the other way around!" Ian was shouting now, but quickly realized all eyes had turned on him so he leaned forward and whispered. "I thought buying up the rural accounts was just going to be a hobby for the old man. Who knew he would try to get his company back. One of my major clients was in such a frenzy, he's pulled all future accounts. He's even considering going with J & R Marketing."

Dave splayed his hands across the table. "Look, Ian, you've got to keep your cool. This is business. You hurled the first volley and now they're firing back. That's how it works."

If Dave weren't his father's decades long friend, Ian might have fired him on the spot, but Ian knew he was just being impetuous, taking it out on Dave when it was Ian's own fault for not reading from his father's playbook. He'd wanted to show him he was smart and talented, to get a pat on the back from the old man. Now he would come off looking like an idiot, and he had no one to blame but himself. He sagged into his seat, feeling like a deflated helium balloon.

"What now?"

The old man steepled his fingers. "For God sakes, Ian. You're in marketing. You market yourself. You go back and bring those accounts in any way you have to. Pull out the stops. Find out their interests and target those interests. Use blackmail, if you have to. Like your old man always said, you have to know more about your clients than they know about themselves. Once you have that, you can get whatever you want."

Ian was feeling two sheets to the wind by the time the steak and potatoes arrived but ordered another martini anyway. This would mean calling on the private detective he had used for the previous assignment. More money drained from the company while he sought to expand his burgeoning empire. He rubbed his temples, feeling as drained as his company.

Fifteen

As Wyatt stood in the middle of the Western clothing store, he tried to untangle himself from Kate, only to peer down and see that she had been crying. Fortunately, at that moment Emajean was busy showing off her purchases to a store clerk because he wanted to grab Kate up in his arms and hold her, tell her everything was going to be alright. It was the man in him wanting to protect.

He lifted her chin and said, "Everything okay?"

Although she nodded, she wouldn't look him in the eye and he could see that she was still troubled by her phone conversation.

"Too much shopping, I see," he said, smiling down at her, "but I have to say, you look mighty pretty in those new duds of yours."

He had learned years ago that throwing in a few antiquated words worked wonders at lifting spirits. It was like talking to a favored uncle *and* it had earned him a few brownie points with the women. But that was beside the point, because he never used it to manipulate people, just to brighten their day. The other thing he had learned about being a favored uncle is that you had to act like one. You had to have respect for the other person or a few words here or there only got you so far.

"What say we blow this joint?" He winked at Kate and, to his relief, she favored him with a watery smile. "Rocky Tops has the best curly fries in town and they make a mean rhubarb pie. What say we head on over and show the new girl around."

Bingo. A full-blown smile. He kissed the top of her head, a brave thing to do since he didn't know her all that well, but what he did know of her he was beginning to like. Motioning to Emajean to meet them at Rocky Tops, he then put a hand on Kate's shoulder and steered her toward the exit. As he did, he noticed Karl on the boardwalk across the street looking both ways in front of J & R Marketing. Afraid Kate might see the man enter her place of establishment, Wyatt planted himself between her and Karl. She had enough worries right now. She didn't need any more.

Still, he couldn't help but wonder what that rattlesnake was up to. The man might look good in that suit and tie of his, but Wyatt had learned long ago that you couldn't judge a snake by its skin. Even a harmless garter snake could cause serious damage if the bite got infected. He wasn't about to let that rattlesnake get anywhere close to himself... more importantly, Kate.

* * *

Still numb from her conversation with Palmer, Kate couldn't help but feel grateful that Wyatt had come to her aid. He had a way about him that calmed her instantly. As they headed down the boardwalk toward Rocky Tops, she wiped away the remaining tears and told him that the photograph she'd seen back at the ranch belonged to Ryan.

"Really?" he said, clearly surprised. "I didn't know the boy had that kind of talent. Let's hope he finds a use for it."

But Kate wasn't listening. Not for the first time, she wondered about her relationships with men. Did they all cheat? Was that just a part of their DNA like being born with blond hair and blue eyes? Or was it simply the insecure ones who had to prove their manhood? She wasn't sure. Sara had given Kate her "survival of the species" lecture, and yet she was the first one to encourage Kate to test her wings. But was it wrong to want to be in a committed relationship with a man who loved her? Who would *always* love her?

She was glad when they reached the big log cabin restaurant, the front entrance flanked by a carved bear standing on its hind legs with a trout in its mouth. Food would give her something to think about other than men. She had thought she understood them. Now she wasn't sure she ever would, she realized with a sigh. They were a complete and utter mystery.

As soon as she and Wyatt were seated and had menus in

their hands, Wyatt said, "So now that you have no job to return to, how long are you planning to stay?"

Although he appeared nonchalant, the gentle tapping of his fingers on the mahogany table revealed his interest in her answer.

"It depends on whether we can make a go of it locally. We don't have much time to get up and running. We have bills to pay." She made note that she would need to look at the books when she went to the office later.

"What happens if you can't get the business going quickly?"

"Small businesses don't have much time to succeed because they require a lot of capital in the beginning with very few returns. New business owners have to do much of the work themselves and put in long hours to survive." Just the thought of it ruined her appetite. What would she do if she couldn't get the new business going? She didn't want to think about it.

Wyatt paused, as though studying his menu. Finally, he looked over at her and said, "What if I could help get you going, and you help get me going?"

"How?" She put down her menu and waited as the waitress came to take their order.

"Let's just say I've known a lot of vets over my time and they look out for each other. Some of them have done very well for themselves. Some, not so good. Each has different demons to face. But I know they would use your services if I asked them. Provided you do a good job for them, of course."

"Of course!"

He smiled and held out his hand to her. She shook it. "Deal," he said.

"Deal."

At that moment, Emajean waltzed in, bags in tow that she stowed at her feet, letting loose a chuff of air from the exertion. Wyatt called a waitress over and Emajean quickly put in her order.

For the next hour as they ate and talked, Kate was on cloud nine. She couldn't wait to get to the office to look over the books and to call Nora to tell her about her recent good fortune, if what Wyatt promised panned out.

They finished up, and were walking out of the diner when Kate caught sight of a former vet with a cardboard sign. He had a three-day stubble and hands that were permanently grease stained and cracked, while his face appeared weathered. His brown eyes had the look of a man who'd been beaten down by life and had no faith in it anymore. It was hard to look at him and yet hard to look away. She didn't know how to fix what ailed him and other former vets. She just knew that someone who had fought for their country shouldn't be on a street corner begging for food or money.

Wyatt leaned over and handed the man a twenty, then nodded toward the door of the restaurant. "Go get something to eat," he said, shaking the man's hand. "And thank you for your service."

She glanced over at Wyatt. Everything about this man surprised her. Here he was, about to go out of business himself, and yet he had bought her clothes--someone he didn't even know--had taken her to lunch, and had given a vet money to eat.

"You have a big heart, Wyatt." He put a hand on her shoulder in thanks. "But one question. Why, when you're so close to foreclosure, are you helping other people when you may lose everything yourself?"

He chuckled and peered down at his hand-tooled boots. "Because that may be me out there someday. In fact, that *was* me for a short time after I returned from the Iraq war. We're all in this boat together, whether we like it or not. You have rich people looking down on poor people, but if they keep making everyone poor there's going to be fewer and fewer of the rich. People who are good with their hands put down people who use their brains, and yet we need brawn *and* brain to make up a society. We're lost without each other."

"Wow!" Kate said, surprised by his vehemence. She would have pondered it further, but just then, she peered down the boardwalk and saw Mr. Ewing coming from... *J & R Marketing*. What sent shivers down her spine was that he wore a cat and the canary grin as if he were about to burp feathers.

* * *

Kate excused herself while the others took care of business around town. If she planned to stay in Wyoming, she would need to purchase a car, but she would deal with one thing at a time. First, she needed to find out what Karl Ewing was doing snooping around her and Nora's new business, or at least it would be theirs. Soon. Her end of the paperwork wasn't yet finalized and it would be a week or more before she could do the final signing, making Nora and Jack majority shareholders, and her the minority shareholder. Until they had finished dividing up the two companies and had the paperwork signed on her end, as Nora had explained, "anything can happen." She picked up her pace, eager to discover what the man was after.

As soon as Kate entered the building both Stanford and Gladys surrounded her, both talking at once until she finally threw up her hands and said, "One at a time. What happened? I just saw Karl Ewing leave here. What did he want?"

They both started in again until Kate said, "Gladys, you first."

"They... they stole the accounts." Gladys wheezed as she spoke, then stopped to grab the inhaler on her desk.

"Who?"

Gladys let Stanford do the talking.

"The thing is," he said, looking even more natty than he had the day before in his tailored pants and vest, his hair gelled to perfection, "Karl removed our client list and won't tell us what's happening with it."

This made no sense. If the company was in the process of selling the business, why strip it? Surely, Ian would have to know that they would back out of the deal or take him to court at the very least.

"Show me exactly what he took," she said, forcing herself to remain calm.

The pair walked her over to the computer on Gladys's desk. Kate stood behind Gladys as she brought up the accounts page. One look at the page, and Kate had her answer. She stood in stunned silence. He had completely wiped out the accounts. Only one name remained… Wyatt Madison.

She paused for a moment to pull herself together. "Okay? Anything else?"

"The work you did the other night on Mr. Madison's account?"

Kate had a sinking feeling. She pulled up a chair and sat down before Gladys could give her any more bad news.

"He said you weren't authorized to work on the account until the dissolution was finalized so he put a hold on any marketing you've done so far on Mr. Madison's account."

Kate threw her head back and sighed. How on earth could she explain this to Wyatt… the same man who had only moments ago promised to help her and her agency? Now she would have to tell him that everything she had done was for nothing. There would be no saving the ranch. She rubbed her eyes feeling suddenly tired.

"I'm afraid to ask, but I need to see the books."

The pair shared a look that made Kate's stomach churn. It was clear now that she would be starting this business from scratch, without money, without accounts or even the ability to do the work needed unless they were new accounts that she brought in herself.

"Well, it is what it is," she said, opening the books. For the next half hour, she went over what was left of the money. They were starting in the hole. The only thing that they had walked away with was the rental properties, the employees, and the office equipment. For what Nora had paid for the business, it would have made more sense to hire all new employees and start a completely new business.

At the realization, Kate's eyes glistened. This hadn't been a sound business decision. Nora had bought the company for *them*. For Jack's employees. To save their careers… and for Jack himself. But they would have nothing if Nora and Kate couldn't pull their fledgling company back from the brink. They all stood to lose if they didn't stand together.

"What should we do?" Stanford asked, his dark brows furrowed.

"Wait here," Kate said, clamoring to her feet. "I need to talk to someone. In the meantime, I want you to cold call every business you can think of and sell your ever-loving hearts out, okay?"

It must have been the pep talk they needed, because though they both looked wary, they also appeared determined, and they would need a lot of that in the upcoming weeks and months.

In the meantime, she found Wyatt at the local barbers getting a haircut. He took one look at her face, removed the barber's cape and paid the barber. He walked her down to a small outdoor courtyard, a bronze horse and rider in the center of the square, and motioned her to a bench.

"Emajean's grocery shopping," he said to her questioning look. "So tell me, what happened."

"Karl wiped us out. Our accounts. He even stopped work on your account until the dissolution is finalized, so I can't do anything for you." She had a hard time looking him in the eye.

He paused, as though thinking. Then with a determined expression that bordered on devilish, he said, "The hell you can't. Tell you what, nothing's to say we can't make a trade, yes?"

Kate cocked her head. "What sort of trade?"

A glint in his eye revealed part anger, part mischievousness. "I'll find you a whole mess of clients, and you teach me how to do my own promotion. Nothin' says I can't do it myself, right? I might not be able to bring your company money until the dissolution is finalized, but they can't stop me from helping you and helping myself, *with* a little help from a friend." He winked at her.

How is it that he could always set things right no matter how bad they seemed?

"Thank you," Kate said, feeling as if a weight had been lifted from her shoulders.

"Now you hang tight, and I'll go find Emajean. I'll be right back."

After Wyatt left, Kate sat there pondering all that had happened today and wondering what tomorrow would bring.

She didn't think her heart could take any more surprises. As she sat there, she noticed a Hasidic Jew in a dark, flat brimmed hat with long curly locks walk past. His face wore years of oppression like a cloak.

Odd.

As he moved out of her line of vision a woman came into view wearing an old RAF uniform. Her hair was also curled, though Kate was certain a curling iron was involved in that. And she wore a bright shade of lipstick that made her appear as hopeful as the Hasidic Jew had appeared hopeless.

Kate blinked to be sure she hadn't dreamt it. She was beginning to wonder what was in her breakfast that morning when she saw an old black man limp along, his back bent, his eyes hooded. He wore overalls and had massive hands that appeared arthritic, years of grime beneath the fingernails. As he passed her, he winked. For just a split second, she had caught a glint of amusement in those eyes before they hooded over again and he was gone. She was sure they all had stories to tell. Stories every bit as amazing as each of the vets she had interviewed. And isn't that really what marketing was? Telling a story that attracted the consumer? So why couldn't her new company market for a cause. Their company motto could be: *change stories, change lives.* If they could write a new story for people whose lives had been difficult, maybe they could change the outcome for those people.

A sudden breeze rushed in, sweeping away leaves and causing her hair to fly, her shirt flapping like a sheet in the wind. Just as quickly as the wind had come up, it died down. As a child on her grandmother's farm, the wind would whip up dust devils and her grandma would say, "That's the spirits of our ancestors trying to tell us something, darlin'. When you hear them calling, you heed their message."

Chilly fingers reached up Kate's spine and she shivered because she'd heard the message, and she would heed the call.

Sixteen

Wyatt sat out on the porch, cell phone in hand, listening to the soft rhythm of the cicadas in the big oak tree out front. He loved the smell of oak in the hot afternoon sun. It gave off a nutty aroma of acorns that reminded him of his childhood. Back then he had climbed the oak, played cowboys and Indians. Only now the Indians were his friends along with the cowboys. He chuckled. Funny how perceptions changed with age and perspective.

He looked again at the old oak, where he and Kate had sat swinging the other night and talking. When he'd asked her if she had a boyfriend, she had paused before answering. Body language spoke volumes, and yet he found her the most trustworthy, honest person he had ever met. That, more than anything, was what he needed after everything he had been through.

For the next half hour, Wyatt sat thinking about Kate and his life on the ranch until finally, he said, "Enough procrastinating." He had promised to help Kate with her client list and he meant to do just that.

Still, Kate had been acting strange ever since she had returned from their afternoon outing. She had seemed fine on the bench after they'd had their talk. Maybe she was still worried about the company and the finances. He could understand the stress that caused, seeing how his own finances were reaching the critical point. He would need to find new money to keep the ranch up and running. The food bill alone for the vets was enormous, even though he bought in bulk and Emajean could stretch a penny as far as the eye could see.

Time to make a few phone calls.

His first call went to a fellow military officer he'd met while overseas who now owned a franchise out west. That netted him zero. He left a voice message on his voicemail. Next, he called a buddy who had gone on to own a janitorial supply business out in Billings. He'd done pretty well for himself. After a brief talk with his wife, she assured Wyatt that it would be days before his old friend could get back to him as he was away on business. Wyatt dreaded the third call, but hit pay dirt when Joe Evans answered in a deep baritone.

"Well, I don't need any marketing at the moment, but why don't I add your friend's name to the vet website I've been chatting on, see if we can drum up some business for her."

Joe reminded Wyatt of James Earl Jones with his barrel chest and throaty laugh. He had liked Joe the instant he'd met him. He knew simply putting a name on a website was a longshot, but it was worth a try.

"Hey, you still got that ranch for vets?"

"Sure do," Wyatt said, cringing at the thought that he might have to answer more questions about it.

"How's it going? You still taking care of our boys?"

"Trying," he said, hoping to leave it at that.

"You got sponsors?"

The dreaded question. "Nope, not at the moment."

"So how are you funding it?" the vet asked, going straight to the nitty gritty.

"Well, now," Wyatt hemmed and hawed, "I've been paying for it out of pocket."

Joe followed up with a long pause that made Wyatt squirm at the prospect of being grilled by his former sergeant.

"Well, can't do that for long," Joe said, his voice suddenly stern.

"Got that right," Wyatt said, truthfully.

"Let me see what I can do." Joe sounded either tired or simply more serious, Wyatt couldn't quite decide. Joe gave Wyatt the link for the DAV website for wounded warriors and promised to touch base later in the week.

For the next hour and a half, Wyatt plowed through one name after another. He felt defeated by the time he'd hung up on his last call with little to show for his effort. Time to give Kate the "good" news. He'd received vague promises at best, at worst, downright rejections. At least he could say he'd given it a thorough go round. He felt stiff by the time he rose to go talk to her.

Just then, Emajean opened the screen door and poked her head out. "I'm going to run the food down to the men. You want to come have dinner with 'em?"

"Where's Kate?"

She fingered the white linen kitchen towel that she'd embroidered with little yellow daisies. "Out back. She's been on the phone. The last I saw, she was taking a walk. Headed toward the cabin. Want to pick her up on the way?"

"Sure."

For the next ten minutes, they brought out casseroles, bread and butter, bowls of watermelon and pickled onions. A salad topped it all off, followed by a blueberry crisp that made Wyatt's mouth water. After he'd secured the food in the back of his Ranger, they set off for the cabin. They'd driven nearly ten minutes before they spotted Kate within sight of the cabin. Next to the gargantuan log structure, she looked small, tiny even. And the forlorn expression on her face made it clear that she'd had about as much success as he had, which was as close to nil as possible. He pulled up beside her, a cloud of dust rising up after him.

"Hop in," he said, taking in the white dress she had changed into which showed her curves and the tan she had developed since being here.

She ran around to the passenger side of the truck and squeezed in next to Emajean. Damn, she smelled good. Sort of a lemon scent mixed with... what? Gardenia, maybe, but he was no expert. Whatever it was, it made him forget all about the food in the back or the miserable failures of the day.

"You headed to the cabin?" he asked, putting his truck into gear.

"I was just out walking." When she frowned, she bit her lip. Funny how he hadn't noticed the few freckles on her nose until now.

"Thinking?"

She nodded, but clearly didn't want to say more. The silver bracelets on her wrist clinked together. For some reason it made her seem more feminine, more desirable. He switched gears again, happy to keep busy thinking of something besides her seated on the other side of Emajean.

As if suddenly realizing that she had been excluded from the conversation, Emajean cleared her throat and cocked one eyebrow. Wyatt chuckled. "Okay, teacher, we'll behave."

This time Kate laughed, her face flushing a deep burgundy. Henry was already waiting for them at the cabin as they pulled up and got out of the truck. The sheepdog ran up to greet them, barking.

"Traitor," Wyatt said. "Ever since the men moved in, Henry comes home for food and that's about all."

"It's because they feed him scraps," said Emajean, pragmatically.

"Better 'n dog food."

Ryan stood on the porch next to Les, looking for all the world as though he'd lost his best friend. Wyatt had avoided him since the shooting. He knew it had been an accident, but he hadn't quite forgiven Ryan either.

"Hey, there, how ya holdin' up?" Wyatt asked Ryan as he clambered up the steps onto the porch.

Ryan shrugged.

"Ryan, here, is going through a rough patch, but he'll be okay. He's got us," Les said, toying with the rim of his black Stetson.

"I just can't stop thinking about my mom," Ryan said. "I'm worried about her, but that's no excuse for what happened the other day." He stared down at his boots, then to Wyatt's surprise, he squared his shoulders, looked straight in Wyatt's eyes and said, "It will never happen again, I swear."

Wyatt knelt down and petted the dog while peering up at the young man. "We'll get you through this. I promise. I can't say it's not going to hurt like hell, but we'll keep you so busy you won't know what to do with yourself. Pretty soon, you're going to meet other people who will appreciate you, find a girl maybe, and you're going to be a better man because you know what it's like to grow up without much parental influence. We'll teach you coping skills, okay?"

Ryan nodded reluctantly, his brown eyes trusting despite

everything he had been through. That was a good sign. It's when they trusted no one that he knew he'd be fighting an uphill battle. Toby was the one he worried about most. He had been standing next to the stall when the gun went off the day that Kate had first arrived. That boy had disaster written all over him. If they couldn't get through to him soon, Wyatt worried he might be a lost cause.

"And you know the first way to learn to cope?"

Ryan shrugged.

"You learn to have fun. You forget to have fun when you're in the military--fun that doesn't involve drinking and hookers--but believe me, neither one of those is going to make you happy for long. And over time, they'll make you damn miserable, so let's learn how to have fun."

"Is that an order?" Emajean asked playfully.

"Copy that," said Wyatt, slipping into his military lingo like a second skin.

"You," he said, pointing at Emajean and duly noting her scowl that warned him to step lightly, "get us some paper plates. We're going to have us a picnic." He turned to Les. "Could you round up a couple of the men and get us all some fishing gear?"

Les stood. Despite his long nose and hair graying at the temples, he had the rugged look of a woodsman. "Sure can. I'll get some firewood, too, in case we stay late." He winked at Kate, who blushed a deep shade of crimson.

"Good." The men must have heard the commotion because, one by one they began to file out onto the porch, excitement gathering as each in turn heard the plan for this evening.

Wyatt frowned. "Where's Toby?"

Les leaned in, his voice low. "Took off. Yesterday. The boy has been trouble... starting fights. We think he may be stealing, too, but we have no proof."

"Do you think we should warn the sheriff?"

"I don't know. He was gunning for bear the way he looked when he left," Les said, wearing a blue plaid shirt with abalone buttons.

Wyatt slapped his leg so hard with his hat, it blew off a showering of dust. He thought about going after the boy, but Les took his arm and held him back. "Toby has to work off some steam. Sometimes you just have to wait until they're ready to come back. You can't save them all."

And that was the hell of it. Wyatt wanted to save every last one, the way he hadn't been able to save Carson. Wyatt wasn't like some of the other men who were inured to tragedy and just figured it was a dog-eat-dog world where only the strongest survived. Sometimes the weakest were the ones to actually change the world, make it better. Take Stephen Hawking or Beethoven. Van Gogh. Or even Roosevelt. Any one of them could have been written off. What would have happened if society hadn't protected those gifted individuals? If those men had only been measured by their brawn?

No, each vet had potential and he wanted them to have the chance to fulfill that potential. He would fight to his dying breath to see that these young men--and that's what they were, really--were given a fair shake.

"I won't give up on Toby, Les. I won't."

"Fair enough." Les dropped his head but not his gaze.

"Anyway, I know you're right. Give him time to run off some steam. Let the boys have fun tonight, then we can go looking for him tomorrow."

* * *

Twenty minutes later, they had the bus packed that Les used to haul the vets around in, with Emajean driving and the boys whooping and hollering in the back.

"I guess it's you and me," he told Kate, who had been regarding him carefully through the entire exchange. The Sheltie gave a bark. "And you, too, Henry."

As they drove down the narrow, rutted road headed for the creek, Wyatt turned to Kate. "Penny for your thoughts," he said, once again noticing how pretty she looked in the late afternoon sun.

"I was just thinking you're a very remarkable man, Wyatt."

He squeezed her hand in thanks. He could have sworn she held his hand a little longer than necessary. It put a smile on his face that wouldn't quit, even when he pulled up next to the bus only to discover that some of the men had gone in for a dip before dinner. A skinny dip!

Seventeen

As the vets sat around the fire, Kate couldn't help but feel connected, maybe for the first time in her life. She relished the taste of the casserole along with the rainbow trout a few of the men had caught, the smell of burning embers and roasting ears scenting the air. Why is it that the outdoors could make her feel alive and part of a bigger community when living among a million people or more had made her feel lonely?

She shivered as the chill night air framed the first stars of the evening. No one had wanted to eat right away. They were having too much fun chasing each other and splashing in the water, swimming or fishing, although the ones fishing had to move downriver to catch any fish with all the commotion taking place.

"Cold?" Wyatt said, taking a seat next to Kate, a plate of warm food in his hand.

"A little bit. I didn't think I'd be gone long when I went for a walk, so I didn't think to bring a jacket."

She watched with a touch of humor as Wyatt scanned his body to see if there were anything he could offer her. "All I have is my arms, if you don't think that's too forward."

"Uh... no," she said, nearly choking on her food. He leaned in and wrapped an arm around her. To her chagrin, he wore the scent of the campfire like cologne. She would take the smell of a good wood fire any day over cologne.

She squeezed in tighter, grateful for the warmth he offered, comforted by the feel of a man next to her. Before, she had taken the simple act of being touched for granted. Now, having lost it, she basked in the heat of Wyatt's embrace and never wanted it to end. But like all good things, the night closed in and the stars twinkled above, reminding her that this too, would come to a close and she would once again sleep alone in the upstairs room, knowing he was in a room nearby, equally alone.

Fortunately, Les picked up a guitar and began playing campfire songs. Soon most everyone joined in. Wyatt's languorous voice washed over her like a rolling brook, its tenor carrying her to a far-off place where the ills of the world lay dormant, unheeded. They carried her to the land of dreams where night jasmine perfumed the air and the lulling song chased away all of her cares. Soon, Wyatt and Kate were dancing, encircled by the men who formed a ring around them, each swaying and singing.

She awoke to Wyatt tenderly shaking her.

"Katy, Katy," he whispered gently. "It's time to go."

It took a moment to get her bearings. She lifted her head off his shoulder, and flushed with embarrassment when she realized that she had fallen asleep against him and their dance merely a dream.

For the next few minutes, he helped her pack up her things and then they drove off in the truck, picking up Emajean back at the bunkhouse once she had the bus stowed and the men safely in the cabin. As they prepared to leave, a warm light glowed from within the cabin, leaving Kate feeling nostalgic and wishing that tonight would never come to an end.

Once they were back at the farmhouse, Emajean excused herself and left Kate and Wyatt all alone in the truck.

"Thanks for coming with me and the men tonight," Wyatt said, turning in his seat to face her.

Kate's breathing grew shallow and her heart fluttered in her chest. It had been so long since she'd... since she'd what? Been in a new relationship? But she was getting ahead of herself. It had been one night and one night only. He hadn't even kissed her.

As if reading her thoughts, Wyatt leaned in and gently pressed his lips to hers. His breath smelled minted and... and what? She could describe his smell as nothing short of intoxicating. Before she knew it, they were in a heated embrace that made her forget all about her job, about her life, about Palmer.

Palmer.

She pulled away. How could she have forgotten him so

quickly? Sure, they had separated. Sure, he had been unfaithful, but she had promised to take this time away to think, to come to a decision about their relationship. She breathed a deep sigh.

"I think maybe we're moving too fast," she said, gasping for air.

Wyatt's expression, which moments ago had been tender and caring, hardened and he looked down at their joined hands. He rubbed a thumb across the back of her hand and swallowed down the lump in his throat she had no doubt caused.

"I'm grateful," she said, hoping to ease the tension... to help him understand it was she, not he, who was at fault here. "Truly. You're a wonderful man."

"But..." He peered directly into her eyes, preventing her from looking away, from absolving her of the guilt she felt. She owed Palmer nothing. She knew that, and yet she had never been the unfaithful type. That was the one thing about her. She was loyal. Loneliness might have made her do stupid things, but she had never, and would never be unfaithful. That was the difference between Palmer and her.

"But, I need time," she said at last. "My life right now is... well, it's complicated."

"Complicated," he repeated, as if that might explain what had happened between them.

"Please understand." At that moment, she wished she could take back everything she had just said and dive into his arms, forget about her past, about her unending loneliness, about all the worries that seemed to shadow her wherever she went. She wished she could take all the mean people in the world and just throw them into the ocean so that she could enjoy her life and the people in it. And she had a strong feeling that Wyatt was one of those people she wanted in her life, if she would let him. But she had been hurt once too often, and she was afraid to let go, to give love a second chance. To risk being hurt again. The pain was too deep, too impenetrable. She didn't know if she could survive another wound like the last one.

"I understand," he said. He kissed her gently on the nose.

"Goodnight, Katy."

She hardly remembered getting out of the truck, entering the house, and climbing the stairs to her temporary quarters. As if of their own accord, her feet moved toward the window where she stood watching him from above. For the longest time he stood looking out over his land, gazing up at the moon and appearing for all the world like a forlorn puppy. It took every bit of willpower she possessed not to run downstairs and launch herself into his arms, to beg his forgiveness and ask him to give her a second chance, but she couldn't do it. Her pride wouldn't allow it.

* * *

Wyatt listened to the crickets playing their sorrowful tune in the meadow beyond. He had always loved the sounds of a ranch at night, the distant howls of the coyote under a harvest moon, the rustling of nightlife amongst the bushes. He especially loved the smells of hay and livestock. He had never felt lonely out here in the dark. Until tonight.

He couldn't say why, but to have tasted love, if only briefly, reminded him of all that he was missing in his life. Without it, he could imagine never needing it. But now that he'd felt Kate's lips, tasted her sweet scent, he knew he had been fooling himself. No man is an island. Emajean had been great company, and he would be forever grateful for it, but it wasn't the same as having a woman beside him, to talk to at night, to hold in his arms and to feel comforted when he'd had a bad day. Even the playful banter made the burdens of his life feel less heavy.

Feeling unsettled and not ready to go in just yet, he wandered over to the barn and found Spirit in her stall, munching on stalks of hay.

"Hey, girl," he said, patting her mane. "I've got problems, wanna hear them?"

The horse nodded her head and he laughed.

"Well, that makes one of you. See, I got girl troubles," he said. "I like a special filly, but she doesn't seem to like me all that much. Got any answers?"

"Yes."

He spun around in time to see Kate framed in the doorway, her silhouette dark against the moonlight. "I thought you--"

"I tried to leave things the way they were, but I can't. I--"

Before she could finish, he'd sprinted the distance between them and had wrapped her in his arms, twirling her around.

"Maybe Spirit does have special powers," he said, looking down at her eyes with twinkled copper flecks that reflected the moonlight. "She brought you to me."

Then he soundly kissed her and felt the world slide away in a swirl of emotions that he'd tucked away for a very long time.

* * *

How had she let her emotions get the better of her? Kate wondered as she dressed to face the morning... and Wyatt. She still felt the kiss fresh on her lips and remembered the taste of him from the night before. The way he held her in his arms and made her feel like she mattered. She closed her eyes, gathering her thoughts before she went downstairs to face him. To tell him she hadn't meant for any of it to happen. To remind him why she had come and that they needed to keep a professional distance while they were working together. Later she might think about a relationship, but right now she needed to focus on getting her life and her career in order. As long as she was in Wyatt's arms, all reason went out the window. Resolute, she wrapped herself tightly in the knowledge that though it might sting when she told him, a pinprick at the first stages of a relationship was far easier to bear than an all-out gaping wound later on. And she knew more than she had ever wanted to know about that.

Just then she heard a chirp on her cell phone and saw that she had a text from the office with the added handle "urgent." She quickly made the call.

"Go to GoFundMe," said Gladys in short gasps.

"But that account was closed."

"I know," said Gladys, "but there's a new account. It's for

the ranch. But that's not all."

Feeling hot, suddenly, Kate plopped down onto the chenille bedspread with its pink chenille roses. Fortunately, a breeze blew through the lace curtain, reviving her somewhat. The entire room reminded her of her grandmother's house. A time when life felt safe, secure. Or had it ever? Maybe she was just fooling herself, wishing for a time that never existed.

"I hope you're seated."

"I am."

"Take a look at the GoFundMe account."

Gladys gave her the information needed to upload the website. Kate watched the page open and read the numbers. Goosebumps ran the length of her arms. She jumped to her feet and nearly dropped the phone in the process. "How?"

"Friends of Wyatt's. Vets. Lots of vets. They contributed to the GoFundMe account to help keep his ranch afloat for a while." Gladys let loose a deep throaty laugh followed by wheezing and gasping.

"Go get your inhaler."

"I will," Gladys said, "but Kate?"

"Yeah?"

"I think we still need to be real careful until the ink has dried on the contract with Ian. I don't trust the man."

Kate agreed wholeheartedly. "I need to tell Wyatt."

"Just be careful who he tells, okay? Let's keep this under our hats for now."

"No problem." Kate said goodbye then hung up the phone and gathered her laptop to go find Wyatt.

For some reason, her excitement waned the minute she'd started out the door. One thing that she had learned in business is that nothing could ever remain secret for long. Someone would always let something slip. And then they could be right back where they had started. Or worse.

Eighteen

By the time Kate entered the big farmhouse kitchen, with its butcher block island, copper pans and ladles swinging from the fixture above, breakfast was over. Once again, she'd been left a cold plate to warm in the microwave. This time it was hash browns with red peppers and green onions, greasy fried eggs, and real bacon, the kind she would have never eaten in Manhattan. She had always maintained a simple diet of whole grains, a boiled egg at best, and a piece of fruit, usually a banana. It was quick, easy, and light on calories, which suited her perfectly.

"Where's Wyatt?" she asked.

Emajean wiped her hands on her red-and-white apron, then pointed out the window above the porcelain farmhouse sink.

Kate saw that he was riding a tractor "in the back forty" as Emajean called it.

"The yard gets a little overgrown this time of year."

Wyatt was churning up dust as he drove around a clothesline lined with clothing and sheets, secured with wooden pins. At the base, sat a pair of old boots filled with hens and chickens, long stems with little pink flowers draping over the sides of the boots.

Emajean eyed Kate's blue laptop. "Got something for him?"

Kate nodded.

"Well, even good news can wait until after you've eaten."

Kate tried to protest, but Emajean would have none of it.

"Sit. You're making me nervous, fussing about. I'll warm your plate."

Kate knew it would do no good to argue with the woman. It was clear that she was used to getting her way and had held the alpha position around here for years. No girl from Manhattan would stand a chance. So Kate did the only thing she could. She sat and ate, all the while looking at her watch and gulping down the food as fast as possible.

Finally, she stood just in time to hear the mower turn off.

"See?" Emajean said, gathering Kate's plate and rinsing it in the sink before she had a chance to offer to do it, a tactical ploy no doubt. As if to say this is *my* kitchen.

"Thanks," Kate called over her shoulder as she rushed to get going. From her position at the door, she could see Emajean shaking her head as if to say *city girl.*

By the time she reached the backyard, Wyatt had moved on to a spot behind the barn and was mowing around a huge oak tree. She raised a hand to get his attention. He idled the mower but instead of shutting it down, he waved her over. Hurriedly, she set her laptop onto the picnic table out back before joining him.

"You want me... on the tractor?"

He moved forward to give her room on the back. She shrugged, then climbed aboard.

Within moments they were whirring around on the tractor, mowing the lawn, both of Kate's hands wrapped tightly around Wyatt's waist. She moaned inwardly. This was not what she had planned. Being this close, feeling the warmth of his back, the lingering wood scent of him from the night before still fresh, only made it that much harder to say what she must.

For the next fifteen minutes, they looped back and forth, laughing as they took bumps faster than they should. By the time he stopped the motor and hopped off, lifting her to the ground, Kate felt dizzy, and deliriously happy. When had she had so much fun? Palmer had liked the Manhattan nightlife, the drinking, the crowds, sweaty bodies rubbing up against each other under the neon lights of the clubs. Clubbing had never been her thing. She'd always come away feeling slightly dirty and exhausted. Empty. Everything had felt fake: fake lights, fake people dressed to impress, but most of all fake happiness. It had all been smoke and mirrors to hide the loneliness of city life, or at least it seemed that way to her. She would take a campfire and a chance to mow the lawn any day over clubbing.

"So, what's up, pretty lady?" Wyatt said, beaming down at her, sweat glistening off his brow.

"Can we find somewhere to sit?"

He motioned to the picnic table at the back of the house. He took her hand and led her over to it. This was *definitely* not going as planned, and yet she was reluctant to end it.

Once seated, she opened the laptop and said, "I have something to show you."

"Oh?" He cocked his head as though unsure whether to expect good news or bad.

She typed in "GoFundMe," then typed in Wyatt's name.

"What's this?" he asked as she brought up the account in his name.

"Remember that sergeant you spoke to the other day?"

"Yeah?" he said, clearly confused.

"Well, he didn't just feed you a line when he told you he would help; he put out an APB to all his friends and the vets came through for you." She pointed the laptop his way. "This won't keep you going for the long haul, but it will keep you going another couple of months. Enough to give you some breathing room until we can find a more permanent solution."

Wyatt jumped to his feet and let out a whoop. Then he pulled her up and brought her around so that she was in his arms in a flash. He twirled her around, just as he had the night before and planted a kiss firmly and squarely on her lips.

She had no time to react other than to allow herself to be swept up in his embrace. When she finally came up for air, she saw the twinkle in his eye and couldn't bring herself to say all the things she had planned. Instead, she decided to tell him about the amazing thing his friend had done for her.

"*And* he put out an APB for J & R Marketing, too. We're getting calls from all over the country. In fact, I need to spend the day at the office. But I'm going to need a vehicle, and it's time I stop sponging off of you and buy my own car."

He raised a brow. "Truck."

"Car."

"I hate to break it to you, but this here's truck country. It snows. We haul things. That's just the way it is," he said, matter-of-factly. "It's a law, handed down by the almighty himself." He winked, followed by a big, toothy grin.

She couldn't tell if he was joking. "We'll see."

"I'll take you into town, but give me a half hour to check on the guys and then I'll meet you back here on the porch, deal?"

"Deal."

Yet, as he walked away, his wide shoulders bearing the weight of the world, she couldn't help but wonder if she might be adding more to that weight by not calling things off before she and Wyatt went too far. She couldn't risk her heart again. It had been damaged almost beyond repair. The next time she might not be so lucky.

*   *   *

Wyatt put the tractor away, then checked his phone before he headed to the cabin. A cryptic message from Les had him scratching his head. All it said was, "He's back." He had a feeling he knew who, and he wasn't sure whether to be worried or happy. Toby. A dark haired, swarthy young man with hairline scars. Horrible home life. Father was a woodman. Toby had worshipped his father, but his father was a tough taskmaster. His mother had died after a long bout with cancer. Toby had never adjusted, not with his homelife, not here. He was one of those wild cards. You never knew what he would do. There was an edge to him that wasn't like the other boys. Some people you could reform. Most of the boys would go on to lead good lives, to get married and raise families and, with any luck, to be happy again. If Wyatt could have even a small hand in that, he would feel good about his life. Feel like his life had meaning.

He switched on the engine and circled the driveway to the dirt road out back. He waved to Kate as he passed. Although she wasn't beautiful in the classical sense, she had a girl-next-door quality that endeared him to her. Beauty he could have any day of the week. Girls threw themselves at him, thinking he was the complete package, property and all. But beauty went so far. That kind of girl didn't stay with you when things got bad.

Oh, they might lift you up for a bit, but as soon as the next guy noticed their looks they were already headed for the door. He wanted a woman with substance. Someone who wasn't a fly-by-night. Someone like Kate.

Damn, he hadn't wanted to think about her or to care too much. She lived a big life, and he wanted simple. The simpler the better. Eggs and bacon in the morning along with a fresh pot of coffee. A late evening ride on Spirit and his horse, Brambles, a buckskin Mustang. Riding her was like riding a Ferrari. She was sleek, fast, and quick witted. Her only flaw was that she could be high strung, but he'd never been put off by high strung, strong women. Kate was proof of that.

Kate.

The heat of the noonday sun was starting to heat up the cabin of his truck and he swiped at his brow. The news she'd given him had made his day. Now, he had a couple of months to breathe while they put together a marketing campaign, which is why he'd wanted to go see the men in the first place, or rather should he say one kid in particular. Ryan had one hell of a knack for photography. If anyone could find the right shots for the photoshoot, he could. And maybe it would get the boy's mind off his homelife long enough for him to form more healthy relationships with someone who could appreciate him and his abilities.

Wyatt rounded the final bend and pulled up in front of the cabin. It never failed to impress him when he drove up to the large log structure. The men had done an amazing job. Whenever he'd told anyone about the project, he'd received questioning looks due to its size and its all-out beauty. Little did they know that most of the wood was either donated or wood that he and his fellow vets had cleared and had debarked themselves. The furniture was made of either repurposed throwaways or log furniture they had made from scratch. Then Emajean had slapped some paint on garage sale finds and voila! They had a genuine decor. Even the chair and loveseat on the porch were made from grapevine they'd salvaged from the garden. He had wanted something the men could be proud of, and it was easy to see by the way they took care of the place that they *were* proud.

Part of Les's training of the boys was to teach them how to clean, how to pick up after themselves, how to take pride in everything around them. Without that sense of pride in self, they could never make good husbands or fathers. Which means they could never make good community members, which in turn reflected on society and how it was molded. That was the thing he had liked about the CCC's. The government had fed young boys, housed them, and taught them pride in what they'd created. Roosevelt had given the young men hope. Made them believe in a better future. Without that, the country might have gone down the tubes.

Wyatt tucked away his musings, took his truck out of gear and got out. Henry ran up, tail wagging to greet him. He had thought about getting another dog, since this one was obviously happier here, but then again who wouldn't be?

"How's it going there, ole Henry? They feedin' you well?" he said, bending down and scratching his ears.

Just then, Toby walked out like an old-time gunslinger, his boots clicking on the wooden porch and his dark brown eyes shooting bullets. One thing Wyatt had learned early on was to never let your opponent get in a power position. It gave them an advantage. Wyatt stood and held out a hand to try to diffuse the situation. For a long moment, Toby just looked at it, then reluctantly shook hands.

"So," Wyatt said, scuffling his feet against the wood and purposely looking away from Toby so that the former vet wouldn't interpret eye-to-eye contact as a potential threat. That was another tool he'd learned for his arsenal when dealing with vets. "Are you here to stay, or just passing through?"

"It depends."

"On what?" Wyatt hazarded a glance at Toby whose eyes were steely and cold, menacing even. *Uh-oh.* The hair on the back of his neck prickled like it did when he'd come upon a grizzly once. Maybe he had been wrong to think he could rehabilitate Toby. No, he needed to get the guy off the property, and fast, before he gave the other guys trouble.

Toby lifted an eyebrow, but Wyatt had caught the glint of

fire in his gaze. "On whether you're ready to accept *my* conditions."

Wyatt put his hands up. "Whoa! Stop right there. This is *my* ranch, and *I'll* be the one making the conditions, are we clear? You are a guest at this ranch. I don't owe you a damn thing."

Wyatt braced for a fight as Toby pulled himself up to his full height--six foot two, minimum. Fortunately, Les, who seemed to have a sixth sense about these things, exited the log cabin at that exact moment and said, "So, how are we doing? Everything okay here?"

The two men stared each other down. Finally, Toby's shoulders sagged and he said, "Mr. Madison here is just reminding me of my manners." He tipped his hat to Wyatt, then strolled past him, but it was a slow languorous walk that spoke volumes about who he believed was in charge.

If Wyatt had done that to his father as a kid, his father would have reached across and clouted him one. However, one thing Wyatt had learned from watching his father was restraint--to know when to pick your battles. And where. Not everything required a response. Some things worked themselves out on their own. But sometimes you had to act. Consequences came with actions though, that much he knew. There were always consequences, and often unforeseen. A wise man picked his battles carefully, used diplomacy first and foremost. But sometimes a man was given no choice.

Once Toby was gone, both men relaxed, and Wyatt broke the ice by saying, "That guy has issues."

"Got that right," Les said. "He walks around the place like a cat on a hot sidewalk. It gives me the creeps. Sometimes I swear he just appears out of nowhere. The only thing I've found that will settle him is the computer. I'm always on edge until he's busy with it. He can play a video game for hours."

Wyatt sized Les up. The first thing that came to mind when he thought of Les was the word "spare." He was tall, thin, and never said more than he absolutely had to. He wasn't laconic, by any means, but he chose his words carefully and never spoke just to hear himself talk.

"Think he's got ADHD?" Wyatt said as he leaned up

against one of the massive posts.

"No doubt about it. But I'd love to know his background. He reminds me of one of those kids with fetal alcohol syndrome. He does weird stuff." Les shoved his hands in his jean pockets.

"How so?"

Les looked around as if to be sure that Toby wasn't in spitting distance then leaned forward and said, "I caught him setting fire to some pieces of hay a while back. He would just watch them float through the air as they burned. Could have set the barn on fire. When I asked him what was up with that, he had sort of a blank look. Then he just walked away."

That sounded like the kid. Wyatt had found him throwing small pebbles at Henry one day. Fortunately, Wyatt had caught him and put a stop to it, but the boy didn't even feel bad about what he was doing. Said he wouldn't have really hit him with them, but Wyatt wasn't so sure.

Just then, Wyatt heard a thwack followed by another thwack. He and Les turned their heads in the direction of the noise. Wyatt could just make out Toby down by the creek. In his hand was a substantial sized branch, which he was using to hit another branch on a tree.

"We're going to need to put a stop to this, Les. I came here to talk to Ryan about doing some work for me. After that, I'd appreciate it if you and I went down and talked to Toby. I would feel a whole lot better if he found another place to be."

Les fingered a scar that ran just under his chin. A guy like Les had probably put out a few fires in his day. Wyatt hated to ask Les to help him with one more, but that was the price of admission to this rodeo, unfortunately. Still, Les had been a trooper.

"I'll keep an eye on Toby until you're done talking to Ryan," Les said. "He's upstairs, in his room."

As if on cue, Wyatt heard the first strains of guitar picking and a soft, melodious voice from an upstairs window. He would know that voice anywhere.

Wyatt put a hand on Les's shoulder. "Thanks. Be right back."

After saying a brief hello to the boys, Wyatt stood in front of the open bunk room. On the top of one of the bunk beds close to the front of the house, Ryan was bent over his guitar, his head swaying to the music as he sang. His thoughts must have been in some far-off place because he jumped slightly when Wyatt entered.

"Sorry, didn't see you there." Ryan bowed his head sheepishly, his long straight brown hair falling over one eye.

Despite the earlier shooting, Ryan was the antithesis of Toby. Sure, the boy had problems, but he also had a softer side that convinced Wyatt that, unlike Toby, Ryan could be rehabilitated and go on to live a useful life. Wyatt wanted to believe that everyone was redeemable, but after years of witnessing carnage and destruction, he knew that some people could be salvaged, some couldn't. He wanted to believe he could help every boy that crossed his path, even Toby, but he was beginning to think that it was time to let the boy go, before something bad happened that affected *all* of them.

Wyatt turned his attention to Ryan, who refused to look him in the eye. Wyatt had rescued an abused dog once who wore the same beaten expression. It pained Wyatt to see anything that browbeaten, so he decided to make the first move.

"Son," he said, squeezing the young man's shoulder, "things got out of hand earlier. I know you didn't mean for me to be shot."

Ryan hazarded a brief glance then quickly looked down, his hand now idle on the frets. "Are you going to ask me to leave?" he said, his hands quivering slightly.

"No, son, I'm not." Ryan's head darted up with a hopeful expression that would have melted even the hardest heart, and Wyatt's certainly wasn't that. "But I do think I've found a way you can repay me."

"Oh?" Ryan swallowed the Adam's apple at his throat.

"See, I need some photographs for a marketing campaign here at the ranch, and Emajean says you're pretty handy with a camera."

For the first time since Wyatt had entered the huge bunk room, Ryan seemed to relax. He set his guitar on the bed and very quietly said, "Do you want to see some of my pictures?"

"Sure."

Ryan climbed down off his rack and reached for one of the twin trunks at the end of his bed with the name Ryan O'Roark on it. He opened it. Packed neatly inside were his clothes, his toiletries, and his memorabilia along with a book about old-style braiding with images of handcrafted Romel reins and braided tack.

"Here they are," Ryan said, pulling out a manilla envelope. He handed the packet to Wyatt who took it and lifted the photographs gingerly from a folder inside.

Wyatt quirked a brow. This was not what he had expected. He handled each carefully, one by one. Finally, when he was done perusing through the entire collection, he placed them back in the envelope.

Ryan waited, his knee bobbing up and down and his arms crossed as though expecting the worst.

"These are amazing, Ryan. Where did you learn to take photographs like that?"

"Self-taught." He shrugged his shoulders as though that explained everything. When Wyatt cocked his head, waiting for a further explanation, Ryan added, "We didn't have a lot of money growing up so I spent a lot of time in the library. Plus, we were homeless for a year and it got cold. The librarian used to give me hot coffee and something to eat."

His face bloomed in multiple shades of red, so much so that he began to cough and sputter until Wyatt had to pat him on the back to calm him down. Why hadn't he realized it before? The boy *was* painfully thin.

"Well, anytime you're hungry, you just get yourself something to eat. Don't wait until mealtime, you hear?"

Ryan peered at his shoes and nodded.

"In the meantime, can I get you to look around the ranch, see what you can find that might make for interesting copy? Shots that show the boys at work, show a bit about the camp, that sort of thing. We need to get something going soon. No pressure."

Ryan smiled for the first time since Wyatt had entered the room. It was a quiet smile, a humble smile. He had obviously heard little praise in his short life. Wyatt meant to change that.

Wyatt stood and shook Ryan's hand. "Show me what you've got just as soon as you get the pictures printed. I'll pay for the printing." He pulled out a wad of cash and counted out five twenty dollar bills. "If you need any more, let me know."

As he said goodbye and left the room, he could swear the boy had tears in his eyes but he was careful not to let on that he had seen.

Moments later, he opened the door to the porch expecting to find Les seated on one of the cane chairs, but he was nowhere to be seen.

"What the...? Oh, hell," he said, and decided to go search for him. Ten minutes later, he came up empty-handed. For several minutes, he stood there, wondering where the ranch manager had gone. Finally, he saw movement out of the corner of his eye as Les came straggling through the bushes.

"What happened? Where's Toby?"

"Gone," he said, throwing up his hands in frustration. "I've looked everywhere, but I can't find him."

Wyatt glanced down at his watch. He needed to get Kate into town pronto if she planned to get anything done today. He'd just have to look for Toby when he returned. With any luck, the boy would have figured out he should leave. But Wyatt had a feeling Toby wasn't the type of guy to leave on his own. No, he liked confrontation. It was his M.O. Wyatt had the uneasy feeling that the boy would never leave without a fight. He just hoped no one got hurt in the process.

Nineteen

Two hours later, and after much wheeling and dealing, Kate was the proud owner of a 2008 Land Rover LR3, a compromise for sure between the truck that Wyatt wanted and the Lexus that she had been eyeing. As she signed the final papers, she glanced over at Wyatt who seemed to be stewing about something. She wondered if perhaps he was regretting the kiss as much as she was kicking herself for not being stronger. True, she had tried to call it off with Palmer, but she *had* accepted his ring even if he had coerced her into taking it, no strings attached. She fingered it in her pocket. It was in a new platinum setting with a rose quartz diamond taken from his grandmother's original ring. She should have given it back the moment he had offered it to her.

Why didn't I?

She wasn't sure. Maybe it was the fear of the future that held her back. Or the fear of failure. She didn't know. What she *did* know is that she needed to make a clean break before she started anything new. She owed that to Wyatt *and* Palmer. Furthermore, she owed it to herself. As long as she had one foot in both places, she could never fully commit to either and that had never been her style. That was what all her exes had done and she *could* never, *would* never hurt a man the way they had hurt her.

"Here's your new keys," the dealer said, handing her a shiny new keyring with the dealership logo on them and the words "live the good life." Was there such a thing? She hoped so.

She jingled the keys to get Wyatt's attention. "Thanks for the lift to town."

"I have to say, I have mixed feelings about those keys," he said, wrapping an arm around her waist. "I sort of liked being the one to drive you around. It gave me the opportunity to get to know you better." He kissed her on her nose.

She looked into those almost translucent blue eyes and felt her resolve weaken. How did she know he wouldn't end up just like the others, having affairs behind her back, or just simply walking away without a word? It was the story of her life, a story she wanted to change. No one told women that in the fairytale the handsome prince went off to rescue some other fair maiden and left the poor princess in the tower to fend for herself until she grew old. Then he would leave her for some other much younger and prettier princess. If they'd shown *that* particular fairytale in theaters most young women would have run for the exit before the final curtain fell.

Life isn't *a fairytale and no one can rescue you!*

Maybe it was time to change the fairytale. Bring it into the twenty-first century. She unwrapped his hands from her waist and squeezed them. Maybe it was time to be the hero of her own story. And with any luck, she would find a man who could appreciate that in her. Enough to want to stay.

"Thanks for everything, but I really had better get to the office and find out what's happening. It sounds like Gladys and Stanford are swamped down there."

"Okay, and Kate..."

"Yes?"

"I've got our photographer... I think."

"Ryan?"

"The young man who shot me," he said, shrugging at the irony. "He does some mighty fine work, though. I'd like to give him a try. Would you mind?"

A smile formed on her lips unheeded. When had Palmer ever asked her opinion about anything? She had always felt like his secretary. *Could you get me the remote, Kate? Bring me that beer, would you?* Why had she never noticed the dynamics before?

"I'll make you a deal, Wyatt. Have Ryan bring me the pictures as soon as possible and I will write the copy for it, deal?"

Wyatt shook on it.

"But Wyatt--"

"Yes?"

"He has to be good. Our reputation is on the line, and as a

part owner of a new company I have to have a good product. I hope you're not offended."

He put his hands up and said, "No problem. Of course." But she could see that she had put him in a bad position. He lived with the young man and wouldn't want to do anything that might create more drama than there already had been this past week. This had probably been his attempt at a peace offering and she was proud of him for that, no matter how it turned out in the end.

"Well, I'd better let you get to work," he said, winking at her.

Henry, who had been waiting patiently in the truck, let out a farewell yip that made both of them laugh.

* * *

Five minutes later, Kate was seated behind the desk that Gladys and Stanford had managed to scrounge up for her.

Stanford covered the receiver and whispered, "The phones have been ringing off the hook."

When the phones finally died down an hour later, Kate leaned back in her chair needing time to think. No way could a small site like hers handle the load they were experiencing. She needed help, and fast.

"Do you have a map of all the sites that Nora and Jack purchased?"

Gladys led her to a wall map with dozens of tiny pins in it, each a small marketing business in locations like Central City, Nebraska, McMinnville, Oregon, or Yellow Springs, Ohio. Stanford, looking dapper in his vested suit, purple dress shirt, and spit-polish shoes, handed Kate his iPhone displaying a map with red dots to indicate the locations.

"This *is* the twenty-first century, Gladys."

She punched him lightly on the shoulder.

"Sexual harassment," he said, then laughed. He zoomed in on different points on the map. "If we distribute these calls evenly, dividing them up according to the nearest location to the customer, we should be able to handle the incoming."

Kate appraised the young man. Along with what looked to be a year-round tan, he wore a silver hoop earring and was in his mid-twenties--one of those boys who hadn't had the confidence beaten out of him, thank heavens. "You're awfully smart."

"That's why you pay me the big bucks." He winked then sipped on his salty caramel frappé.

"Okay, I'll phone Nora. You start calling these locations, then we'll coordinate who gets what. Do you think your phone has an organizational chart for that?"

"Of course," he said, offering a toothy grin.

Through the course of the day, it became clear that although Stanford was the brains of the operation, Gladys was the organizational task master who kept everyone moving in the right direction. Kate stayed long after they had left, finishing up all the details until she was too hungry and weary to stay any longer. What she hadn't accomplished here she could accomplish back at the ranch. With tired limbs and swollen joints from sitting too long at a computer, she grabbed her sweater and headed for the door.

As she drove away in her new SUV, she saw a dark car pull out of a side street, its lights off.

That's odd.

She peered through her mirror and could almost believe she'd imagined it, but then saw a glint of a car reflected off the dull light of a passing building. The car was following her.

You're being ridiculous. Why would anyone want to follow me?

She decided to test her theory. She sped up, going faster and faster, convinced now that she was being tailed. Abruptly, she slammed on the brakes and watched the other car swerve around her and careen past with a screech of tires until it was no longer visible. For a brief moment, relief washed over her. Then a sudden thought came to her, making her pulse race and her hands shake.

What if he's up ahead, waiting?

She hadn't thought of that when she had pulled that last maneuver. *How stupid.* She might have just made things worse. For the next half hour, she searched fruitlessly into the dark, expecting to see the shadow of a car, one of those black muscle cars she'd seen advertised in a magazine. Fortunately, all she could see were the outline of trees as she neared the ranch, the trees thinning the closer she got to the rock stanchions bearing the new **R&R Ranch** sign that read: *where veterans come to rest and heal.*

That's it, she thought excitedly. That would be her byline for the ranch's marketing campaign. As she inched up the driveway, she noticed a sole figure silhouetted against the sparse moonlight. Wyatt had waited up for her. It felt comforting to know that someone was there for her, that she wasn't alone. How many times had she come home to an empty house with Palmer nowhere in sight? She had become so used to it that it had become the norm. She hadn't known it could be any different. For the first time in her life, she wanted a home, family... really wanted it. A husband whose life wasn't spent elsewhere. Someone to protect and love her. And she might just need that protection, she realized, after what she'd witnessed tonight.

<h1 style="text-align:center">Twenty</h1>

Wyatt yawned and looked down at his lighted watch as he waited for Kate to park the Land Rover and to come up on the porch. He'd been feeling unsettled all night. Toby was nowhere to be seen on the property, which should have made him feel better, but there was something about the boy that worried him. Worried him so much that he had gone online to see if he could find out more about him. Sure enough, Toby had priors. A whole string of them. A few for assault and battery, one for arson. No one had died, but he'd sent a couple people to the hospital. Wyatt didn't want to wait to see what further damage the boy could do. Tomorrow he would go to town and get a restraining order to keep him off the property. He should have done that in the first place. He rubbed his eyes, tired suddenly.

Kate came slogging up the steps.

"You're late there, lady."

"I didn't know I had a curfew," she said with a slow grin.

For some reason she looked more fragile tonight. He could almost picture the little girl in her, playing dress-up in her mother's dress and high heels, putting on lipstick, smearing it all over, but proud of the way she looked despite the fact that nothing fit just right. He felt like that sometimes, like nothing fit anymore. When he was with Kate, though, he forgot all about that. Forgot about his loneliness, about his many losses. It was as though he'd found his other half, the half he had lost in the war. The half that still believed in love, faith, hope. She made him believe again. But beliefs could be shattered just like dreams... or lives. He thought of Carson, pictured his crumpled body, the life draining from him along with the blood until all that was left was an empty shell. The hell of it was, he'd seen the body rise, felt his friend's spirit flow through him and out the other side as it ascended toward the heavens. He had never told anyone what he had witnessed, and he never would. They would want to know what he'd been smoking.

He sighed, tired of loss, real tired. Feeling way older than his years, he stood to greet Kate. "How'd your day go?"

"Okay. Lots to do, but I think we're getting the workload hammered out. How about you? Everything okay at the O.K. Corral?"

"Like I haven't heard *that* one before," he said, lifting a wayward brow.

He offered her a seat on the top porch step and sat down beside her, eager for the warmth she provided... and the solace.

"Actually," he said, "I'm having a problem with one of the vets."

"Oh?" She leaned forward and stared up at him. "What problem?"

He scratched behind his ear. "There was a fight, before you came to the ranch, between Toby and his girlfriend. Les and I settled him down, but there's something about the boy..." He shook his head, wishing he could pinpoint what exactly bothered him about the guy. "He's a loose cannon," he said, finally. "As long as he's here, I worry about the safety of my men and my staff."

"That's odd."

"What?" he said, seeing her troubled expression.

"Okay, I hope you don't think I'm being paranoid, but I could swear someone was following me on the way home from the office today." She clasped her hands together, running her thumb nervously against her palm.

"What did the car look like?" he said, her fear catching like a wildfire.

"Now, I'm not that good with cars, but it looked to me like one of those muscle cars--black. We didn't have much of a moon, so I can't be sure. Does Toby have a car?"

Wyatt steepled his fingers. He would have had to own a car to have shown up so suddenly and then disappeared just as quickly. Or someone would have had to bring him to the ranch. He would ask around in the morning.

* * *

The silver-haired man gave a nod from across the lounge and Ian rose to meet him. He had been nursing a highball in anticipation of today's meeting. Everything rested on what this man could accomplish in the next forty-eight hours.

"Hello there, Karl." Ian shook the man's hand and peered down at the folder he had under his arm.

Just then the barmaid came by and stooped over Karl's shoulder. "What'll you have, hon?" She smiled a little too readily at the older gentleman. Then turned to Ian. "Need a touchup?"

He tapped the bottom of his glass on the table in answer, the universal blackjack response for "I'll take another one." She winked and was gone.

"So, who have you got?"

Karl opened his folder and tapped on a glossy eight-by-eleven photograph of a very tough looking guy. Although he was thin and wiry, he had scars in his hairline and on his cheek. His swarthy skin produced small freckles from overexposure to the sun along his cheekbones and the swell of his nose.

"Who is he?"

The barmaid returned and lay down two coasters then set two glasses filled with rich golden liquid onto the table. Karl gave her a tip then patted her on the bottom. Ian felt a rise in temperature. Even *he* knew you didn't do that anymore; it could be seen as sexual harassment. A guy could get his ass sued if he wasn't careful, but Karl was old school. He hadn't received the memo that the world was changing and you couldn't just paw a woman because she earned less. Well, he'd figure it out someday.

"His name's Toby McKenzie. Was in and out of juvie as a kid. Went on to bigger crimes later, mostly assault, but arson, too."

"Good," Ian said, the highball giving him just the right buzz.

"He's been living at the ranch of a Mr. Wyatt Madison." He laughed at the name.

"So, this Toby fellow, he's not there anymore?"

Karl shook his head. "He went to the property last night to

scope out the place and set things up. The owner got wise to
him so he decided to make a quick exit, but he'll be back. I
guarantee it."

"Good. How about the girl?" Ian asked, shifting in his chair
and soaking in the good news.

"We've got him on her tail. She caught wind of him last
night, so we'll have to switch cars out periodically to keep her
off balance, make her think there's more than one person out
there."

Ian let that sink in. He needed to play his hand carefully.
Give away too much, and he put himself and his company in
jeopardy. The less anyone knew, and the safer he played it, the
better.

"I don't want her hurt, Karl. Just scared. Scared enough
that she'll drop out of the business. Find herself a nice quiet job
as a waitress somewhere."

"Or a barmaid?" Karl winked at the woman passing by
and gave her leg a squeeze, nearly tripping her in the process.

Ian hated to admit it, but the guy was a sleazeball. The only
reason he got away with it was because he was handsome and
charming. And he had money... Ian's money in particular.
Karl was a chameleon. A quick-change artist. A con man. He
could be suave and sophisticated one minute, then turn like a
dime if the circumstances were right. That's why so many
companies had hired him over the years, to handle any
unsavory business. In fact, that's why Ian had hired him, even
though he didn't like the guy.

"Let's let her worry about her next job," Ian continued.
"Just make sure you avoid mistakes and that none of this comes
back on me."

"That's why you hired the best," Karl said, fingering a
large gold band with an equally large diamond surrounded by
black onyx.

Ian sank back in his seat and drank down another sip of his
drink, savoring the afterburn of the whiskey. It warmed his
limbs. As he stood to leave, he gave the guy one final long, slow
appraisal. He just hoped the guy was as good as his mouth.

Twenty-One

Kate's heart raced when she glanced into her rearview mirror as she left her office for the second time in two days. She was still reeling at the thought that the car following her yesterday hadn't been a coincidence. And yet here she was again, an old beater caddie on her tail. "Okay, now I'm just being paranoid," she decided.

Get a grip.

She was letting her imagination get the best of her. Swerving over, she slammed on the brakes and watched the car whir past. Her heart pounded as she determined what to do next. *Why would someone follow her?* she wondered for the second time in two days. Surely, Ian wouldn't waste his time on her, considering how small the odds were of the new company succeeding. Maybe it was this Toby fellow from Wyatt's ranch. Maybe he didn't want to see the program succeed.

Or maybe you're just being ridiculous.

Either way, she needed to be vigilant. If it turned out to be nothing, then she could chalk it up to an overactive imagination, and if not... well, she would cross that bridge when she came to it.

She breathed in the smell of the newly mowed fields. The wheatfields around her had just been cut and baled, reminding her that time was slipping away. It was mid-August and she had zero to show for Wyatt's marketing campaign. He deserved better and she meant to make it right by him.

She thought back to the night before. She and Wyatt had talked late into the night about anything and everything. Never had she felt more comfortable with a man. It was as if he filled some hole she hadn't even realized was missing, a hole that no one before him had ever been able to fill. He made her believe in men again, and that was the most dangerous kind of man, because if he failed her then who could she trust? No one, and that was the crux of the problem. She knew her heart could never take another rejection, another gaping wound. There had been too many, each taking a notch out of her heart. A man like Wyatt would take much more than a notch, she felt certain.

Slowly, she pulled back out onto the highway headed toward the ranch. As the miles drifted past with nothing but cattle and lodgepole pine to block her view, she had started to become complacent when she saw the same blue-and-white caddie tucked into a copse at the side of the road. She could just make out the silhouette of a man. She watched her rear-view mirror to see if he would follow. Just as she was about to go over a rise, she saw the car creep out onto the road. Panic set in and she stepped on the gas. One thing she had learned while in Manhattan was how to drive... fast, if need be. She'd had to be a good driver to survive city driving.

Kate didn't start breathing again until she saw the ranch off to the right and had turned into it. She flew down the dirt driveway, certain she had finally lost the caddie when she saw it pull up at the front of the drive, slow, then nearly come to a stop before speeding up and disappearing from sight. Her breathing was heavy and her hands shaking by the time she entered the old farmhouse.

Emajean appeared from the kitchen in an old-fashioned apron with ruffles that looked incongruous to the "tough as nails" persona she gave off. She frowned. "You look like you've seen a ghost. Anything wrong?"

The room smelled like breaded chuck roast and mashed potatoes along with other savory smells, a berry pie maybe. Normally, that would have had Kate thinking back to her days at her grandmother's farm, but now all she could think about was that menacing caddie.

"Where's Wyatt? I need to see him right away."

"He's down at the barn feeding the animals. Don't you want to wash up for dinner?"

Kate didn't wait to hear what else the woman had to say. She dropped her purse and her jacket onto the ottoman in front of the LazyBoy and ran out to find him. The afternoon sun was low on the horizon as sunset neared, shining bright rays against the silvery clouds that made her think of heaven and angels.

Inside the barn, musty dust motes swirled in the air, the smell of earth and manure strong. Toward the back of the barn she heard the scraping of a shovel inside one of the stalls. She ran and flung the stall door open.

"Wyatt, I--"

The man bent over with a shovel stood and turned.

"Oh, you're not Wyatt," she said with a start.

"No, Ma'am. Wyatt's out on the combine beyond the pasture." He pointed toward the east. Now that he was standing, Kate could see that the man had numerous tattoos, one rather large one on his forearm, a silhouette of a woman, like the ones truckers often displayed on their grills. That, and a rose. On his chest was a tattoo that she could only surmise was some sort of gang symbol. Definitely *not* Wyatt.

She thanked him then hurried toward the sound of the combine. By the time she reached the giant green behemoth, she felt sure she looked like a crazed woman running through the wheat field, her legs stinging with each new scratch and tear at her legs from the chaff that had yet to be turned into the soil.

Wyatt idled the engine then reached out a hand to pull her up. He scooted over so that she was behind the wheel.

She frowned, confused.

"She's all yours," he shouted over the roar of the engine. "Put her in gear."

Kate followed his directions, the rumble and shriek of the engine as it set off doing nothing to quell her fear.

"It's like riding one hell of a big bike, yeah?"

Sweat dripped down his brow and beneath the collar of his shirt, the top buttons open to allow in air. He removed his hat and wiped the sweat from his brow, his wide smile making her feel safe again. For one crazy minute, she thought of asking him to cradle her in his arms, to tell her everything was going to be okay, that this had all just been some awful nightmare and she was going to wake up now. Everything would be okay. But that wasn't real life and this wasn't a novel. She had to face

it, whether she wanted to or not. As her friend Sara would have
said, "It's time to put on your big girl panties."

Within minutes, she began to feel comfortable at the wheel.
For some reason, it made her feel more in control. If she could
handle this, she could handle anything. Kate had the brief
suspicion that Wyatt had sensed her feelings of helplessness and
had determined to help her feel strong again, capable.

He draped an arm over her shoulder, pointing out
mountain peaks where he had hiked with friends as a teen, to
the brook that ran the length of the property where he had
gone frogging as a child. He talked easily about a childhood
with brothers and a sister that seemed idyllic.

"How about you?" he said at last. "What was your
childhood like?"

Where to start? Long before her brother Eric had gone off
to war, there had been a war brewing in her home between a
mother and a father that were like oil and water. They had
tried, for the sake of the kids, and she had appreciated them for
that. But in the end, the war had taken its toll. They had parted
not really as friends, but with respect for each other. She
couldn't have asked for anything more. Still, it had left her
feeling as though family was transient. Eric had gone off to war,
her mother had turned in on herself and Kate had gone to
college, her childhood obliterated with the swipe of a pen. She
had spent the rest of her life trying to recapture a sense of
family. Of belonging.

"My childhood was normal," she said with a shrug.

For the next half hour, she drove the combine up and down
rows and was filthy and tired when she finished, but happy...
happier than she'd been in a long time. As he helped her down,
he said, "Okay, why don't you tell me why you came running
all the way out to the field. I know you didn't decide you want
to be a farmer, all of a sudden, so what's up?"

She explained what she had seen over the past two days. "I
know you probably think I'm being a flake, but I just have this
feeling..."

He took her hand and ran his fingers along each of hers as
though divining every secret she might have. At long last he

said, "Les found a lighter in the barn last night."

"Could one of the guys have dropped it in there when they were helping you with the animals?" She recalled the beefy young man with tattoos, a former gang member, she felt certain.

"No. We have a strict policy at the ranch. No weapons of any kind, and no smoking paraphernalia near the barn or next to the wheat fields." He ran a hand over his brow as another drip of sweat rolled down onto his shirt sleeve. "It's just common sense."

To him, maybe, but she had a sneaking suspicion that these vets were young and didn't always think about the consequences.

"Let's go inside and get some dinner," Wyatt said. "Then give me the descriptions of the two cars and I'll get the sheriff to check them out. It could be nothing, or it could be something, but we're not going to know until we do some research. Okay?"

He wrapped an arm around her shoulder and, despite everything she had promised herself, she leaned into that wide shoulder, grateful for the warmth it provided. No man before had offered her that sense of security. With the others she had learned independence, how to be capable... and alone. She was tired of being alone, of being lonely. She wanted a man who would be there for her. Who would be *with* her. Was that so wrong? To want a man she could face the world with together? All this thinking was making her head ache.

She was grateful by the time she sat down to dinner at the wide oak table. The chuck roast smelled sinfully delicious and she hadn't had that kind of gravy since she was a kid.

By the time she wiped her mouth with the linen napkin, her stomach felt fuller than it had for some time. Usually she was too busy to do anything other than grab a quick bite on the run. Kate and the others were just getting ready to retire in the living room when someone knocked on the door.

Emajean reached the door first and opened it. "Ryan, come on in."

She held the screen door for him as he entered, the squeak

of the screen door and the crash it made against the door jamb just one more sound that reminded Kate of her grandmother and days gone by.

A thousand bits of wonderful.

The memory of those words popped into her head unheeded. Was Wyatt her thousand bits of wonderful, the one bright star in the sky that was meant for her and her alone? She didn't know, but a piece of her prayed that he was and that he would see her as that one shining star in the night sky meant for him. She hoped so, but better not to overthink it.

Frustrated, she ran a hand through her curly brown hair. She wished her emotions would quit seesawing and that she could make up her mind whether to trust a man with her heart again. She turned her attention to Ryan who was settled on the recliner. He reached into an inside pocket of his jacket and pulled out an envelope that he laid onto the table, careful to avoid eye contact.

"There they are," he said, venturing a peek at the threesome before quickly lowering his eyes. "The photographs."

"Well, let's just take a look at these." Wyatt spread them out over the hand-hewn coffee table that had faces of animals carved into it. Kate wondered if Wyatt had carved it and made a mental note to ask him about it later.

Wyatt whistled and drew Kate in closer for a better view of the photographs. With obvious pride, he pointed to one with him on a horse in the wheatfield, the Sawtooth Mountains behind. Another was of the log cabin itself, the cobalt blue sky framing it. Still another was of the ranches' sign, the iron filigree that topped the pine posts against a flaming sunset that caused her to take in air, it was so breathtaking. What vet wouldn't want to stay here after seeing these pictures? But who would, or better yet, *could* afford to pay for that opportunity? That's what she had yet to figure out because most vets returned home penniless and with great need. She could write the copy. She had no doubt about that, not after seeing these vets and knowing Wyatt the way she knew him. What they needed was a continuous stream of income that would keep both these vets *and* the ranch afloat for the foreseeable future.

"These are fantastic," she said, excitement causing her words to spill over each other like water over a dip in a burbling stream.

Her excitement was contagious. Even Ryan hazarded a glance at her.

"Wyatt, what if you provide workshops that teach each of the boys a skill they can take into the real world so they can earn a living? Give famous artists and craftsmen an all-expenses stay at the ranch, take their family boating, horseback riding, and on campouts. The artist agrees to half-day sessions, they have the afternoons free to do fun things as a family. In return, they stay a month."

Wyatt frowned, not the reaction Kate was expecting, leaving her feeling suddenly deflated.

"Don't get me wrong," he said, fingering the photos, "that's a great idea, but how does that help us with income for the ranch?"

"You can partner with schools and public buildings all around the country to work on major works of arts or crafts like they did in the Great Depression. Wait here!" she said, holding up a finger as she ran upstairs and grabbed her laptop, then ran back downstairs.

"Here," she said, barely able to contain her excitement as she opened a window in her computer to display an eight-foot by twelve-foot pair of doors that fronted a lodge.

Upon seeing the craftsmanship, Wyatt whistled. Even Ryan rose and came over next to them to take a look at the massive doors. Carved into them were mountains, a lake, and a beautiful egret with a trout in its talon. Off to one side, on either edge of the panels, stood white pines. The door would have cost thousands of dollars.

"We could get woodworkers and metalworkers to teach the boys how to make hand-scrolled gates for vineyards. Can you imagine the pride? Plus, they would be earning their keep through the sale of these masterpieces while apprenticing at a new skill. Maybe we could even find jobs for them once their apprenticeship is up."

Wyatt peered up at Ryan whose brown eyes held a shimmer Kate had never seen before in this shyest of young men. But she knew it wasn't just shyness. The kid had been beaten before, that much was clear. The only time she'd seen anything that skittish of people was a dog she'd once befriended, who had been beaten and starved by its owner. She had never quite won its full trust, no matter how hard she tried.

"What do you think, Ryan? Do you think it could work, that the men would go for it?"

"Hell, yes," he said in a low, gravelly voice, then immediately apologized for swearing in front of Kate and Emajean.

Wyatt squeezed Ryan's shoulder. "Then that's good enough for me."

For the next hour and a half, they talked and planned the future, each of them becoming more and more excited as the night wore on. Finally, Ryan excused himself, leaving the photographs behind so that Kate could work up the copy on them. In the meantime, Emajean feigned some chore she needed to finish up in the kitchen to give Kate and Wyatt some time alone together.

"Feel like going for a swing?" Wyatt said, giving Kate's hand a gentle tug.

"I have work to do."

"That can wait," he said with a twinkle in his eye. "Come on out with me, Kate."

How could she deny him that when he had made her feel like a human being again after everything that had happened?

When they were seated on the swing under the oak tree, a full moon blazing across the stubbled field, he pulled her close. The moon illuminated a flock of geese that had taken up residence there in pursuit of small insects and rodents.

He lay his head on hers, the whiskers on his chin digging ever so softly into her forehead, and yet she wouldn't have changed it for the world. Next, he twined the fingers of his left hand with hers while trailing the fingers of his right hand down her arm creating shivers of delight as she finally gave into the feelings that had been fomenting for days in her treacherous heart.

"Kate?"

"Hmm?" she said, not wanting to break the spell of the silence, punctuated by the occasional sound of crickets in the field or a tree frog in the canopy above. Even the geese had settled in for the night and were enjoying the silence at the end of a long hot day.

"I know it's too soon, but..." His voice trailed and he peered down at her as if hoping to catch a glimpse of her answer in her eyes.

"It is," she said, swallowing down the emotion she felt in that moment. "But I'm glad all the same."

She hadn't realized how tense he'd become until she noticed his muscles relax as he sat back in the swing once again. He pulled her tighter into his arms, as though grateful that she had made at least that much of a commitment.

"Kate?"

"Yes?"

"I'll protect you. I won't let anything happen to you, I promise."

Her throat felt dry as she choked back the emotion she felt. No one had ever told her that before. Had ever cared enough. Or if they had, she'd never known it. It made her feel good to hear that, to know she mattered. To know that there was someone who thought enough of her to *want* to protect her.

He pulled her chin to him and gave her a deep, lingering kiss. Then he threw his head back and said, "I think we'd better get back to the house before I do something that is very ungentlemanly."

Together, they laughed. Nevertheless, she was relieved to be headed to the house before she did something that she was decidedly not ready for yet. To give her heart away to a man that may, or may not, have her best interests at heart.

Once she was back upstairs, she couldn't stop thinking about Wyatt, about the kiss, about how she felt when she was around him. But could she really trust her judgment? She'd been wrong before. She had believed in a man that hadn't earned her trust. How did you get past that and learn to trust again?

Well, she couldn't dwell on it all night. She decided it was time to get busy and begin writing the copy that would hopefully one day help save the ranch. And she also needed to start contacting partnering organizations that could sponsor works of art. And lastly, she would need to begin contacting artists around the nation to see if they would be interested in coming to the ranch to apprentice these kids. It would be a full night's work and then some. Before she could get started, she decided to check her email to see if either Stanford or Gladys had contacted her... or Nora.

What she hadn't expected when she opened her email was the message she'd received from Palmer.

"I love you. I miss you. I'm sorry for everything. I'm flying up on Saturday to bring you home and I won't take no for an answer."

Twenty-Two

When Kate finally awoke after only three hours of sleep, her eyes were swollen and her head felt heavy as though she'd partied the night before and was nursing a hangover.

But this was no hangover.

The words Palmer had written kept coming back to her in painful detail. *I'm flying up on Saturday to bring you home and I won't take no for an answer.*

How could she stop him from coming? She didn't want him here. He was the last person she wanted to see right now with her feelings about Wyatt so new and so raw. She needed time to figure out what was right for *her*.

At least she had made headway with the marketing campaign. That much was obvious by all the paperwork and leftover snacks she had strewn around the room from last night's orgy of work and caffeine to keep her awake.

She yawned and stretched, still feeling the aftereffects of a hard night. No doubt, she had bags under her eyes. Just to be certain, she peered in the mirror above the dresser and sighed. Maybe she could wear sunglasses.

Fortunately, she now had most of her copy for Wyatt's promotional done. Also, she had emailed too many organizations to count, telling them about the ranch and its plans, and had yet to hear back. Even if only two percent of the people she had contacted responded, she would have done her job.

Her final act before heading off to bed in the wee hours of the morning was to email Palmer to tell him in no uncertain terms that she needed more time to figure out what she wanted. He had called her at eight a.m. to tell her how disappointed he was but that he understood and would wait, no matter how long it took. Still, she couldn't get over the idea that the only reason he wanted her back was because he couldn't have her. For him it had always been the thrill of the chase. Once the chase was finished, he was on to a new conquest. That's how it had been with all the men she had dated. Still, maybe that was simply the makeup of men and she was just now figuring that out. She hoped not.

She quickly took a shower and went downstairs. To her chagrin, she had once again missed out on breakfast, as witnessed by the stern set of Emajean's lips.

"Sorry I'm late," Kate murmured. "I was working on Wyatt's marketing campaign but I've made good headway. Where's Wyatt?"

"Don't you smell it?"

Kate lifted her head and sniffed, the latent odor of smoke in the air. Emajean walked over to the window and opened it. Thick smoke came pouring in. She quickly shut the window and closed the curtains.

"What's it from?"

"Not a forest fire, I can tell you that. Fortunately, it was just the stubble from the leftover wheat and hay. If it had reached the barn, it would have been an entirely different story. Wyatt could have lost everything, his animals, his hay, the wheat. He planned to take it into town today to sell to the local mill. He stood to lose a pretty penny."

"And the ranch," Kate added, to which Emajean merely nodded, her expression severe, yet stoic. "How did it happen?"

"Not sure yet." Emajean set a plate of rewarmed eggs, hash browns, and a bowl of peaches onto the table then urged Kate to come sit and eat. "The sheriff is supposed to be here any minute to take a look at the place. The fire chief is here already. He thinks it's arson."

The lighter.

Kate wondered if Wyatt had talked to Les the night before as planned and if he had learned any more about who might have left it. Was the lighter a warning? Her thoughts drifted back to the faceless driver in the muscle car and the one in the caddie. Could *they* have any connection to the fire? Furthermore, were those two separate incidents with two separate drivers, or were the drivers one in the same? She didn't know. She only knew she needed to be more prepared the next time; *she* needed to be the one to pursue *the driver*. It was the only way that person would ever stop. She couldn't let whoever was behind the wheel intimidate her.

She hadn't realized she'd been picking at her food until she looked up and saw Emajean with hands on hips and arching a brow as she nodded toward the plate.

"I'm not very hungry," Kate protested, but decided there was no use in arguing. She gulped down the food, barely tasting the delicious eggs or hash browns. She washed it all down with orange juice, which left her stomach feeling unsettled, then hurried out to find Wyatt.

The sun was already high in the sky by the time she reached the wheatfield, the charred ruins still smoldering. Only yesterday, this pastoral setting had looked like something out of a picture postcard. Now it looked like something out of *Dante's Inferno*. Wyatt wore black smudges all across his face, and his skin appeared blistered in places. Sweat dripped down the sides of his face, the waning fire still sending shimmery waves of heat into the air.

Kate rushed to his side. "Are you okay?"

"I've had better days," he said with a tired laugh. "And you?"

She had all but forgotten her disheveled appearance once she'd learned about the fire. Now, she looked down at herself, at her rumpled clothing and felt the bags beneath her eyes.

"Looks like it has been a rough night for both of us," she said with a wan smile.

"You know my story," he said. "So, what happened to you?"

For a brief moment, she pondered telling him about Palmer, about him wanting to come here to collect her, but now was not the time. Wyatt had plenty on his plate already. Better to keep things light and to tell him the good news, what there was of it.

"I was up late writing copy and contacting artists and craftsmen. I have Gladys working on a website using the photographs Ryan gave us. The woman is a wunderkind with a website. Just amazing. And Stanford has the gift for art, so between them both I think you'll be more than happy with the end product. And it's all gratis, so Ian can't come back on us. We'll just call it a gift, a fair exchange for all your help getting us clients."

"Thanks," he said, but she could see the defeat in the tight set of his lips.

Just then, the fire chief, who had been standing next to the barn beside his fire truck, clipboard in hand, began heading toward them, hand upraised. He was a tall man, medium build with sandy brown hair. As he walked their way, Kate wondered why she hadn't heard the rumble of the engine when the fire truck came through? But then again, she *had* been tired and she *had* worn earplugs so she could sleep in late, not to mention taking melatonin to help her sleep.

"We think we found the ignition point," the fire chief called out and then waved them to follow him as he moved toward the left side of the field closest to the trees.

"Whoever did this either knew something about fire or was darn lucky, because if there had been a backdraft this entire mountainside would have gone up in flames. It would have taken us days to put it out."

"How do you know it was arson?" Kate asked.

"We don't, for sure, not yet. But we have a strong suspicion." He knelt onto the ground and pointed at the blackened stubble. "See how the fire fans out from this point and then spreads sideways?"

They both nodded.

"That means the wind was coming from behind us and moving southwest. It usually flows more northerly. We're having the stubble here tested to see if there's any lighter fluid, but my guess is that it will come back positive. You can tell because there's a slightly oily sheen right here. Again, it doesn't confirm my suspicions, but I've been at this long enough to hazard a fairly safe bet."

Kate and Wyatt exchanged glances. Was it too soon to bring up Wyatt's suspicions? Apparently, Wyatt was thinking the same thing because he offered a small shake of his head. She wondered why he would protect the boy, if he'd had a hand in the fire. She vowed to ask him later, when they were alone.

"When Sheriff Benson comes, he'll ask you some questions about any potential suspects, if indeed this is arson, so you'll want to begin thinking about that." The fire chief stood, looking as rested and jovial as his crew appeared weary and tired from battling the hot flames. "I'm going to head out. If you need anything else, let one of the guys know. I'll leave two of them here to make sure that if anything flares up, they'll keep an eye on it and put it out right away. Any other questions, give me a call." He handed Wyatt his card, nodded to Kate and then headed to his four-wheel drive pickup, dark blue to match his uniform.

Only moments later, the sheriff's SUV came barreling down the road, bouncing against the washboard path, dust flying in its wake. The sheriff stopped to talk to the fire chief through the partially opened window of his SUV, then sped toward them. He drove just to the edge of the field and parked.

The man who got out of the SUV could only be described as swarthy. Big-boned, her grandma used to call men like him with plenty of roast beef and mashed potatoes under his belt by the looks of him. It didn't take much to see that he was the exact opposite of the fire chief, who was quick to laugh and a people person.

"Looks like we got us a problem, eh Wyatt?" Sheriff Benson said, hitching up his belt. "And who's this pretty lady?" he added with a chuckle that sounded more gruff than appeasing.

Wyatt made short work of the introductions.

"I'll leave you two to talk," Kate said, seeing her cue to leave. She needed to drop some paperwork off in town anyway.

As she was walking back, she noticed something lying on the ground close to the oak tree as though someone had been standing under it watching the wheatfield... or her window. She picked up the cigarette butt. A Marlboro. Whose could it be? Certainly not Wyatt's. He didn't smoke. She tried to recall if she'd seen any of the men smoking one of these at the picnic the other night but couldn't. They were all too busy swimming, eating, or sitting around the campfire. This might be something important. But then she thought of how Wyatt had reacted when she had planned to tell the fire chief about Toby. She decided to hold onto it until she could talk to Wyatt. She looked one last time at the two men out in the field and at the two firemen who were monitoring any outbreaks, then turned to go inside.

From where she stood, one would have a perfect view into her bedroom, to the desk where she worked. The thought sent a shiver through her. No matter how hot the weather, it was time to keep her doors and windows locked.

* * *

Once the sheriff was gone and after the two firemen had promised to call Wyatt if anything came up, he took the Ranger and went in search of Les. His foreman and most of the vets had come down early to help Wyatt put out as much of the fire as they could until the firemen could arrive. Afterwards, they'd gone to wash up and wolf down some lunch that Emajean had ready and waiting.

That was the thing about Emajean. She'd been a farmer's daughter her whole life and had helped her mother in the kitchen anytime the farm hands needed to be fed. The woman was a champ when it came to "mustering the troops." She could feed an army, if necessary, and without a lot of prep time. He'd never been more grateful to his father than for leaving him Emajean. He didn't know where he would have been without her.

He thought to that day, several years back, when she'd pulled him out of a bar by the scruff of his neck and drove him to the ranch, yelling at him the entire way.

"Your father didn't work his entire life to see you drowning your sorrows in a bar, Mister," she had said, never once looking at him as she drove. "Now you're going to pay him your respect by cleaning up and taking care of the ranch that his father, and his father before him, worked so hard to keep going." Finally, she'd turned to him and said, "Do you hear me, Mister?"

130

He had felt like he was five years old and getting a tongue lashing from his mother, though his mother would have never spoken to him like that. She was a far different person. She was the Amelia Earhart of his family, always looking to the future with a sunny outlook. Always cheering on the troops, assuring them that despite most family farms going under, they would find a way to make theirs work. She had instilled in him a belief that he could succeed no matter what life threw his way. She just hadn't counted on Iraq or Afghanistan. Or the 2006 economic crash. Every time his family had thought they were finally making headway, a new disaster would strike. They had almost lost the ranch that time. Ironically, it was his parents' deaths that had saved the ranch. Their life insurance had bought him time, but time had been running out, until Kate had arrived.

Kate.

Like his mother, she had helped him believe again. Believe in the goodness of people, in the promise of tomorrow. She had offered him hope. Just then, a dark cloud drifted over as he parked his Ranger in front of the wide double doors of the log cabin's garage.

What would Kate think when she found out he had been married before? That he had a child, a daughter Emily, who was ten. Or that he had been the one responsible for the breakup of the marriage.

He sat in his truck, reliving those moments when Charlotte had caught him in the arms of another woman, in their own bed, for Christ's sake. What had he been thinking? He sighed. He *hadn't* been thinking. He'd just been so angry at everyone, the world, the army, even his wife. Most of all at himself, for not being able to save his friend.

For so many years he had risked his life, every waking moment regimented: when to sleep, when to get up, where and when to eat. He'd wanted to cut loose, to taste freedom again, to remember what it was like not to have to answer to anyone... including his wife.

The weight of what he'd done rested heavily on his chest, a guilt that could never be squelched. He rubbed his chest, remembering.

"When will you be home?" Charlotte had asked, her tanned face haggard after a late night tending to Emily's ear infection and a full day of work before that. "We have a parent-teacher conference tonight at 7:00."

"It's my life and I'll be home when I damn well please." Emily had been crying in the background, but all he could hear or see was yet another person relying on him, depending on him, and he'd been a damned big failure at that. He hadn't even been able to keep his friend alive. He had promised Carson's mother he would keep Carson safe. But he hadn't. He hadn't. And now he was tired of playing hero to everyone, including his family. He had just wanted to forget about it... *all* of it. But the only way he could forget was in a bottle... or in the arms of a woman.

He realized now he'd been selfish and that Charlotte just wanted a partner, someone to love and support her, but his cup was empty. Until he filled it up, he was no good to anyone, least of all himself.

Even now, he recalled the look on her face, the utter and total devastation. She had grabbed Emily and then ran, and had never looked back. It was a betrayal she couldn't forgive. And he had only himself to blame. She had been a good woman. Oh, he had tried to villainize her, to make her out to be the bad guy, but in the end, after he'd become sober, he just couldn't do it anymore. She had loved him--he knew that-- utterly and completely, and he had screwed up. Afterwards, he had spent the rest of his life trying to make amends.

He knew now he couldn't fix the past, but he *could* fix the future and that's exactly what he intended to do. Yet, he couldn't do that until he told Kate about his past... and about his child... who had called last night to say she wanted to come stay with him for a month.

"It'll be so much fun. Mom's gotta work so she said I could stay with you and ride Spot until school starts."

Spot, who Kate had renamed Spirit.

Wyatt didn't know how Emily would respond to the name change of her horse. Worst of all, he didn't know how his

daughter would react to his budding relationship with Kate...
at least he hoped it was a budding relationship.

You can't start a relationship founded on lies.

He had to tell her about himself, about his past... soon. If
she found out what had happened by anyone else, she would
never trust him again, and that's what he needed more than
anything in his life. Trust. To trust, and to be trusted. But he
knew now he had to earn that trust; it wasn't just handed to a
person.

As he opened the door of his truck, he felt a burst of wind
and peered up at the sky. He hoped those were rain clouds. If
ever they needed rain it was now, to keep the dying embers at
bay. If the wind came up with no rain, the embers could pick
up, head the opposite direction and end up taking out a whole
hillside of trees. It would put the fire too close to the log cabin
for comfort. Maybe he'd talk to the guys and see if they could
help him build a fire line. He was already exhausted from this
morning's fire fight, but rest was something he could ill afford
right now. That would have to wait until they were sure the
danger was past. And what if Toby decided to come back
tonight? Surely, he would lay low for a while, especially with
the firemen on watch. Just to be safe, Wyatt would have the
men do rotating shifts to watch the cabin, the house, and the
barn.

He trudged slowly to the cabin, every joint in his body
aching. Les must have been watching through the window
because he met Wyatt out on the porch.

"Let's go for a walk," Les said, hat in hand.

As if he'd just been waiting for his cue, Henry showed up
on the porch, tail wagging, and ran ahead of them to where
lines of fencing corralled cattle that they would butcher for
meat in winter to feed the vets. Anything left over was sold,
bringing in meager earnings toward the upkeep of the ranch. It
was a labor of love, but even love could only go so far. Without
the capital to keep the ranch afloat, they would all be out of
luck. Wyatt couldn't let that happen.

"So," he said, plucking a long blade of grass and sucking
the sweet inner juices, "do you think Toby was behind this?"

"Of course," Les replied without hesitation. He kicked a boot on the ground and seemed to revel in the wake of dust that it stirred, while a flock of geese flew overhead, honking as they flew. "Ryan said that Toby circled back and threw a pebble at his window. Asked him if he would sneak him up to his room. Said we were picking on him."

"And Ryan told him...?"

"No, of course. He doesn't like Toby any better than we do. Said he saw him hit a woman once. He and some other guys had to pull Toby off the girl. She was pretty messed up when it was over. A guy like that has a hair trigger, and I don't want to be around when he pulls it, know what I mean?" Les fingered the blond stubble on his chin, the beginnings of a beard.

"At least the sheriff knows all about him now," Wyatt said, tossing the chewed piece of grass. "I wasn't sure how much to say because... you know."

Les's eyes darted up and, for a moment, they just stared at each other in silence. "So, Toby knows about your prison time?"

Wyatt nodded.

"Holy you know what, Sherlock. You are screwed."

They both laughed without mirth. If anyone got wind of Wyatt's time in prison, that would be the end of any help he could hope to receive for his ranch. He would never get a sponsor again. It didn't matter that he had cleaned up his act, or that he had gone straight for the eight years afterward. All that anyone would hear was the word ex-con and that would be all she wrote. He rubbed at his temples to stifle the burgeoning headache.

"How did he find out?"

"Internet. Criminals Caught In The Act." Again, they laughed. Sometimes that's all you could do.

"And you think he would use it against you?" Les asked.

"I know he would."

"How?"

One of the cows meandered over and Wyatt petted its head. "He told me."

"He threatened to blackmail you?"

"Not with money. That's not what he's interested in."

Wyatt checked the cow's ears for mites as he spoke. No matter what was going on in his life, the ranch still took precedence.

"So what bug's he got up his rear?" Les asked.

"Feels I owe him. For his service and all. He wants a place to stay, three square meals a day, and to do whatever the hell he pleases, even if it means causing havoc for the rest of us. I'm not going to let that happen."

Wyatt watched as Les pushed his straw hat back on his head and peered out over the broad valley and to the hillside beyond. Once again, Wyatt thanked his lucky stars that this hillside hadn't gone up in flames.

"The guy is trouble," Les said, "that's all there is to it."

Wyatt rubbed the cow's haunches and then patted it on the rump to get it moving back with the rest of the herd.

"Hey, Les, before I forget--Toby smoked, right?"

"Yeah, he smoked anything he could get his hands on. Even vapes, on occasion, some hippy name like Tibetan Paradise, or something like that."

"Yeah, but you couldn't light a field on fire with an e-cigarette, right?" Wyatt asked, frowning.

"No, but you could with a cigarette. He was looking for them the other day."

"Good to know. I'll let the sheriff know, too. Do you have any idea what kind he smoked?"

Les pursed his lips while thinking. "Can't recall at the moment."

"Okay, well I need to go to town," Wyatt said, letting go of the fence. "In the meantime, keep an eye on the place for me, would you?"

Les squeezed his shoulder and said, "You can count on me."

Twenty-Three

By the time Kate entered the ranch house, her thoughts still on the burned wheat stubble, she was out of breath. Emajean was gone, no doubt up at the cabin feeding "her men." Kate trudged to her room upstairs to collect her things before heading to the office. In the mirror over the dresser, she once again noticed the bags beneath her eyes. Well, nothing she could do about them now.

She thought of leaving a note for either Emajean or Wyatt, but they were all so busy that she'd probably be back before they noticed her missing. She just needed to go into town to check on business and to mail off a few flyers. Also, to see how the website was progressing.

Before leaving, she felt the cigarette in her pocket. She pulled it out and set it on the dresser, determined to show it to Wyatt when she returned. In the meantime, she changed into a pair of white capris and a halter top, with a light floral patterned shirt to go over the top. She added strappy sandals, the kind that Wyatt would undoubtedly tease her about, but she would be in an office today, not playing farm girl, though she had to admit she enjoyed being out on the farm soaking up sunshine.

A half hour later, she found a spot in town next to a brand new Lexus with license plates from Iowa, of all places. Must be the lure of the West that brought people to Cody. The brochures boasted great skiing in the winter. She wondered if she would still be here by then, or if Nora would want her back in New York. If Kate was to help run the company, Nora would want her there, most likely. And yet, Kate couldn't get over how comfortable she felt here, with the wide-open vistas, the lack of traffic... and Wyatt.

Every time she thought about him, her heart would skip a beat. When he wasn't around, she found herself wishing he was. Had she ever felt that way about Palmer? Not really. She had just felt lonely, as though something was missing but she couldn't say what. Even the Manhattan skylines gave her an unending sense of isolation in a sea of faces. Cities had always done that to her... made her feel alone, lonely. She never really felt connected until she was at her grandmother's house, on the farm, touring the small town, her grandmother introducing her to the many people from her church. She had felt welcomed. Part of a community. Those had been the best times of her life.

Here, once again, she felt that sense of connection. Sure, she knew Emajean would always view her as an outsider, but even that was part of the charm. It just made Kate that more committed to winning the woman over and to prove that she wasn't some priss from the city who thought she was better than everyone else.

She turned the engine off and headed for the office. As she walked toward the door, an old woman wearing a headscarf greeted her. The woman looked like a gypsy, with her thick body and baggy dress that hung down over compression socks and clunky black shoes. The loose brown sweater completed the look.

"Don't go in there," she said, pulling on Kate's shirt.

"What?" Kate said, confused.

"Not today, don't go in there."

"But I have to, that's my office."

The gypsy woman scowled, then hummed like a cat. "Don't say I didn't warn you."

Kate felt a chill run up her spine. What was it with these old women and their warnings? Her grandmother was purported to have "the gift," had said she could see into the future. And there were times when Kate had listened to her predictions and they had come true, or worse, had not listened and had suffered the consequences. She turned to the door. If something *were* to happen, the very least she could do was to warn the others, to give them the day off. Inwardly, she groaned. They all had so much work to do.

She turned back to the gypsy only to discover that she was gone. Frowning, she peered up and down the street. "This is too weird," she muttered to herself. "And now you're talking to yourself. Hurray!"

Before anyone could begin staring at her for her odd behavior, she decided to make a quick stop inside, to suggest that Stanford and Gladys work from home today until things were a little more settled. Then she could decide about tomorrow.

The bell rang as she entered.

"Hey, Kate, come here!" Gladys said excitedly as she pulled up a chair next to her computer. "Let me show you the new website."

"Okay, but just for a minute. I thought maybe you and Stanford could take the day off early, go home and do a little work from there."

She was trying not to scare them, but she could see that she had by the way they turned to her, eyes wide as they glanced nervously at each other.

"Why?" Stanford asked, smacking on his cherry flavored gum.

"We had a fire out at the ranch. Arson, we think." Kate decided to leave out the part about the gypsy lady and just stick to facts. "Until we're sure what's going on, I think it might be a good idea if we closed up for the day."

"Hey, I don't mind working from home," Stanford said, fingering his silver hoop earring.

"Yeah, because no one will be there to stand guard and make sure you work!" Gladys raised a brow, undoubtedly hoping to intimidate him, but Stanford wasn't the type to be easily intimidated. Not with that wicked grin.

"Let's just make this quick," Kate urged. "Show me what you've got."

Gladys and Stanford talked over each other as they each showed her what they had done so far. Kate could only declare them miracle workers. The end product looked amazing.

"Good job, you guys, now get your stuff, pronto."

Instead of being upset by the intrusion into the day, the pair jumped to their feet and bantered back and forth about who would get the most work done at home and who could expect to be found slacking.

"Hey, no one said I couldn't take your laptop with me down to Joey's Fine Dining," Stanford said as he gathered his purse. "I can kill two birds with one stone."

Gladys stopped what she was doing. "You better not get pizza drippings on that laptop."

"*Fine* dining, I said."

Kate stood between them and held up her hands. "No more bickering, you two. Go home and I'll close up."

The moment the pair were gone, Kate felt that same familiar prick down her spine that she had when she'd spoken to the gypsy. She quickly closed the office and locked it, but she couldn't get over the feeling that someone was watching her. And that this particular someone had a plan.

* * *

Wyatt searched the house, calling Kate's name, but the house merely hummed with the sound of the refrigerator. He looked out the window and realized that her SUV was gone. Prior to Kate's arrival, he had never thought much about the house before, but suddenly it felt empty, cavernous. He could swear that he had heard an echo when calling her name.

Maybe she had left a note in her room or his. He marched up the stairs and was about to turn away from her door when he saw that it was slightly ajar. Frowning, he opened it. Even though it was his house, he felt funny walking into "Kate's" room.

It was amazing how quickly the room had taken on a more feminine appearance with Kate here. Bottles of makeup were strewn across the vanity, and her camisole--or at least he thought that's what it was called--was draped over one end of her mirror. He felt his cheeks flush. Kate would be angry if she caught him snooping through her things.

He turned to leave. That's when he saw it. The cigarette lying on the dresser. He rushed over to it. She didn't smoke, and especially not Marlboros. Where had she come by a cigarette? Was she an accomplice... using the marketing campaign as a ploy to steal his ranch? She *was* from the city after all. They had different ethics, though he could beg to differ on that one. He was just about to pocket the cigarette when he heard movement from behind and turned quickly.

"What are you doing in my room?" Kate demanded.

Guilt mixed with indignation and he flinched. "You may have forgotten, but this is *my* house and *my* ranch." He couldn't help the dig, but she deserved it, if indeed she'd been behind the fire in some way.

"As a matter of fact, I *haven't* forgotten. But I would have hoped that while I was here you would afford me some privacy."

"And why do you need so much privacy?" he said in challenge, chin lifted.

"Because," she said, making quick work of the space between them, "I have earned it." She grabbed the cigarette out of his hand. "I suppose you're wondering why I have this."

He nodded, but stayed silent, giving her the chance to exonerate herself.

"If you had trusted me, you would have waited for me to give this to you. I found it under the oak tree, near the charred field."

"Why didn't you show it to me before you left?" he challenged.

"Because you had already left for the cabin and I needed to get to town to take care of a few things. I thought it could wait an hour until you got back. But I can see you had other plans," she said, blistering him with those lovely gray-green eyes.

"Oh," he mumbled, peering down at his feet. "Why didn't you leave me a note?"

"Because I wasn't planning to be gone long and I thought it would be better if we talked in person."

"So you're not--" he blurted out and quickly realized his mistake.

"Not what?"

"Nothing." He felt the temperature in the room rise by at least a good fifteen degrees.

"No, you started it, so finish it. I'm not what."

"In cahoots."

"In cahoots?"

He splayed his hands. "With that Ian guy. To take my land."

She laughed outright at that. In fact, she laughed so hard that it nearly brought tears to her eyes which made it feel that much warmer and muggier in the cramped quarters.

"Why would I *ever* do such a despicable thing like that? Do you really think I'm the sort of person who would steal from a man who has worked hard all his life and who is helping a bunch of vets with his own money? Do you?"

Her laughter had turned to anger faster than sunshine to rain. He glanced at the door, wishing he were on the other side of it. Whether he liked it or not, they were having their first fight. This would be a make or break moment, only now he wished he could make a break for it until things calmed down.

"Well, I've got news for you, buddy, I just spent the last twenty-four hours working my behind off to save this farm for *you*." Her voice caught. Suddenly, she was in his arms crying and he was soothing her, patting her hair and whispering encouragement.

"I'm sorry. I should have never gone into your room. I made assumptions--"

"*Wrong* assumptions."

He could still hear the anger in her voice. "Okay, *wrong* assumptions. And I'm sorry."

"I'm sorry, too, for not showing you the cigarette sooner. I was just afraid to take it out to you while the sheriff was here. After all, you were so adamant about not telling him about Toby that I was afraid I might mess something up. I found it under the tree out front."

How ironic, because, after much consideration, Wyatt had been the one to talk to the sheriff about Toby. Well, none of that mattered now.

"So, could it be his?"

"More than likely," Wyatt said, combing through her soft auburn hair with his fingers. "I'll let the sheriff know that you found the cigarette."

He took a thumb and wiped away her tears. Yet she still

wore a pensive expression.

"I have a feeling you haven't told me everything."

She bit her lips, then finally nodded. "You're going to think this is crazy, but a woman came up to me while I was heading into the office. She warned me not to go inside the office today."

"Why?"

"That's just it, I don't know." She bit her lips again. "But the odd thing is, she sort of looked like a gypsy."

"We don't get many gypsies in Wyoming," he said with a laugh. When she didn't laugh, too, he knew she wasn't kidding. "You're serious?"

She nodded sheepishly.

"Hmm," he murmured.

"Do you think we should tell the sheriff?"

He stepped back so he could get a good look at her, then took her hands in his. They felt so small. He rubbed the back of her hands with his thumb and said, "No. I think we should keep this to ourselves for now."

Reluctantly, she concurred. "So, what do you think that meant?"

"I don't know. What did you do about it?"

"I didn't know how serious to take the woman's advice, but to be on the safe side, Gladys and Stanford are going to work from home for the rest of the day. I closed up shop."

"Did you notice anything suspicious?"

Kate shook her head, the sides of her hair still damp from tears.

"That's good. Maybe when I go talk to the sheriff, I'll feel him out about anything else suspicious." Wyatt was about to excuse himself, when he stopped. "Do you want to come with me to town? It might be a good idea to stick together until we know what's really going on around here."

A look of relief washed over her. "Give me a minute, and I'll be right down."

Ten minutes later they were on the road. Fortunately, no car was trailing them that Wyatt could see. Maybe his earlier assumption had been right. If Toby *was* behind all this, maybe he was lying low for a while. He hoped so.

When they arrived in town at the sheriff's office, the sheriff was nowhere to be seen.

"He got a call," the dispatcher told Wyatt. "A burglary in process. They caught the guy, but nothing to do with the ranch."

"Thanks," Wyatt said.

He was about to leave when the dispatcher got a call that crackled over the dispatch. "We found the guy inside J & R Marketing. Said he was only trying to steal some files, but we found him with baling wire and duct tape. We're bringing him in for questioning, over."

Wyatt exchanged glances with Kate, whose eyes had grown round with shock and surprise. So the gypsy--if indeed that's what she was--had spoken the truth.

Twenty-Four

Inside Sheriff Benson's office, Kate heard a commotion and peered up in time to see the sheriff enter with a handcuffed, scruffy-looking man in his early twenties. He had wide-set eyes, wide cheekbones, and narrow eyes. Shifty was the first word that came to mind.

"Is that Toby?" Kate whispered to Wyatt.

Wyatt nodded and stood, his gaze never wavering from the young man's face.

The sheriff seemed surprised to see them in the lobby of the sheriff's office, but quickly gathered his wits and said, "Come with me."

He held onto Toby's arm as he ushered them down a long, narrow hallway and into a side room crammed with three chairs, two on one side of a large desk, and one on the other side. Behind him was a glass trophy case with photographs of him and fellow officers in uniform. Below that was a display of awards, ribbons, and trophies that he and his fellow officers had received over the years in their line of duty.

On his desk sat a picture of his wife, two strapping young sons fresh out of junior high and high school, and a daughter who appeared around elevenish, if Kate were any judge.

The sheriff put the handcuffed young man on a chair in the corner and called for two of his junior officers, who appeared almost instantly as though waiting for their cue. The sheriff steepled his fingers and nodded to the potential felon in the corner.

"This here fellow was found in J & R Marketing. We caught him with a flash drive. He was downloading files from your computers. Do you know why he might be interested in your files?"

Toby appeared sweaty and wild-eyed from the apparent struggle he'd had with the officer when captured. His black t-shirt still bore the marks of a scuffle from the collar being twisted into a ball by one or the other of the officers.

"No, I don't," Kate said truthfully.

"That's the guy I believe set fire to my field this morning," Wyatt added, glaring in Toby's direction. Dipping into his pocket, he produced the cigarette that Kate had found earlier and lay it on the table. "And this is what he was doing before he set the fire, isn't that right, Toby?"

Toby grunted, then merely turned toward the wall so he wouldn't have to face Wyatt. *He's awfully smooth for someone who is new to crime.* Kate bet that he had a rap sheet a mile long.

"Is this cigarette yours?" Sheriff Benson asked. "And don't lie, because we can do DNA testing."

"I want an attorney," Toby mumbled, refusing to face them.

Sheriff Benson ignored him as though the boy hadn't spoken. "So, do you have a beef against both these people?"

Toby didn't even bother to answer this time.

"What'd they do to you, huh? You can answer now, or you can answer later, but you *will* answer."

"Not without a lawyer."

The sheriff stood so abruptly that his chair scraped against the smooth gray-tiled floor. In response, Toby trembled and put his cuffed hands in the air as if to deflect a blow. Kate wondered how many times the boy had been hit over his lifetime. Funny how one kid could come away from a childhood of abuse with the determination never to abuse anyone else, whereas another kid in the same household would simply perpetuate the abuse. Not for the first time, she wondered what made people "go bad."

"We've already read you your Miranda rights. Now get him a damned lawyer," the sheriff told the junior officer.

"Okay, buddy, come with me," said the taller officer, the more fit of the two.

Together, the pair ushered him out of the room. Once they were alone again, Sheriff Benson returned to his seat.

"So, you tell me, why do you think this boy would set fire to your place then turn around and break into *her* place of business? What's the connection?"

Kate turned to Wyatt who seemed just as puzzled as she was, under the circumstances.

"Well, I know this boss of hers, this Ian--"

Kate filled in the last name for him.

"He wanted me to stay with his company," Wyatt said, pulling at his chin.

"Ian was involved in a hostile takeover of the company I worked for," Kate added in explanation. "He sold the rural offices to my former boss. He went after all the rural accounts when the company split."

"I refused to go with him," Wyatt said. "I opted to stay with Kate here."

Kate's heart melted to think that he had put such trust and faith in her after knowing her for such a short time.

"So, you think this guy may be trying to sabotage the business, *and* your farm?"

It was clear by Wyatt's surprised expression that, like her, neither one of them had thought of that before, or at least not considered it a real possibility. But could he? Could Ian try to sabotage *both* of their livelihoods? The thought was chilling.

"Well, the good news is he wasn't able to get any of your files, but there are many ways of getting at those if someone really wants to. All you need is a fifteen-year-old with a bunch of time on his or her hands, someone who would like a little play money, and you've got yourself a hacker."

That was a cheery thought. "Good to know," Kate said.

The sheriff laid his hands on the table, palms up as though showing he had nothing to hide. "I'm just being realistic."

Wyatt stood, clearly done with more bad news. He shook the sheriff's hand and said, "Keep us posted if you hear anything, would you?"

"Will do."

Once outside, Wyatt rubbed his face and stared at the crystal blue sky before returning his attention to Kate, who was feeling a growing knot in the pit of her stomach.

"What now?"

"I say we keep a sentry posted at the ranch," Wyatt said

"Yes, but Toby will be behind bars. Do you think we'll

have to worry after this?"

Wyatt squeezed his eyes shut and then opened them. "You never know what people are capable of, especially when they're trying to protect what they consider their territory."

"Yes, but we paid for nearly half the company. And you have the right to choose whomever you want to handle your account."

He rubbed his jaw. "*You* may think so, and I may think so, but not everyone thinks like you and I."

"So, what now?" she asked, her shoulders slumped in defeat.

"We wait."

"Wait for what?"

He smiled and took her hand. "For the next shoe to drop."

* * *

For the next two days, an uneasy silence settled over the ranch. Contrary to Wyatt's earlier fears, nothing happened. Kate had returned to work, and the website was set to go live in a week, accompanied by a news story both locally and nationally. A reporter would interview Wyatt later that day and, if all went well, the story was to be shown by sister stations nationally on Labor Day. Even as he sat on the wicker loveseat Emajean had the boys place on the back porch and sipped his morning coffee, black with just a hint of chicory, he felt the jitters coming on. After all, he was a simple man who liked simple pleasures. He'd never been one to clamor for the spotlight.

Fortunately, Bobby Sue Perkins was to be his interviewer and he'd known Bobby Sue for years. Since she was a toddler, actually. Still, he'd never been interviewed by her before in front of the cameras, and he was already freezing despite the fact that the sun was just coming up in the east. By the time she arrived at ten, he could only imagine what he'd be like. He would be lucky to put together a coherent sentence.

"Knock, knock!" Kate opened the screen door and ventured outdoors. "Would you mind a little company?"

He scooted over and made room for her on the wicker

147

loveseat. Her hair was still wet and folded into a French braid. She wore white capris and a clingy black-and-white sweater that showed off her curves. It reminded him that it had been awhile since he'd been with a woman and he missed it. Especially now.

"How are you holding up?" Kate said, taking a seat next to him.

She smelled of warm honey and vanilla, an aroma that reminded him of his mother's baking, a happy time, back when life seemed full of possibility. He had cobbled together a life with Emajean, but it wasn't the same as having a family of his own. He couldn't help but wonder if he would mess up again. After the divorce with his first wife, he'd kept a tidy emotional distance between him and everyone he had ever dated. Safer that way. That way he couldn't hurt the woman and she couldn't hurt him. And that plan filled his basic needs, but not the core one. Love. He had thought he could live without it... until now. Seeing Kate, he wasn't so sure anymore.

"Not well, I take it?" Kate said, eyeing him carefully.

He'd been so lost in thought, he'd forgotten the question. "Oh, right. Got a touch of the nerves, and you?"

"I do this for a living, and once in a while I'm in front of the camera, so it's not as stressful for me," she said, her gray eyes glistening.

"Lucky you," he said with a half-hearted laugh.

"Well, it'll be over soon. Hang in there." She paused and appeared hesitant. "After the interview, I need to go to the airport. Nora and Jack finally got a flight in. They're going to be here for two nights on a layover before they head out to Utah and to one of our forty-five other offices. I'm going to meet with them and then..."

Her voice drifted off. Wyatt had been gazing over the landscape at the five acres of pines and scrub oak that bordered the south acre of their property and stood between his ranch and the cabin. When she stopped, he turned his head.

"Then what?"

"Then I think it's time I look for my own place. I've overstayed my welcome and then some."

Wyatt had known this time would come, but it took him by surprise nonetheless. He had enjoyed having her here. Wanted her to stay.

"Can I say anything to change your mind?" He gathered her hand in his, feeling the tender warmth of it and wishing he could say something, *anything*, to make her stay.

"This is a beautiful place, and I've enjoyed being here tremendously. But I'm living here rent free, and I've been here longer than we'd agreed."

He peered down at her tapered fingers and rubbed his thumb on the back of them one by one. "You do what you have to," he said, his throat constricting, "but you're welcome to stay as long as you want."

At that point, he ventured a look into her beautiful almond-shaped eyes and saw an expression of what he could only hope was longing, the same longing that he had been feeling for her the past few weeks. He kissed the back of her hand and felt her stir. Within moments, she was in his arms and the worry of the past few days melted away, replaced by a well of emotion so deep that it took all of his strength to keep from lifting her into his arms and carrying her off to bed.

Finally, he pulled back at exactly the same time she did and they both laughed. "Could I at least pay rent?" They laughed some more.

He tweaked her nose. "We'll see. I would do anything to keep you here."

Those last words had spilled out so quickly that it was too late to retract them. He immediately tried to backtrack, but finally gave up when he saw that it was only making things worse.

"Wyatt..." she said, cupping her hand over his. "There's something I've been meaning to tell you."

"No," he said, "there's something I've been needing to tell *you*. Let's go for a walk."

They had walked no more than fifty yards down the dirt path that led to the cabin when Wyatt heard Emajean yell out the back door. "Wyatt! Phone for you."

He groaned as she held up his cell phone.

"Can it wait?" he yelled, but he knew the answer by her dark expression.

"It's Bobby Sue."

He turned to Kate and could read the disappointment in her eyes.

"I've got to take this, but I'll be right back, okay? Hold that thought."

Although she nodded, he could see she was biting her lip, a sure sign of anxiety if ever there was one. He squeezed her hand, then hurried to reach the phone. The news wasn't good, at least not from his perspective. Bobby Sue was on her way over. She was almost here. He balled his hand in frustration.

When he was done with the phone call, he ran to catch up to Kate. By the time he reached her, he was panting and out of breath.

"We're going to have to hold this conversation until later." He explained the cancellation of another appointment. "Bobby Sue was forced to move up our interview. I hope you don't mind."

"Of course not," Kate said, but he could read the discouragement in her voice.

He squeezed her hand. "In the meantime, would you provide backup in case I get tongue tied?"

"Sure," she said, appearing more at ease now.

They'd barely walked to the front of the farmhouse when Wyatt saw a cloud of dust in the distance preceded by a white sport utility vehicle.

"The word lead foot was made for that girl," he said with a laugh.

*　*　*

Within minutes, the SUV was parked in front of the house, a lingering cloud of dust choking the air. Out from the vehicle popped the shortest newscaster Kate had ever laid eyes on. She was plump, black, and had a 120-watt smile that radiated through her like a firefly. Her shoulder-length hair lay flat against her head and shined as brightly as her smile. As if to further prove what Kate had already suspected--that she was perky--she bounced over to where Wyatt and Kate stood, hand held out to greet them. Kate shook her hand. She instantly liked Bobby Sue.

"Hey there, Wyatt," the reporter said, ignoring the professional greetings. "Who've you got here?"

"My new assistant." He winked at Kate. "My marketing agent. She's the one helping me set up all this." He waved his hand toward the ranch. Then he stopped and frowned. "Where's your cameraman?"

"First of all, this is the twenty-first century and we say camera*person*, since we have both cameramen *and* camerawomen. Secondly, I am the camerawoman *and* the newscaster. We have to set up our own cameras these days. It's cheaper."

Kate laughed. Somehow she had expected Wyoming to be less progressive. She was happy to be proved wrong. With this attitude, the country might actually elect a woman to the White House one of these days. A girl could only dream.

For the next hour, Bobby Sue traipsed with them all over the ranch, taking pictures of the men talking in front of the log cabin. Many of the young vets wore hats with insignias from their service, while a few of them waved flags.

"We want to put this on for our Labor Day airing. It would fit in perfectly. If the big networks like it, they'll show it nationally, so fingers crossed," she said, entwining two stubby fingers. "We're going to market it hard. For Wyatt here. *And* for our boys."

Bobby Sue winked at the guys who let loose with howls and wolf whistles. Well, some things hadn't changed, Kate realized with a smile.

After Bobby Sue had left, and Wyatt and Kate were standing alone on the porch, Kate had to admit that the interview had gone amazingly well, which made it harder to say what she had to say to Wyatt. Ever since she had told Palmer she wasn't ready to see him, he'd become increasingly persistent. It was as if he were in it for the hunt alone and that bothered her. She wanted someone who would be in it for the long haul, someone who would stay no matter what circumstances were thrown his way. To put it simply, she wanted someone who would love her, wholly and unconditionally. She knew she was asking for the moon to expect someone to be there forever, to love her and her alone, but that's what she wanted. What she *needed* to thrive.

"Ugh!" she said, not realizing she had spoken aloud.

"What, you didn't think that went well?"

Wyatt's blue eyes were amazingly clear, like looking into twin pools of water. And like water, they drew her to him. She wanted to dive in, to explore this person who was new to her, and yet seemed like someone she had known for years.

"It went amazingly well."

"Then why the sigh?"

She looked over to the oak tree standing off to the left of the porch. The oak represented strength, stability. A place for shelter in a storm. She wished it had the power to give her strength to say what she needed to--to let Wyatt know about Palmer, about the ambivalence she felt for him. And about her growing attraction to Wyatt. But would he understand? She couldn't risk pushing him away. Not until they got to know each other better.

"It's just that I guess I would like to see how things go before we have some heavy talk."

If Wyatt were a smoker, she would have said he could use a cigarette right about now. To prove her point, he rolled his thumb and forefinger nervously together and frowned, peering down at his boots as if he could find the answer to what he wanted to say there.

Finally, he lifted his head and stared off into the distance. "You're right. We can save our talk until later."

She could tell that she had upset him, so to make amends, she said, "Why don't you come with me to pick up Nora and Jack tonight? I'm sure they would love to meet you."

"Better yet, why don't you invite them here for the day?" Wyatt offered. "That way they'll get a chance to see the place. Learn what the campaign is all about."

Kate felt a welling of excitement. Nora would love it here,

she felt certain, and Jack, too, if Nora could talk them into coming.

"Tell you what. I'll ask Emajean to set up extra plates for dinner. In fact, why don't they spend the night here? Emajean could prepare one of the guest rooms."

The screen door squeaked open and out popped Emajean wearing a red-and-white checkered blouse with a white t-shirt under it and a pair of Wrangler blue jeans over some of the oldest, dustiest boots Kate had ever seen. "What will you ask me?"

"Ole Big Ears here," Wyatt said with a lift of his brow and a twinkle in his eyes, "has been horning in on our conversation. So you already know that we're gonna have guests tonight."

Emajean moaned and grumbled something about ingrates who invited people without her permission, then promptly disappeared behind the screen door, but not before Kate had read the excitement in her eyes at the idea of company. Now she would have something to gossip about with the ladies at church next Sunday.

"So, fill me in on this Nora lady," Wyatt said.

For the next twenty minutes, Kate told him everything she knew about Nora and Jack. When she was through, he said, "So do you think she's got the right stuff?"

"The right stuff?"

"To keep this ship afloat."

Kate smiled. "Oh, she has the right stuff alright."

Nora may have lived in Jack's shadow all these years, but Kate felt sure it was his wife's time to shine. And shine she would, given half a chance. But in a man's world, she would need more than half a chance, because good didn't cut it. Only an *exceptional* woman would be allowed into that exclusive world of business. No, the doors had been firmly closed to women for centuries. But with any luck, the exceptional women of the world would help pull the rest of their kind through the barely opened door to allow women into the rarefied world of men.

Twenty-Five

The morning had turned cloudy with a chance of thunderstorms in the late afternoon. Kate stood out on the porch, peering nervously at the sky and hoping that Nora's plane wouldn't be delayed due to inclement weather. Poor Wyatt had long since tired of Kate's badgering about the time and the weather, about whether or not they would need to arrive at the airport earlier than planned. Frustrated, he had gone off to feed the horses, but she felt certain he was looking for peace and quiet. She couldn't blame him. She was driving *herself* crazy with all the incessant worrying.

She paced back and forth across the porch, relieved when she finally saw Wyatt exit the barn and yell, "Okay, we're heading to the airport as soon as I change into a clean pair of boots."

Kate didn't know whether to run out and hug Wyatt or to run in and grab her belongings. She had so many questions for Nora and so many things to tell her about the company and what had transpired since the sale, the latest news about Toby first and foremost on her mind.

"What do you think will happen to Toby?" Kate asked Wyatt as soon as they were buckled up in Kate's SUV and on their way.

"I talked to the sheriff this morning. This isn't Toby's first offense by a longshot, but he's probably not going to do a lot of time either. It's up to the prosecutor and the defense attorney."

"Did the sheriff say when, or if, his case will go to court?"

Wyatt shrugged. "The courts are so backlogged these days that it will probably end in a plea bargain."

"Which means?"

"Which means he'll serve a small amount of time, weeks, maybe a month or two and then be released."

Kate frowned as she peered out over the landscape, so different from New York and its skyscrapers. Cars honking, people cursing her if she didn't move quickly enough. Here, everything was different. It was like comparing a waterfall to a babbling brook. One was noisy, sometimes frightening, and filled with smells, both delicious and awful. The other was quiet, peaceful, and smelled of freshly tilled earth and pine. And yet both had their undertow. A turbulent, churning rhythm of undercurrent that could run deep and carry snags set to pull a swimmer under, if the swimmer wasn't careful. Toby was a perfect example of that.

Why, *why* couldn't Ian and Toby just leave things alone, move on, give Kate and Wyatt their space? There was plenty of work to go around. But some people needed to win at all costs. When that happened, it left no choice but to fight.

"I just can't believe they'll release Toby after all he did," Kate said, scowling.

"It's the way things work in our justice system."

Again, Kate peered out of the windshield at a field of buttercups, searching for answers, wishing that she could secure those answers as easily as plucking flowers from the meadow beyond. Her eyes searched the stand of lumber pine on this side of the road, while on the other side of the road lay open field, dry from lack of water. According to Wyatt, the weather had changed dramatically over the past few years, global warming, by his estimation, causing drought and deforestation through lightning strikes and uncontrolled burning.

As if to prove his theory right, Kate heard the first rumbles of a brewing storm and felt a matching rumble in her chest.

"What will happen once Toby's released?"

"I had a restraining order placed on him. They're still looking into his ties with Ian. Not much will happen with the fire because they can just say he was careless, that it wasn't intentional."

Despite Wyatt's outward calm, worry lines creased his forehead and his mouth was set in a thin straight line. Kate reached out and squeezed his hand.

"And what about the burglary?" she asked.

"The sheriff's office is still investigating. If they find anything that could tie him to the farm, then at that point he could get more time. We can only hope. The longer he's locked up, the better."

Kate couldn't agree more. Maybe once things had settled down, and with enough time and distance between them, Toby, and indeed Ian, if he truly was involved, might move on and that would be the end of it. She hoped so.

They drove in silence for much of the rest of the journey, choosing to talk about the more mundane aspects of their day. An hour later, they reached their destination. Nora and Jack, always punctual, were standing in front of the terminal, suitcases in hand and looking out of place in this rural setting.

Whereas Nora wore a sleek yellow dress suit with black high heels and a gold wristband, Jack wore shorts and a Hawaiian shirt. Nowhere could you find a more incompatible pair physically, but emotionally they were soulmates. Nora was Jack's strongest advocate and God help the man or woman who did anything to hurt him, while Jack was as easy-going and laid back a person Kate had ever known. His face had grown a bit jowly over the years, and he had basset hound eyes. But when he smiled, and he smiled often, he was like a kind uncle, everyone's friend.

That wasn't to say he didn't have a tougher side. Woe to the marketing agent who didn't do his or her job correctly. But mostly, Kate and the rest of the staff worked hard for him because they loved him and knew that he cared deeply about his profession and all the people in it. For that reason, they had grown together like a family. In short, Jack was everything Ian was not.

"So this is the man who has been keeping you so busy these past few weeks," Nora said, arching a brow in Kate's direction.

Kate instantly flushed, heat rising to her cheeks. She quickly recovered, making brief introductions.

Jack hugged Kate then reached in to shake Wyatt's hand. "Has my girl here been talking your ear off? She sure has mine, over the years."

Again, Kate felt herself flush, wishing the topic of conversation would move away from her and on to something else. Fortunately, Wyatt read her discomfort and offered to load their bags.

Afterward, he invited them out for dinner where they got to know each other better. All Kate's worries slipped away in increments so that by the time they were done with dinner and nearing the ranch, she had almost forgotten them completely until she heard another ominous rumble of thunder.

"Wow! We're going to get quite the introduction to Wyoming, it appears." Jack grinned, obviously relishing the storm that had gone from simple rumbling to an all-out ear shattering roar followed by lightning that lit up the night sky and a downpour of rain.

"This is what we call a gully washer," Wyatt said as Kate pulled into the long driveway.

They were almost to the farmhouse when lightning filled up the entire night sky behind the house. Emajean must have seen Kate's headlights because she came rushing out onto the porch in an apron, her hair frothing as though caught in a sea breeze. Frantic, she gripped the porch railing as if to stave off the storm.

"Something's wrong," Wyatt said, leaping out of the SUV as it rolled to a stop.

Kate parked the SUV and ran after him, feeling nearly as vested in the ranch as Wyatt, after everything that had happened.

"They set Toby free," Emajean yelled over the storm. "I just got word from the sheriff that they let him go an hour ago. They put him on a bus out of town, but the bus had a flat tire a few miles out. While the bus driver was working on the flat, Toby took off." Her words spilled over each other like rushing water. "According to several of the passengers, they saw him running toward town. The bus broke down a half mile from here."

Kate froze at the words and peered over her shoulder. *A half mile from here*. That meant that he could already be on the property, maybe even in the barn.

* * *

The news that Toby had been freed washed over Wyatt and left him feeling anxious. Even now, Toby could be out there somewhere hiding in any number of places: the barn, the shed, even in the cabin for all he knew. That thought sent a chill through him as he stood out on the porch, both Emajean and Kate at his side.

"Did you let Les know?" Wyatt asked.

"Of course I did," Emajean said, turning surly at anything that challenged her competence.

"And what did he say?"

"He has the men combing the cabin and its surroundings now."

Jack stepped forward. "Do you want me to come with you to check out the barn? Make sure he hasn't holed up in there?"

Wyatt didn't take long to come to a decision. Two hands were better than one in a fight, and even though Jack was from New York, he had a feeling he had seen action more than once in his life and could pull his weight, if need be. He quickly explained the situation with Toby to him. Then he said, "I'm going to go around the back of the barn. You go through the front door and I'll meet you inside. If you see him, shout, and I'll come running."

Emajean handed Wyatt a forty-eight Colt that she pulled from her apron pocket. Fear registered on Kate's face.

"It'll be alright. Wait here," Wyatt told the ladies.

The only one who appeared amused was Nora, who seemed to be revelling in the situation.

Just then, Wyatt heard another clap of thunder followed moments later by a root-like network of lightning bolts. Another sharp crack sounded and the sky lit up.

"Over there!" Emajean yelled. "The tree."

Sure enough, one of the larger pinyon pines behind the barn was on fire. The rain might slow the progress of the spread of the fire, but the wind could counteract it. Plus, pines had resin, and that resin could act like a mini explosion that could set off the trees around it if they didn't get the fire under control, quickly. Worse yet, it could set the barn on fire with the animals and hay from the latest harvest still in it.

"Change of plans," he yelled over the storm. "I'm going to need all of you. Emajean, you go call the fire department."

"Will do."

"Nora." It took only a second to decide she would be no use in a crisis, not with those designer clothes and high heels. "You can wait inside. Emajean will make you comfortable."

"Kate and Jack, I could use your help. There's a hose by the side of the barn. You take that, Jack. Kate, come with me. I need you to help me clear the horses out of the barn in case it catches fire. With any luck, this rain will help douse it," he said, fat wet raindrops dripping down his face.

For the next ten minutes, they worked feverishly to get the animals out of the barn. The horses were spooked by the lightning and reared up, nearly clipping Wyatt numerous times. If he hadn't worked with horses all his life, he might very well have sustained a serious injury.

While he opened the stall doors, he had Kate open the gate for him, then he maneuvered the horses into the paddock. Once there, they roared and bucked their fear, white eyes shining in the night as both man and beast sloshed through the quickly forming mud.

Behind him, Wyatt heard a thud and saw that Kate had fallen in the mud, face first. He would have laughed at how ridiculous she looked, but at that moment it was as if the cavalry had appeared because truck after truck full of neighbors arrived to help put out the fire.

"What the...?"

Everett was Wyatt's closest neighbor from the first contingent of arrivals, his bushy, mountain-man beard flowing over a large barrel chest and belly. "Hey, Wyatt!" he yelled. "We heard from that city girl that you had yourself another fire."

"City girl?" He turned to Kate, who only shrugged and wiped mud from her face.

"That Nora somebody or other from New York."

Kate laughed, then shrugged again. "She's an organizer."

"How the hell...?" Wyatt said, shaking his head. "Never mind." At that moment, another neighbor arrived, Frank

Forrester. Frank was as lean and spare as Everett was bulky. "You and Frank are handy with an axe, no?"

"Sure are!" Frank said. "Got one right here." He pulled one out of the bed of his gray GMC pickup truck.

Wyatt pointed to the forest that edged his property. "The pine behind the barn is on fire. We need to bring it down before the fire spreads."

Felling the tree would be tricky and would require a steady eye so that it didn't land on the barn and set the whole thing aflame.

Wyatt nodded in the direction of the forest. "You're going to need to thread the needle so the pine lands exactly between the oak tree and the barn."

Everett pushed his red ball cap back on his head and whistled. "You believe in miracles?"

"Don't know. But I'll believe one if I see one." Wyatt flashed him a toothy grin.

"You owe me a pint for this one," Everett said. Then he headed toward the pine with the axe in his hand, Wyatt and Kate trailing beside him and Frank not far behind.

"Tell you what. I'll make that two pints, if you can pull it off." Wyatt winked.

"You must think I'm Santa Claus and the Tooth Fairy all rolled up into one," Everett groused, but kept up his fast pace nonetheless.

Wyatt was panting by the time they reached the back of the barn where Jack was valiantly squirting the tree with the spray nozzle on the end of the hose. By now, the pine was almost fully engulfed and the wind was sending hot embers flying into the air. Any minute now, the fire would spread to the trees around it and, instead of a single tree, they would have an all-out forest fire. Wyatt couldn't let that happen.

"Hurry," he urged. "You get on that side of it," he told Everett. "And Frank, you chop just below it on the opposite side. I'm going to try to hook the tree with a grappling hook from the hayloft so that we can pull it the direction we need it to fall."

"Kate," he shouted. "Go let the horses out of the paddock

and into the pasture where they can run while we get this under control."

Then he raced off toward the barn, leaving the men to begin the arduous task of felling the tree. He made quick work of the ladder. Before he could gather the hook, he saw that sparks were flying through the air, a couple of them landing dangerously close to the hay. He removed his shirt and smothered the embers with it. Then he grabbed the hook and swung it once, twice, three times. On the third try it finally caught and he threw down the rope. He quickly raced back down the ladder. He didn't know how Kate had done it, but she had already moved several of the horses and was racing to get the last of the horses out. For the next few minutes, he helped her until the last of the horses was in the pasture.

By the time the pair arrived at the rear of the barn, the yard was awash in a sea of men and women there to help. Two of the neighbor men had a hold of the rope and were pulling. Seeing that they had everything under control, Wyatt looked over at Kate who seemed small and frightened against the warm glow of the tree. He reached an arm around her to comfort her and felt her gratitude when she lay her head on his shoulder.

"Do you think they'll be able to get the tree down without setting the barn on fire?"

He shook his head. "I don't know."

For the next few minutes, they huddled together watching. Just then, the horses must have caught wind of the smoke and fire because a loud thud of hooves against the pasture's wooden fences reverberated among the other surreal sounds of fire licking at the inky sky and the quiet murmur of voices in the gathering crowd.

"Did you hear that?" Kate said, shivering suddenly.

Wyatt pulled her in closer. The terrified sound of the horses shrieking in fear lent the scene an eerie quality that wouldn't soon dissipate.

As Wyatt and the others stood there, watching and waiting for the tree to fall, the vets appeared soaking wet from their trek down the road toward the barn. It felt as though the entire community had turned out. From where Wyatt stood, he could see women standing out on the porch with food they had rushed to provide, in case this turned into an all-nighter.

The sound of the fire engine chugging up the road added to the almost circus-like atmosphere as it struggled past the quickly abandoned trucks and cars up and down the road. The horn tooted several times to get past the people who were lingering on the sides of the road, waiting to be called into action if necessary.

At last, the big red truck arrived just as the tree let out a giant crack, teetered precariously and fell in slow motion with a loud and resounding thud that reverberated several times before it finally came to a rest behind the barn.

Immediately, the firemen set to work to put out the flames. As they did, Wyatt remembered the embers that he had seen flying through the hayloft and said, "I had better go check the hayloft, just in case there are any remaining embers."

"Let me," Kate offered. "You're needed here in case the firemen have any problems or questions."

Wyatt hesitated. He didn't like the thought of her in the hayloft alone, but she was right. He might be needed here.

"There's a bucket next to the sink in the barn. Fill it up, then hook it to the pulley I have rigged for that use. You can pull it up once you're in the loft."

"Got it she said." Then she was off.

He wondered if he had made the right decision sending her up there alone. He was about to call her back when one of the firemen yelled to him. He watched her enter the barn and felt a tug of anxiety. He was just being overly cautious. She would be fine.

Twenty-Six

The barn felt a good ten degrees cooler, yet a leftover mugginess from the outgoing storm created a cloying dampness that made Kate's clothes stick to her skin. It took a full thirty seconds for her eyes to adjust to the lack of light in the barn.

She scanned the gloomy interior until she found the sink and then made quick work of filling the pail that hung on a nail next to it. Though she was careful not to slosh its contents, her jeans managed to get a healthy dousing anyway. Soon she found the pulley next to the hayloft that Wyatt had spoken about and set it gently onto the hook. Then she climbed the ladder to the hayloft above.

For some reason she couldn't quite explain, her heart began to flutter and her skin grew clammy at the idea of going up by herself. After all, Toby was still out there... somewhere.

As she neared the top of the ladder, she forced herself to be brave. If she was ever going to be a successful businesswoman, she would face many challenges and this was just one of them. At that, she placed a hand over the lip of the loft ready to lift herself up the final way when she felt something on her hand and screamed. There, peering down on her from the ledge was a medium-sized rat, its nose twitching and its eyes glowing bright against the shadows.

"You scared the..."

She didn't finish her sentence. Instead, she willed herself over the lip and onto the solid wood floor of the loft. For a moment, she waited for her eyes to adjust to the changing light. It gave her heart time to return to a more normal rhythm.

Finally, she pulled herself upright and stood. From the opening to the loft, she could see below. The firemen had doused the pine and were now concentrating on any embers that might have flown up into the surrounding trees. No doubt they would stand watch again tonight. Now to do her part.

She walked over to the edge of the loft and began ferrying

the bucket up the pulley. Prickles of fear trickled down her spine. She had always hated standing too close to a ledge of any sort. Frowning, she looked behind her. Nothing.

"Afraid of a damned rat," she muttered to herself, glad that no one could hear her.

She had just managed to haul the pail up when she heard a rustle. Piles of hay had been stacked into rows of varying heights creating any number of places to hide.

"Who's there?" she demanded.

Another noise, this time louder, set her heart to hammering like a piston. She was about to make a quick exit when an orange and yellow manx came sauntering from behind one of the hay bales and ran to her, rubbing its body against her and purring.

She reached down to scratch behind its ears. It purred louder.

"I scared off your breakfast, didn't I?" Kate said, rubbing a hand along its back.

The cat stared at her with unblinking yellow eyes, little flecks of gold winking up at her when the light hit them. The manx arched its back, and stretched its front legs, releasing knife-like claws.

"Well, c'mon. Help me check out the loft. Then I'll find you something to eat. Deal?"

It might seem foolish to some, but it felt comforting to have the cat with her. She knew the manx would be no help in a crisis, but at least it provided her a tiny sliver of calm.

Shaking her head to dispel any lingering worries, she hefted the pail onto the wooden floor, sloshing it in the process. Then slowly, methodically, she checked behind each haystack, finding only one small ember that was easily doused.

She was just about to leave when the cat let out a loud screech, its hair standing on end as it peered at something behind her. Before Kate had a chance to react, she felt a hand clamp down over her mouth and felt a mouth next to her ear.

"Shut up and listen," the voice hissed. "Find another job, do you hear me?"

Her abductor put a choke hold around her neck and

repeated his warning. Just before she passed out, she heard the added threat "if you want to live."

The man was gone by the time she awoke to the sound of Wyatt's voice calling to her from the ladder below. It took a moment to orient herself and to remember what had happened before she passed out.

"Wyatt," she called weakly. "Is that you?"

Within seconds, he had bolted up the ladder and knelt down next to her.

"What happened? Are you okay?"

She tried to speak, but in the end only nodded. Finally, she was able to squeak out the words, "He was here."

"Who? Toby?"

She nodded, to which Wyatt's jaw set in grim determination. Kate had to say, she wouldn't want that look turned on her, yet it felt good to know Wyatt was in her corner.

* * *

Anger gripped Wyatt as he thought about what Toby had done to Kate. When had tormenting women become fair game? Probably since Adam and Eve in the Garden of Eden, he decided ruefully. Still, it didn't make it right. It took a coward to pick on women and children, and he didn't like cowards.

Once Wyatt had brought Kate down from the hayloft, he sat her on a haybale and checked her over to make sure she was alright. "I'm going to hitch up my horse and go after Toby."

"How do you know where he's gone?"

"He had to have left a trail."

Outside the barn door, the rain began to fall again, the rumbles of thunder much lower now and in the distance.

"The rain will help me as long as he keeps to the road, but if he's gone into the forest, it's going to be much harder."

Les appeared at the opening to the barn, his hair soaked and his chambray shirt clinging to his chest.

"The fire's out. The chief has been called to another fire a few miles up the road. He needs to leave. He asked us to keep an eye on any remaining embers. Hope you don't mind, but I told him we would."

From outside, Wyatt heard the truck fire up its engines and rumble to life. The fire chief gave a blast of the engine's horns as he passed. Wyatt loped to the door in time to wave his hat in return. People were starting to move toward their vehicles, so he quickly rushed to thank them and shake a few hands before they were gone.

In the meantime, Kate had filled Les in on what had happened and he had the big mare saddled and waiting by the time Wyatt was finished. With all that had happened, Toby would have had a decent head start on Wyatt. Plus, the rain was undoubtedly washing away any remaining tracks.

"I'll put Ryan in charge of the boys," Les said, his boots caked in mud. "They'll keep an eye on the women and the cabin. I'll saddle up and join with you shortly."

"Thanks," Wyatt said, gratefully. "Will you have one of the boys help Kate inside before I go?"

"I'm fine," Kate said, attempting to stand.

"Ignore her," Wyatt said with a wink, then set off.

First, he rode around back, certain that Toby would never have risked leaving through the front of the barn. Even with all the commotion, someone would have spotted him. However, with the focus on the tree, he could easily have slipped out back and gone west into the forest. If Wyatt were a betting man, that's where he would place his odds.

Sure enough, wet, muddy tracks led up the hillside and into the brush. They were easy enough to follow. For some time, he was able to track Toby up the hillside as the trail twisted and turned, moving ever further to the west. There would be no homes or buildings for miles in this terrain. Eventually, the forest would lead toward town, so odds were he was following the tree line. Wyatt tracked the boy as far as he was able until the slick rain and wet vegetation had cleaned Toby's boots of any mud.

Wyatt slowed, peering down, looking for signs of broken branches or smudged trail. Gradually, all signs faded. Now what? The only thing left to do was to follow the tree line and hope that his hunch was correct. For the next half hour, he rode just east of the tree line, occasionally entering the forested area to see if he could find any sign of the boy.

When he reached town, he asked around, but nobody had seen Toby. He told everyone he spoke to, to keep an eye out for him and then went to speak with the sheriff.

"Looks like we have more ammunition on the boy now. I'll put my feelers out," the sheriff said.

As he escorted Wyatt out of the office, he patted him on the back. "Sure am sorry about this, Wyatt. You know I would have kept the boy locked up longer if it were feasible."

"I know, Sheriff. It's not your fault."

Wyatt felt dejected as he made the trek back to the ranch. By the time he arrived, he was so tired that it took some doing to unsaddle his mare and put oats out for her. Furthermore, by the time he entered the house, he was wet, cold, and his eyes were gritty with fatigue.

Kate took one look at him and barked orders. "Quick, Emajean, get him a blanket."

"Looks like he needs a bath, first," Emajean said, eyeing him as she would an errant bull who'd had to be rounded up from the back forty.

"I'll get a hot toddy going," Nora said.

Everybody stopped to look at her in her white Vera Wang dress suit and black Jimmy Choo shoes.

"What?" she said with a sly smile. "You have your way of doing things and I have mine. Besides, I have all the ingredients with me. I picked them up at that store on the way here. Who says a guest can't be a good host, too?"

They all laughed.

Jack took the blanket that Emajean handed him and laid it on the back of the LazyBoy. Wyatt sat down, grateful for the warmth of the fireplace. They pumped him full of questions, but he had little to reveal. He had lost all signs of any tracks. For all he knew, Toby could have doubled back and could be on the property right now. He hoped the boy was smart and was miles away, hitchhiking and putting as much distance as possible between him and the ranch.

Twenty minutes later, Les appeared looking as exhausted and muddy as Wyatt. For the second time that day, all hands appeared ready to give yet another straggler the royal treatment. They sat Les up next to the fireplace with a hot toddy in his hand and regaled him with questions and thanks for all that he had done to help the ranch. Then they offered a round of plates piled high with food leftover from the buffet of meals brought over by the neighbors.

By the time they were done talking and eating, everyone was tired, Wyatt included. They were just saying their goodnights, when Wyatt heard a knock on the door and they all turned. Emajean opened the door cautiously.

On the porch stood Ryan, who looked everywhere except at Emajean as he spoke. "I have some bad news," he said. "Some things have turned up missing at the cabin."

"Wyatt!" Emajean called. "I think this is for you."

Wyatt walked stiffly to the door. "C'mon in, Ryan."

Emajean immediately began a plate of food for the boy and thrust it into his hand then ushered him to a seat at the kitchen table.

"So, what is this about missing things?"

Between ravenous bites, Ryan said, "Well, at first we thought one of the guys had misplaced his tobacco, so no big deal. But then one of the other guys said he was missing money from his sock drawer. We've never had a problem with theft."

Wyatt had always been proud of that fact and thankful that Les had been so good at instilling values in the men.

"What else is missing?" Wyatt asked as both Jack and Les drew up seats around the table.

Ryan peered down at his food. When he finally looked up, it was through hooded eyes, a dark strand of hair hanging into his eyes.

"A knife... a kitchen knife."

A murmur ran around the table as the women hovered over the men.

"Jesus!" Wyatt said, then quickly apologized to the ladies present.

So, Toby *had* doubled back. All the while Wyatt was searching in the wrong direction. Some tracker he was. It would clearly be a long, sleepless night of wondering and worrying.

"We'll need to post sentries. Ryan, you gather your men and decide who will take the cabin, who will watch the barn."

"No disrespect, sir, but we really should have two men posted at all times in case of attack."

"Good point," Wyatt said.

"How are the men going to protect themselves?" Kate asked, her brow knitted into a single straight line. She seemed small to him, fragile, and yet he was convinced she had a fighting spirit.

All eyes landed on Wyatt. Should he give men with PTSD guns? And what would be the legal ramifications if one of them were required to use it to protect himself or one of the others? Most states allowed a homeowner to fight back if attacked *inside* the home, but what about in the barn? And the cabin wasn't owned by any of the men. It was Wyatt's. He didn't want to wake the sheriff this late at night to ask about legalities. He would just have to hope that nothing happened between now and tomorrow morning.

"Have Les pass out guns to the men standing watch." He looked the young vet in the eye. "But whatever you do, tell your men to use their guns only if they have to, do you hear?"

"Yes, sir."

Ryan finished his meal and wiped his mouth with the linen napkin provided, then stood. He held out a hand to Wyatt.

"Thanks for having faith in me."

A warmth flooded Wyatt as he shook the vet's hand. He'd never had a son, but if he did, he would want him to be like Ryan. He had made mistakes, but he just needed someone kind and caring to believe in him, just as Emajean had believed in Wyatt when he was at his lowest.

He patted him on the back and wished him luck. Emajean excused herself as she led Nora and Jack to their room and showed them where the linen was for tomorrow morning's shower.

That left Wyatt and Kate all alone. A disquiet had come over them, though Wyatt couldn't say why. He wanted to grab Kate up in his arms and tell her everything would be okay, that the world wasn't really as ugly as it seemed, but the truth was far different and he couldn't shield her from it, try as he might.

"You probably thought you were coming to somewhere safe, after New York," he said with a mirthless laugh.

"Even small towns have their secrets, I see," she said with an equally mirthless laugh.

"But no secrets between us, okay?"

He drew her close and felt her tremble beneath his touch. He knew he would have to tell her about his ex-wife and daughter soon. His daughter was young but tenacious, and he knew he couldn't hold her off much longer. But he wouldn't tell Kate about her... not tonight. Tonight was for healing today's wounds, for comforting Kate and making her feel safe again. Tomorrow, he would tell her. Tomorrow there would be no more secrets.

* * *

More than Kate would ever care to admit, Toby had frightened her... frightened her in a way that ran deep, to the very core of her. Would she be putting others in danger by continuing her career path? She feared the answer was yes.

Wyatt kissed the top of her head as they stood in the living room, then lifted her into his arms.

"What...?"

"Kate, I've wanted you since the day you arrived," he said, kissing her fiercely on the mouth.

When she came up for air, her heart pounding wildly in her chest, he said, "I don't want to sleep alone tonight."

The truth is, she didn't either. She wanted him like she had wanted no other man, especially after today. Before, she'd thought life lasted forever. Now, she knew there was an hourglass counting out the grains of sand and time was passing, and with it her life, her hope for happiness. What was a life without someone to share it with?

"Please?"

No one had ever pleaded for her affection. It felt good to be wanted, needed. She nodded slowly, but before she could get the words out, he swung her around, kissed her deeply as he carried her to his room. Fortunately, Emajean's room and the one that Nora and Jack were staying in were all upstairs.

Wyatt pushed the door to his room open with his hip, shutting it behind him. Then he lay her carefully onto the bed as though she were a great gift that he wanted to take his time unwrapping.

He kissed her deeply, passionately, as he slowly unbuttoned first her blouse, then her pants, kissing the swell of her breasts as he did. His lips trailed down her stomach to the curve of her hips and beyond. Never before had she felt such passion, such need.

With each new touch, his kisses became more frenzied until she could hold back no longer. She helped him pull his shirt over his head and returned his passion kiss for kiss, moving quickly to remove his pants.

For the next twenty minutes, her hips rose to greet his as they explored each others' bodies, the smoothness of each other's skin, and the scars, each touch more needy than the one before. At last their lovemaking reached a climax that ended in spasms of delight that left her feeling spent and satisfied. Afterward, she cuddled in the crook of his arm, her head on his chest, listening to his heartbeat that slowed as he drifted to sleep. She could lay like this all night.

Yet their lovemaking had created a dilemma. Now, she would have to tell Wyatt about Palmer soon. Though she had known that it was over with Palmer the moment she had boarded the plane, she had kept a foot in the door rather than allow it to go completely shut, but why? For security? So she wouldn't have to be alone? And what did that say about her that she didn't want to step out into the world by herself? Yet, other cultures lived among tribes. Even primates lived among others. Was it so wrong to want someone at her side? To want someone who loved her and whom she could love?

No, she would not apologize for wanting to love and be

loved. It was in the human genetic makeup.

She peered over at Wyatt who was now fast asleep. Tomorrow she would tell him about Palmer. Then there would be no more secrets.

Twenty-Seven

When Wyatt awoke the following morning, he felt groggy and disoriented. He peered down at Kate and recalled last night, the passion, the tenderness. He kissed the top of her head and felt her stir in his arms.

How did I get so lucky?

Before last night, he had almost convinced himself that he could go through life alone with just a series of one-night stands to keep him happy. That way he could live whatever life he chose. He would have to answer to no one, and yet it hadn't made him happy like he thought it might. It had just made him selfish and more set in his ways. He didn't want to be like that anymore. He wanted to share a life.

A life with Kate.

He knew it was too early to be thinking such things. Every time he had jumped into something without thinking, he had paid for it. But this time he'd done a lot of thinking, and he was ready. Ready to commit. Ready to be in it for the long haul. Ready to love again. He hoped she felt the same way too.

His thoughts soon turned to Toby who was out there somewhere with a kitchen knife. What he planned to do with that was anyone's guess. Maybe he just wanted protection, but somehow Wyatt doubted it. Toby had already shown himself to be ruthless and unwilling to let sleeping dogs lie. No, he had an agenda, and that agenda seemed to center around this ranch and Kate, and Wyatt was territorial about both. He pulled Kate tighter into his arms.

"I'll keep you safe," he whispered.

Once again, she stirred. This time her eyes fluttered open, and, like him, she glanced around as though unsure of her surroundings.

"Good morning, sleepyhead!" he said, cradling her to him and kissing her full, moist lips. "Sleep well?"

"Best ever," she said with a smile.

He tamped down a roguish grin, but in the end couldn't hide the pride he felt in satisfying this woman that he hoped to keep by his side forever, if possible.

"Heard anything from Ryan or Les?"

"Oh, not since... say eleven or so last night." Again, he smiled, unable to contain the joy he felt at this new turnaround in his life. He hadn't had a more perfect day, despite what had happened yesterday, and it was only eight-thirty in the morning. He stretched and yawned, eager to see how the rest of the day would unfold. If it were up to him, he would lie in this bed all day and get to know everything about Kate. But duty called.

He rose on one elbow. "I would love to spend the day here, but we'd better check on the boys, see if they spotted anyone last night."

Still groggy from sleep, she simply nodded her head and he could swear that she purred. He could listen to that sound all day.

"Okay, sleepyhead," he said, extricating himself from their tight embrace and coming around the other side of the bed to help her out. "You take a shower while I call Les, then I'll meet you for breakfast. Emajean's beginning to take it personally that you're not down on time. I think she thinks you don't like her cooking." He winked.

Kate merely laughed.

"Okay, slavedriver, I'll take a quick shower and then come down, but have that coffee handy because I'm going to need it."

He patted her on the back with one last reminder. "Don't keep Emajean waiting... or me."

* * *

Kate was just drying her hair when her cell phone chirped. She scrolled down on her phone and saw that Palmer had texted. She groaned inwardly. It was clear he had no intentions of giving up trying to win her back. It was time she nipped this in the bud, tell him they were through, that she appreciated everything he had done for her and their life together--what there was of it--and then wish him well with the rest of his life. It was probably better to do it by phone than by text. She started to make the call, then thought she'd better read his text first.

Before she had even finished reading, her hands were shaking and her mouth had gone dry.

Hi, Babe. I decided to surprise you. I'm in Cody at an Airbnb. I'll pick you up in an hour. Love U!

She dropped the phone on the dresser and covered her face with her hands. When she lifted her hands she could see that her face had gone ashen and her lips were trembling. How could she possibly explain this to Wyatt? Furthermore, she couldn't just leave Nora and Jack who had flown all this way to see her.

This can't be happening. Think, think, think!

Some people under stress grew calm and centered, only falling apart after the event. She wished she were one of those people. Instead, her mind went totally blank. She could think of nothing that would change the outcome of the situation.

Then it came to her.

She texted back.

Nora and Jack are here on business. They leave in the afternoon. Then I can come out to the Airbnb. Send directions.

Moments later she received another text.

Too bad about the meeting, but can't wait to see you. We'll make up for lost time.

He followed it up with a smiley face wearing Devil's horns.

She closed her eyes and groaned. *This can* not *be happening.*

How was she going to convince Palmer that there was no "us"? There was only Kate and Wyatt, at least she hoped so. Last night had been... wonderful. She had never felt so immediately connected to a man. She knew if she were ever to marry, it would be to him. There was something about him. He was strong, and yet tender, too. And his work wasn't his life. It was a *part* of his life, a valuable part, but she was convinced that they would work as a team. That she would be included in that life and be made to feel worthy.

She just had to get through today, first.

She quickly dressed, checked her face in the mirror, then descended the stairs to breakfast. Nora and Jack were already seated at the table. Fortunately, Wyatt had been called away to the cabin, so she didn't have to put on a false front of cheerfulness. The tension was still lodged firmly in her stomach, but at least she didn't have to hide her feelings from him.

"So," Nora said, having changed into a pantsuit this time, a crisp pale linen that made the gold necklace and earrings stand out that much more against the lighter pantsuit. She paired it up with black loafers, real Italian leather, no doubt. "Do you mind talking business over breakfast?"

Emajean seemed to recognize their need for privacy and excused herself to the back porch.

"So, it seems we have the same idea that you do. We're going to promote our company via the internet, set our sites in small towns where we can start with cheaper labor until the business is up and running fully, supply jobs for the community, and who knows... We get big enough, we might be able to pay these people a decent wage."

Nora wore a sly smile that reminded Kate of the cat she had once owned as a child after eating the family parakeet. Yet, Nora was the very antithesis of the evil boss. *She*, like Jack, cared for her employees and wanted to see them thrive rather than see them squirm and miserable like some bosses. What a breath of fresh air she was after dealing with someone like Ian.

"So, any idea who could help set up these outposts for us as we move forward?"

Kate's thoughts immediately turned to Gladys and Stanford. She couldn't imagine a more unlikely pair than that duo, but they complemented each other beautifully and each brought something unique to the table. Plus, they were just fun.

She filled Nora in on her ideas.

"Perfect," Nora said. "You find the locations and set up their travel. And you'll work from here?" She raised an eyebrow, but it was clear by her knowing smile that she had no objections.

"Will do."

"Good. Just one more thing. We've got word from one of our former workers that Ian is gunning for you. He doesn't like the fact that you're an upstart and that you're working with us. And he especially doesn't like that you're a woman and you're smart, so be careful, okay?"

Nora didn't have to convince Kate. She was all too aware of Ian's oversized ego and knew he would never accept a woman as his equal. Caution would be her mantra from now on.

"You got it."

Nora looked over at Jack who made a point of not returning his wife's gaze. "And Jack's too chicken to tell you, but we're going to have to make our time here short. We have a lot to accomplish, and the quicker we get at it, the sooner this company will be viable."

"You're leaving?"

Kate felt guilty for getting her hopes up.

"We're taking a short flight into Idaho Falls. One of the locals will take us."

Kate felt like doing a little dance right here in the middle of the dining room.

Nora steepled her fingers. "I hate to ask this, but could you give us a ride into town? We're all packed. We would like to stop off at the office first and meet with Stanford and Gladys."

While they went to gather their things, Kate informed Emajean of their plans and asked her to pass the message along to Wyatt.

As they were packing Kate's SUV, Nora said, "Don't you think we should wait and say goodbye to Wyatt?"

"I'll say goodbye for you," Kate promised, eager to steer clear of Wyatt until she had talked to Palmer. "Besides, he's had a tough few days. I'm sure he's busy sorting things out."

Jack, still in shorts and a Hawaiian shirt, said, "Tell him how much we appreciated him taking us in, and tell him I'll talk to some veterans associations when I return to New York."

If only Jack knew what had happened to her last night when Toby had threatened her, he might not be so forthcoming. Hopefully, by the time Wyatt had backing, all the kinks would be worked out and Toby would be behind bars, this whole episode simply a bad memory.

* * *

For the next few hours, seated at an oak table located in a separate room near the back of the new office, Kate went over everything with Nora and Jack and her staff of two. No organizational detail had been left untouched, including the office's accounts. By the time they were finished, Kate felt drained.

"Let's have lunch down the street at that little diner. What was it called? Oh yes, Rocky Top," Nora said. "Then Jack and I will be off."

"That sounds good." Kate said farewell to Gladys and Stanford. Then Kate, Nora, and Jack exited the building and crossed the street.

They were almost to their destination when Kate heard her name and turned, her heart coming to a near standstill as she realized who had called to her.

Palmer...

"Uh-oh," Nora said with a smirk. "Looks like Thanksgiving is coming early."

"That putz?" Nora elbowed Jack.

Before Kate could process the fact that her boss had never cared for her ex-boyfriend--or soon to be ex--Palmer was upon her, arms outstretched, grabbing her up in a huge bear hug.

"There's my girl! I'm so glad I caught you. Where are you all headed?"

If anything, Palmer had a deeper tan than when she'd last seen him, one that had undoubtedly come from Chateau d'Lauren's tanning studio. And his hair was slicked back in an oily pomade.

"We're headed to another state," Nora said, with a touch of glee in her voice. When Palmer finally released Kate, Nora leaned in and whispered in Kate's ear, "And I bet you wish you were coming with us right about now."

178

Then to Palmer Nora said, "Actually, we're going to lunch. Care to join us?"

Kate's vision clouded and, for a moment, she was struck mute. Nora was obviously having a great deal of fun at her expense. Until now, she had liked her new partner. She was beginning to rethink that.

"You don't mind, do you Kate?" Nora said, her laughter tinkling like wind chimes, but like wind chimes, they could be downright annoying.

"Um, no," Kate said, scratching behind her ear, an obvious signal that she was feeling uncomfortable, but either Nora wasn't getting her cues or she didn't want to, probably the latter.

Totally clueless, Palmer threw an arm around Kate, pulled her tight and whispered, "I've missed you, Kate."

Kate attempted a half-hearted smile while they walked to the diner and entered. As she looked around, she prayed that no one would remember her. Worse yet, that someone would recognize her and tell Wyatt that she was with another man. She could just imagine what he would think after their intimate evening. Even recalling it now, made her flush with a warmth that left her feeling breathless.

To her dismay, the waitress who had waited on Kate and Wyatt the other day was on duty. "So, you're back. No Wyatt today?"

Kate groaned inwardly.

"Wyatt?" Palmer frowned.

"Her client," Jack offered. He gave Kate his best fatherly look that spoke volumes, the most probable advice being *you need to have a talk with that young man. Soon.*

And she would... as soon as she could get Palmer alone. She couldn't possibly break the news to him that they were no longer a couple, and would never *be* a couple, here in a diner with a room full of people *and* her partners.

"Actually," Nora said, lifting her briefcase and placing it on the table, "part of the reason we wanted to see you, Kate, was to have you sign documents. I'll understand if you want to have a lawyer present before you sign partnership papers."

"*I* am a lawyer," Palmer offered.

Kate cringed. Could this get any worse? She would seek legal advice from the guy she planned to dump as soon as lunch was through. She felt like crawling under the table and out of the diner on her hands and knees so no one would see her.

"Here, I'll look them over. I'm sure we can find a way for you to repay me later," he said with a wink.

Okay, now she felt just plain feverish. She was sure she was coming down with something. She felt her forehead and face. Hot. Definitely hot. Was that sweat making her hair stick to her forehead?

"So," Jack said after Palmer had finished reading the papers. "What's the verdict?"

"I say sign them. They're being very fair to you."

Jack pulled out a pen from his pocket and handed it to Kate. She took a deep breath, then signed the papers.

When she was finished, the waitress took their order. After she was gone, Palmer said, "I was trying to find the right time to do this, but I can't think of any more perfect time than now."

Nora and Jack flashed a look of trepidation between themselves, then at Kate, who was having heart palpitations. Surely, he couldn't mean what she thought he did... No, this must be a mistake.

But it was no mistake.

As the diners looked on, Palmer knelt down on one knee before her and pulled a square, silk black box from his pocket. He produced a band that matched the engagement ring he had already given her.

"Kate, will you do me the honor of becoming Mrs. Palmer Jackson?"

The entire diner erupted in applause with a wolf whistle and a few cat calls thrown in for good measure.

Every moment of Kate's life seemed to flash before her eyes. But before she could frame an appropriate response, she blurted out "No! I can't." She threw up her hands and scooted past him to the collective gasp of the diners and was out the door before the hushed whispers and the "oh my gods" could ensue. She didn't know what she was doing or where she was going. She just knew she had to leave, to run as far and as fast as she could.

Before she could form a plan, she found herself in her SUV, driving much too fast down Main Street, not stopping until the pines rose up to meet her and the town lay far behind. Then she pulled over to the side of the road and cried.

What have I done?

She had just humiliated a very kind man. Not the right man, but he didn't deserve the way she had treated him. Already, her phone had rung numerous times, the first incoming call made by Palmer, then by Nora and Jack, and lastly by Wyatt. Oh dear God, did Wyatt know, too? He would want nothing to do with her after he found out what had happened. He would think she was a fool around. Someone who got her kicks out of having one night stands with men she barely knew.

Why is this happening? When she had finally found someone she truly cared about. Some women went a whole lifetime without ever finding their soulmate. She didn't want to live like that. She wanted a partner, a true partner. Not someone like Palmer, whose career came above everything. Who differentiated between sex and love and found them mutually incompatible. She wanted the whole package: sex, love, friendship... and commitment.

The sky once again filled with clouds, the first specter of rain beginning to fall in soft, wet plops. They mirrored the tears on her cheeks that were now dripping onto her blouse.

She heard a chirp and checked her phone. It was a text, this time from Palmer.

Nora told me about Wyatt. I think we should talk. It's only fair. Meet me at the Airbnb.

He gave her directions. She stared at them for a very long time before coming to a decision. Despite everything, she owed him her honesty if nothing else. Reluctantly, she typed the address into her GPS and put her SUV in gear.

Twenty-Eight

The narrow road tilted slightly upward into the hillside, a lush canopy of cedar and pine overhead. Alongside the road a deer and its fawn stood idly nibbling on the grasses below, the adult looking up at Kate only to twitch its ears then rotate them, satellite fashion, to listen for the oncoming vehicles.

The higher Kate's SUV climbed, the worse she felt. It was clear that Palmer had gone to a lot of trouble to make this surprise meeting special. And, true to form, as she mounted the clearing, there stood the most breathtaking house she had ever seen: three stories fronted by massive windows and a deck. Abundant flowers of all shapes and sizes trailed in tendrils down a variety of pots, most blue. Above the third floor was a turret with an egret on top. It reminded Kate of something out of a fairytale. So like Palmer to want the best for her. Yet that only made what she had to say so much harder.

As per the instructions, she pulled up behind the house. They were to have stayed on the top floor with a deck of its own that overlooked the most beautiful garden Kate had ever seen, topping even the one out front of the cabin back at the ranch. A lush display of lavender mixed with delphinium, foxglove, and hollyhock in shades ranging from pink to blue and purple bordered a rock path. In front of all of that were Austin roses in shades of pink and salmon. Lime hydrangeas acted as the centerpiece of this lovely creation and it was all topped off by a fountain that sprayed water caught by shafts of light so that it gave off beautiful rainbow arcs. Birds flitted in and out of it, delighting in the free shower, afterward fluttering to a nearby fence where they would take turns shaking their feathers and fluffing up into little round balls.

"Up here!" Palmer called.

There, on the balcony, stood Palmer, his eyes still swollen and his mouth trembling slightly. To any other woman he would have made the perfect Prince Charming. She would have lived in luxury: a nice home, the perfect two children at the perfect schools. She would have had a nanny to help, and probably even a housekeeper. Furthermore, she would have attended company functions and kept an expense account for clothing so that she could compete with the other wives.

But she would be alone most of the time. And Palmer would be off slaying dragons for other women as her life became more mundane until she all but disappeared as a person. She would be someone he kept for appearances, their love withering like a dying rose. That might be a tradeoff for some women, but it could never be a tradeoff for her. She wanted someone whose life she could share, someone who wanted her by his side, not as a showpiece but as a true partner. Someone to love and who would love her in return.

"I'm glad you came," he said, taking a deep breath as she marched upstairs and halted at the top of the landing.

"I know this isn't how you planned it," she said, forcing her gaze to meet his. "The marriage proposal, everything."

"You can say that again," he acknowledged with a rueful laugh. "Do you want to at least see what you missed?" He nodded to the sleek glass loft doors to the Airbnb.

Kate hesitated, but just then the landlord of the Airbnb came out of the sliding glass door below. She couldn't very well talk to him out here. No doubt the woman had already heard the news making its rounds and wanted to know more. "Okay, but I can only stay for a moment." She prayed he wasn't assuming anything from her acceptance of the offer.

"C'mon." He squeezed her hand briefly and then took her inside.

The place took her breath away. Never had she seen anything so beautiful. An artist must have designed the loft space because everything about it spoke of originality. Amazing succulents hung floor-to-ceiling, some with huge bright pink, almost fluorescent, blooms. On the floor lay a faux zebra rug with crisp, white, overstuffed sofas and a huge, floor-to-ceiling rock fireplace.

On the opposite wall, a loft had been built up above with a ladder to a bed that lay beneath the turret that she had seen driving in. Windows were built into it so that whoever slept there would have a three-hundred-and-sixty-degree view in all directions, including toward the garden.

The bathroom was open to the main room, separated only by a colorful silk-screened Manet curtain that parted to display a rock wall that looked like something out of the Amazon rainforest. The floor was a beautiful mosaic of ferns and flowers. And to further the effect, more blooming succulents--this time in orange and yellow--trailed the walls giving it a lush appearance. No woman in her right mind would turn this down.

Except me.

Every time she looked at the place, all she could picture was her and Wyatt. He would love this room, this place.

The tile backsplash in the kitchen was a menagerie of jungle animals, artistically drawn, topped by a deep green jungle tile. Above the cabinets were more plants: staghorn fern, African violets--some of the biggest she had ever seen--and Zebra plants with large yellow bracts and a red stamen to offset the yellow-and-green stripes.

Next to the island countertops were chairs that had been handcrafted and hand painted so that they looked like a lion, tiger, giraffe, and zebra. An exotic display of pink protea, red hibiscus, and Bird of Paradise was placed in the center of the island countertop.

"I had them ordered from a place in California. I thought that maybe if you knew how much I cared..." His voice drifted off and he looked down at his feet.

"I am so sorry," she said. "If I had known you had gone to all this trouble..."

He looked up with hope in his eyes. She had forgotten how handsome he was, and still that didn't open the floodgates of feeling she should have for the man who had asked her to marry him. Instead, she compared him to Wyatt, who had a rugged handsomeness, so different from Palmer. Wyatt's face bore scars and lines from overexposure to the sun, and he was graying at the temples. Yet those were all the things that made him more interesting, made him more lovable in her eyes, because it represented a full life filled with ups and downs. Not a charmed life, the kind that involved no inward soul searching, no self-examination or inner growth.

Palmer's hope appeared to fade as he no doubt read what she was thinking in her expression. He'd always said her eyes were a giveaway, that she could hide nothing, and she knew that was true. She wore her heart on her sleeve and that hadn't changed over time.

"Will you at least spend the day with me? Give me that. Then you can go on with your life and I'll leave you alone."

Hurt and disappointment laced his words, but she knew that he would move on. He had always been the type of guy to saddle up quickly after a fall.

Great, now she was even *thinking* in cliches.

"I can't..." she said, her words trailing off.

For a moment they stood in awkward silence.

"I'll never forget you, Kate," Palmer said, giving her a light kiss on the forehead.

"We can always be friends," she added, the words ringing false, even to her own ears.

Palmer winced. "The old 'let's be friends' standard."

Kate laughed. "Sorry. I guess that sounded trite."

"How about this for a farewell? I'll name my first kid after you."

Kate nudged him, which got him laughing. She was glad she had come. Things had gone much better than expected, and although she hated that tried-and-true word "closure," she now understood how important it was to deal with the past, to bring it to an equitable conclusion.

"Thanks for the last couple of years. I hope you find the woman you're looking for."

Tears brushed his eyes, causing hers to well up, too.

"Take care, Kate. And if Wyatt is ever mean to you, you just call me. Agreed?"

"Agreed."

She waved farewell.

As she drove away, she couldn't help but have mixed feelings, a feeling of loss for what she'd had and joy for what she hoped lay in her future. Even though her relationship with Palmer hadn't been right for her, and she had never been truly happy, they still had shared history and that would never change.

Now, she just had to pray she hadn't burned her bridge with Wyatt. If he hadn't heard about "the proposal" by now, he would hear about it soon. Better that she tell him instead of the other way around. But how? How did she tell a man she'd just slept with that on that very same day she had been kissed by another man, had been asked to marry him, and had spent a half hour at a place that could only be described as Shangri-la?

How, indeed.

* * *

Wyatt was having a hard time wrapping his mind around what Les had told him. It was the talk of the town: Kate, some man named Palmer... and a proposal. The only thing that made any of this bearable was the fact that Kate had turned the man down.

Then why didn't you come straight here, Kate?

He had been pacing the front porch, waiting for her since he had heard the news, all thoughts of Toby shoved aside as he struggled to understand why she had slept with him last night, then had gone to meet a former boyfriend the very next morning without telling him. Too many questions, not enough answers.

Off in the distance, he saw a gray SUV turn off the main road, followed by a cloud of dust. For a moment, he panicked. He didn't want to play the jealous lover like Toby. If he did, what kind of example would he set for the boys? No, he had to go inside and wait patiently, talk reasonably. He rushed inside only to find Emajean taking stock of him with a furrowed brow.

"Okay, Mister. Something's up. Spill," she said, hands on hips.

"This is none of your business," he snapped, then instantly regretted his lack of tact. It wasn't Emajean's fault that he had

186

spent the last hour with his hand balled in a fist, feeling every bit as angry as he had when his wife left him, even more so this time around because he really felt that he was falling in love. That this was a woman he wanted to spend his life with, to have and to hold forever.

Why? Why had Kate done this, and how could he forgive her? After all, his wife hadn't forgiven *him*.

"Look," Emajean said, her voice softer and kinder than he'd ever thought possible. "I heard what happened in town today."

"It means nothing to me. Kate's just here on assignment."

Emajean cupped her hand over his and looked him squarely in the eye, waiting until he returned her gaze despite how uncomfortable it felt.

"You and I both know that's not true, Wyatt. I know when a woman is in love, and that woman is in love with you, no matter what happened this afternoon at the diner."

"You're wrong."

Emajean squeezed his hand and her expression hardened, congealing into a cold look of disdain.

"For years, you have shielded that damn hard heart of yours in work and with the boys, but it's time to let go of the past. Your wife never gave you a chance to earn back your forgiveness."

Wyatt felt the sting of her words, the memory of how crushed his wife was when she'd found him in the arms of another woman. She had taken their daughter and fled that day. She hadn't asked for anything except her freedom. He'd somehow managed to turn the events on her, as though she had been the unfaithful one for not giving him a second chance, when he should have run to her, begged her forgiveness.

"Give Kate a chance to earn her forgiveness. She's a human being, just like you. We *all* make mistakes, Wyatt. Each and every one of us." She stared at him pointedly.

Sweat trickled down his shirt. He had known Kate only a short time, but she'd been the first person he'd really felt comfortable opening up to. Maybe Emajean was right. Maybe he should at least hear her out.

He heard the SUV pull up in the driveway and heard a car door slam. Emajean patted him on the back and nodded toward the screen door. But to his surprise, Kate didn't enter the house. Instead, he watched her walk past the window toward the barn, head down as though she'd been crying and appearing more defeated than he'd ever seen her before.

When he turned to see what Emajean made of Kate's behavior, she only shrugged.

"Better get out there. That girl needs a hug." Her expression made it clear that he had better do as told if he planned to eat tonight. Funny, because Emajean didn't take to strangers, and particularly female ones who might possibly want to usurp her position in the household.

"You surprise me sometimes, Emajean."

"I surprise myself, now get."

"Aye-aye, sir!" He saluted.

"You're not too old to spank," she said with a laugh.

Looks like they were all changing in unexpected ways.

* * *

Wyatt slowed as he neared the barn, afraid to enter, afraid to confront Kate, afraid that he might say the wrong thing that would end what they had only just started. And he was good at that... saying the wrong thing. He never meant to, but it was a curse of his, or at least that's what his ex had always said. Maybe he could change that, too, over time. He hoped so, because he wanted nothing more than to have Kate by his side.

Inside the barn, he found her next to Spirit's stall running fingers through the mare's mane and talking to her as though she were counselor, confessor, and friend. She was telling the horse her woes, pouring her heart out to the young mare, when she must have heard Wyatt because she turned with a start.

"Oh! I didn't hear you."

Her eyes were swollen and she seemed smaller than before, as though the events of the past day had made her shrink into herself. Emajean was right. She needed a hug. Quickly, he traversed the distance between them and swept her into his arms.

At first, she merely sagged into him. Then she reached out and hugged him tight.

"I heard about what happened."

"Oh, God!" She pulled away from him and covered her mouth.

"It's okay." He brought her to him and placed her head on his chest, surprised at his own reaction. Surprised that he wasn't more upset. "Tell me about the other man."

"It's not like you think," she said, looking up at him with tearful eyes. "We broke up when I came here, but at the last minute he gave me an engagement ring, told me to think about it. And I did. But it wasn't what I wanted. *He* wasn't what I wanted."

Those were the words he had wanted to hear. He wouldn't let her off the hook completely, but for now, they were good enough.

"So why did he come here?"

She shook her head. "I don't know. I guess he thought if he came in person, made the effort, that I would change my mind."

"But you didn't."

"No, I didn't."

"Were you in love with him?"

She paused. "I've loved people, but I was only in love once, until..."

"Now?" He waited, hopeful, the length of her hesitation making him anxious.

Finally, she nodded.

He picked her up and spun her in a circle, setting her down just long enough to throw his hat in the air and let out a whoop.

"Truth from now on, agreed?"

"Agreed."

But as he looked into her eyes, he realized that if he expected her to be truthful, he needed to be truthful, too. He felt sure she would understand about him being married before, and even about having a child. What she might not understand, what she might find impossible to forgive, is that he'd had an affair--more than one. That he had given up his wife and daughter for a series of one-night stands. How could he expect her to forgive him for that when he hadn't forgiven himself?

Twenty-Nine

As Kate stood inside the confines of the barn, muted light cascading through the door from the loft above, she felt as though she'd been given a reprieve. The slate was finally clean and she and Wyatt could start fresh. *No more secrets.* To her relief, Wyatt grasped her hand as they set off for the house. They had just stepped onto the porch when a red Jeep Cherokee came flying down the driveway and pulled up next to the garden.

Wyatt muttered an oath and his breathing grew rapid.

"What is it?" Kate asked, her brows furrowed.

But before Wyatt could answer, out of the jeep popped a beautiful woman, much younger than Kate, and a small child, nine or ten by Kate's reckoning. The girl had bright red hair and a one-hundred-watt smile. Kate wished she could have said the same for the mother, whose face appeared taut, as though ready to do battle.

"Wyatt."

"Charlotte."

The two seemed to square off. And then it came to Kate. The girl with the red hair looked nothing like her mother. However, she did have Wyatt's nose and a sense of confidence, although Kate hazarded a guess that this girl wasn't nearly as subdued as Wyatt.

The girl quickly proved Kate right when she came running over to him and launched herself into his arms, hugging him tightly.

"Why didn't you text me, Daddy?" she said, her eyes now mirroring her mother's.

"You know I don't like all the gadgetry." He fidgeted, refusing to glance over at Kate despite the questions he must know she had for him.

"You could have called," the woman said, coldly. "Are you going to introduce us?"

By now, Wyatt's face had gone from shock, to embarrassment, to him licking his lips, a nervous habit he had used only on rare occasions.

"This is Kate. Kate, this is my ex-wife Charlotte and my daughter, Emily."

Kate held tightly to the railing to keep from teetering. Could this day get any worse?

"Where's Emajean?" the little girl asked.

Emajean, having heard the commotion, came out on the porch. Emily wriggled free from her father and went running to Emajean, launching herself in Emajean's arms just as she had Wyatt's, only Emajean let out an "oomph" of surprise.

"Well, haven't you grown," Emajean said, putting Emily down on the porch and taking a good look at her. "Why, I would say you've grown a foot since I last saw you." She winked at Wyatt.

"Emajean," Charlotte said, coldly.

"Charlotte," Emajean replied, the feelings they had for each other clearly mutual.

As they stood there making small talk, Kate felt like a third wheel to a group of people who had obviously spent much time together and knew each other intimately. It reminded her of how little she knew of Wyatt. Why had she ever believed that in a few months she could truly know another person? It often took years, and sometimes you never really knew a person at all. She had learned that in her relationship with Palmer.

"Wyatt, why don't you take Emily riding?" Emajean suggested. "And I'll get tea going for us ladies. It will give us time to chat."

It was clear Wyatt was searching for a way out of leaving Kate alone with his ex, but Emily already had his hand and was pulling him down the porch stairs past Charlotte, whose quiet fury was evident in the firmness of her stance.

"I suppose it's time the two of you should meet," Emajean said with a smirk.

Kate turned back to see Wyatt being tugged along by his daughter, an apology written into the lines on his face.

"Come along," Emajean said, holding the door open for

Charlotte and Kate.

Ten minutes later, they were seated out back around a table with a bright blue umbrella. They each had dripping glasses of ice cold sun tea and plates set out with a surprisingly feminine tea tray filled with an array of desserts. How Emajean had come up with them on a moment's notice was anyone's guess, but it was clear she was comfortable playing hostess.

Charlotte turned to Kate, dark eyes brimming with anger. The woman wore jeans, an Ann Taylor shirt, and a watch that could have only been a Rolex. To top it off, she sported what looked like a year-round tan.

"So, how long have you and Wyatt been together?" Charlotte asked as she fingered her iced tea.

"I'm really just here on an assignment. I'm doing marketing for the ranch."

Emajean seemed to think she hadn't answered Charlotte correctly, because she quickly added, "She's been here a month and a half now."

"That seems a bit long for an... *assignment.*"

Kate bristled at the implication, and yet the woman was absolutely right. Kate should have been gone weeks ago. Furthermore, a businesswoman didn't sleep with a client. She had definitely crossed some invisible line. Like it or not, she had to accept that things were not the same as they had been before.

"So, how much do you know about Wyatt?" Charlotte asked.

Emajean gave a warning cluck of disapproval.

"She should know." Charlotte took out her sunglasses and placed them on her head, wearing them like a crown.

"Know what?" Kate looked from Charlotte to Emajean but neither seemed forthcoming.

Finally, after enough time had elapsed to make Kate sweat despite the cool breeze, Charlotte leaned forward, her hands spread out before her as though prepared to lay it all out for Kate.

"About all of the women. You're not the first, and you won't be the last."

"Charlotte!" Emajean scolded.

"What? It's true. You know it and I know it." The smirk Charlotte flashed her was nothing short of a touché, a thrust and parry.

Kate shrank into her seat. *What have I done?* She groaned inwardly. She had just told a man who had asked her to marry her that she was in love with someone else, and the man she had been holding out for was a womanizer. She stood up so fast, she nearly knocked her chair over.

"That was uncalled for," Emajean told Charlotte, but that's all Kate heard because she was walking as fast as she could down the dirt road toward the cabin. Once out of sight of the house and Charlotte's gloating eyes, she began running. She wasn't sure where she was going or what she would do once she got there. She just knew that she needed to be as far away from here as possible.

Before she could reach the cabin, she saw a rutted trail that ran off toward the river. She veered to the right of the road, traipsing through bracken and thick brush, sharp spikes of teasle clinging to her clothes as she passed.

For the next twenty minutes, she trailed the river as it flowed southward from the colder Sawtooths above. Here, the temperature had dropped a good fifteen degrees. Still, she felt sweaty from the exertion, her clothes damp.

She had just begun the trail that would take her deeper into the forest when she heard a laugh. Before she had a chance to process what she'd heard, Toby jumped from a large boulder above her and landed directly on top of her. She fell to the ground with a thud as her body hit the dirt trail, the wind knocked out of her. Every inch of her body ached from the jolt as she struggled to register what had happened. She recoiled at the smell of garlic on Toby's breath as he lay atop her.

"Keep quiet!" he growled.

"Wha... what do you want from me?"

"If it weren't for you, I wouldn't have half the county out looking for me," he hissed into her ear.

"Why go after me? Who put you up to this? Was it Ian?" Her breaths came in short gasps, his weight crushing her ribs.

He dug his fingers into her arms. "What does it matter? You're here, and you're my ticket out of here."

"What do you mean?" she said, feeling his nails dig into her.

She knew that if she didn't get him off of her soon, she was going to pass out. While she waited for him to catch his breath, she plotted a way to get him off her. Using an old maneuver she had learned in a self-defense class she had taken in New York, she looped his leg with hers, pressed her hip into his and flipped him.

"What the...?"

"You're not the only one who knows how to pin a person." She just prayed that the training she received would be enough to hold him.

Before she was able to plot her next move, Toby head-butted her in the chin, then elbowed her in the ribs giving him just enough leverage to roll her off of him. In a flash, he unsheathed a knife from inside his boot and held it to her throat.

He smiled at her, sending shivers through her.

"Like I said, you're my ticket out of here."

* * *

Emily had climbed down from Spirit and was picking wildflowers: Summer rose, Indian Paintbrush, and even a few Skyrocket Gilia. Wyatt was just preparing to get down from his horse when Emajean came tearing up on her brown-and-white appaloosa, its sides swathed in sweat from the exertion.

"What is it?" Wyatt demanded, reining in his Mustang. "Have the men found Toby?"

Emajean reined her horse in, the horse snorting and stamping. "It's Kate."

Wyatt's heart sank.

"Baby girl," he called down to Emily, "we need to get going, pronto."

"Why?"

He could see so much of himself in the girl, her natural

curiosity, her love of nature. Even the way she took her time about things that interested her. Except for the red hair, she was his clone.

"Kate's missing. Charlotte..."

Emajean's voice trailed off. Wyatt could only infer from what little she'd said that his ex-wife had done something to upset Kate, and Kate had left.

"Is she on the property? Did she take her SUV?"

"Yes, to the first question, no, to the second."

What neither of them acknowledged, but which was no doubt as much on Emajean's mind as his own, was that Toby was probably still on the property, too. If he had found Kate once, he could find her again.

"Why would she go off alone?" Wyatt asked, moving his Mustang closer to Emajean's Appaloosa.

Emajean glanced nervously at Emily.

"We can talk later."

By that time, Emily was saddled up, but had refused to give up the handful of flowers she had collected, making the ride painfully slow.

Wyatt waited until they were out of earshot of Emily then moved his horse closer to Emajean's once more. "What happened?"

Normally so stoic, Emajean actually flushed with embarrassment. "Charlotte brought up your...your...affairs."

Outrage settled in the small of Wyatt's stomach at the thought that after all these years, Charlotte would hold so much anger at him that she would jeopardize his budding relationship with Kate. He had changed. People did sometimes, if they'd done enough soul searching, and he'd done enough for several lifetimes. Yet still he was being punished for his past.

"Emily," he called, falling back so he could be close to her, "do you think you can remember how to make your pony run?"

By the end of the previous summer, he had taught her to race the pony, but to a child, a year was a long time. Before he could receive an answer, she produced a smile so wide it lit up her cheeks and then she tapped hard on the reins. The pony immediately rode off at a gallop, flowers flying and Emily screeching in delight, oblivious to Wyatt and Emajean's cries of concern.

For the next fifteen minutes, Wyatt galloped to keep up with his daughter, Emajean close on his heels. They had barely reached the dirt road to the house, when Les came out to meet them. Frown lines etched his features and made him appear older than his thirty-five years.

"I've had the boys out looking for Kate. From the look of it, there's been a scuffle down by the river. I'm pretty sure Toby's got her."

Wyatt pulled off his hat and slapped it on his pommel, upsetting his horse and nearly causing him to bolt. A less seasoned horseman would have had trouble calming the horse, but he'd raised his horse from a colt, and they were as bonded as father and son.

"Were the men able to follow their trail?"

Les bit his lip. "Apparently, Toby doubled back, and while Emajean was up here collecting you, he hijacked Kate's SUV."

"And Kate?"

"Gone."

"Did you contact the sheriff's office?"

"They're on it, but..."

"But what?"

Les scratched the stubble on his chin, looking everywhere except at Wyatt.

"But what?" Wyatt repeated, feeling his blood pressure rise.

"Toby has the knife. They're afraid he'll use it on Kate so they're taking this very seriously."

Wyatt leaned in so that Emily couldn't hear more than she had. "You don't know. He could have ditched it. He could..."

Les held up his hands, preventing Wyatt from any further extrapolations.

"They *know* he has it."

"How?"

"Because one of their off-duty officers found the SUV with Toby and Kate in it."

Wyatt blew a short blast of air to relieve the tension. "And?"

"And, he had a knife to her throat. He said that if the officer followed them, he would kill her."

Thirty

"Park here!" Toby gestured to a spot that led to a canyon.

Kate had a sinking feeling about where the abduction was headed. She'd always been told that a woman stood a better chance of survival if she fought than to let herself be drawn into the woods, yet that is precisely what had happened. The entire drive over, Toby had held the knife so close to her throat that even breathing had been difficult. For one brief moment, she had thought she might be saved when an officer had caught up with them and pulled up beside them as they drove, yelling for them to pull over.

But that hope had been dashed when Toby had warned the off-duty officer to stop following them or else. To prove his point, he had nicked her throat, the blood having eventually congealed at the base of her neck.

Only now, as they pulled up to a trailhead and parked, did he release his grip as he shoved her out the door with him in close pursuit.

"Wait!" He reached for a backpack he'd brought that he had secreted away on the property, fully loaded for an obvious escape, should he ever need one. Then he released the brake and rolled the SUV into the brush.

"Where are you taking us?" she demanded, forcing her voice to remain even. She just hoped he planned to take her with him instead of dumping her somewhere as he had the SUV...

"You'll see," he said. "I spent most of my life in these woods, hunting, fishing. I know every brook and stream. I even know the perfect hideout, for now."

"They'll track us," she protested. "They'll use dogs. You'll never get away with this."

He laughed. It was then that she noticed he was missing a tooth, a molar. "You don't understand, do you?"

"Understand what?"

"I only needed you to help me get this far. You're no longer useful."

Kate felt her world spinning. She had to remain calm, to think fast.

"Oh, but you *do* need me," she said to buy time.

"That so?" His eyes shot up and the glimmer of evil she'd read in them earlier had returned.

Think! Think!

"Because if you kill me, Ian won't pay you. He'll be an accomplice to murder and he'll go to prison. And you need money to run, right?"

Toby frowned. She could see that she had snagged him. Now to reel him in.

"But you'll get nothing if something happens to me. I can tell the police that kidnapping me was all your idea, that Ian had no hand in this ruse. He'll be off the hook, I'll be free, and you'll have your money. And I'll make sure you're long gone before I talk to the police. You can change your name, take a nice vacation on the Riviera and no one's the wiser."

He paused, fingering his backpack which he had slung across one shoulder. "Okay," he said, his eyes narrowing as if in challenge. "I'll take you with me, but only if you close your business."

"So that's Ian's condition?"

He bit his lip and looked away. She could see that she had trapped him, caused him to reveal too much. If she were to get out of this alive, she would need to walk a very fine line.

For several minutes, they stood staring at each other until, finally, Toby cursed beneath his breath to let her know how stupid he was being by agreeing to take her with him. "Okay, lady, if you plan on staying alive, you're going to stick close and do exactly as I say."

Still, he grumbled and cursed as he led her deeper into the forest.

* * *

A day had lapsed with still no word about Kate and her

whereabouts and Wyatt was feeling uneasy. Charlotte had been sent packing for her part in this mess, and as for Emily, Emajean had taken her under her wing, only too happy to have something to occupy her thoughts so she wouldn't have to think about Kate. The two were out picking green beans and shelling them, something Emily got to do but once a year as she lived in Cheyenne, in a townhouse with just enough of a yard for a table and chairs.

Now, as Wyatt listened to the sheriff, who had come to the ranch with news, the hairs on Wyatt's neck stood on end. They were seated in the living room, which felt uncomfortably small, suddenly. To make matters worse, the day had turned off sweltering. An early morning rain had given way to a blistering sun that made the rock and dust from the driveway shimmer with heat. Wyatt took out a handkerchief and wiped his neck.

"So, what's the verdict?" Wyatt said, treading lightly to keep from feeling more tense than he already did.

"It's not good, son," the sheriff said. "We found Kate's SUV a half hour ago, hidden in some brush."

Wyatt whistled. "Where?"

"In the Teton National Forest. They're headed into the mountains, looks like."

Even in the summer, those mountains could be treacherous. Only an experienced hiker would know which paths were safe to take this time of year. From what Wyatt knew of Toby, he probably had enough experience from hunting those woods to keep them alive for a while. But they would have had no time to pick up supplies, no food, no water. How did the boy expect them to get by on such short notice?

"Do you know anything about Toby's family?" Wyatt asked.

"I know where you're going with this, son," the sheriff said, hat in hand. "His father's a real good hunter and trapper. The boy learned a thing or two from his dad, that's for certain, so if he has her... "

"You think he doesn't?"

The sheriff licked his lips and steepled his fingers together as though determining how to word what he had to say in such a way that he wouldn't rile Wyatt.

"Just give it to me straight. No beating around the bush."

"Let's just say if I were in his position right now, Kate would slow me down. He's in *his* territory, so he'll be playing by *his* rules. Kate's a wild card. Unless she plays her hand very well...then all I can say is let's hope she's as smart as she looks, because she's going to need every ounce of wit she has to stay alive."

Wyatt sank back in his seat. He was not a man given to crying, even in the face of death--the military had taught him that--but now, for the first time in years, he felt all the grief of one loss upon the other welling up inside of him, threatening to spill over. Abruptly, he stood and peered out the window toward the oak where he and Kate had once stood, where he had formed the beginnings of a bond that was just revealing itself in all its complexity. He wanted her to see him as honest and true, as someone who was loyal, who would have her back in any situation. Someone who would never betray her. He prayed that Charlotte hadn't ruined that for him.

"What can we do?" Wyatt said, his back to the sheriff.

"We've got an experienced crew up there now, on horseback. If anyone can find her, they will."

Wyatt turned to face the sheriff, whose thinning grey hair curled at the ends. "I'm going, too."

The sheriff tapped his cap on the palm of his hand. "Wait a minute here, Wyatt. We don't need to risk any more lives by having you go out there half-cocked."

The sheriff withered under Wyatt's steely gaze. "I'm going. I'll pack a couple horses. Tell me where to start."

"I'm coming with you." Les had apparently been standing unnoticed by the screen door, but he now entered and it was clear by his expression that he meant to harbor no objection.

"Who will look after Emajean and Emily?" Wyatt asked.

"Ryan and the boys will keep an eye on the place. I've already given them instructions."

"How did you know...?" the sheriff started to say.

"I have my friends in town," Les said, leaving it at that. "And I know where your men found the SUV. How soon can you be ready, Wyatt?"

"Half an hour. I'll get the horses loaded. Get Emajean to pack for us. She's going to need to make it quick, but if anyone can do it, she can."

The sheriff threw up his hands. "Okay, but you boys better damn well keep yourselves safe. I don't need a bunch of you getting lost up in those woods. And take something warm. It can get damned cold at night, even this time of year."

"You're not talking to some greenhorns," Wyatt said, to which Les gave a muted laugh, then quickly looked down at his boots as though inspecting them for dust.

"Well, okay," the sheriff said. "I guess we could use an extra set of eyes. By the way, they aired your segment about the place on the news today. The big networks have picked it up. I have a feeling this abduction is going to add a new dimension to the story, don't you?" The sheriff put on his hat and tilted it back so he could rub the sweat off his forehead.

It was Wyatt's turn to mutter a curse under his breath. How could all this be happening on the same day? And how would it look to know that one of the vets had abducted the very woman that had been hired to help save the ranch? If he had ever hoped to save the ranch and to help the vets, his odds were quickly dwindling.

"Is it too late to put a stop to the segment?"

"New York is three hours ahead of us. The story has already aired once, and will get a second airing this evening. So, I would say..."

Les finished for the sheriff. "We're screwed."

"Yes, I'm afraid so."

For some reason, Les's words made Wyatt laugh. All eyes turned to him. "When you've got nothing left, the only thing you have is your sense of humor. The truth is, I can't worry about what happens to the ranch right now. I've got to find Kate. Whatever happens, the world isn't going to come to an end. But it will if I don't find her, so let's get moving."

Before Wyatt could say any more, Les said, "I'm on it."

Wyatt placed a hand on Les's shoulder. "Thanks."

The sheriff prepared to leave, but before he did, he turned

to Wyatt and said, "Son, I promise I'll do everything I can to bring Kate home safely. You've got my word."

Choked with emotion, Wyatt merely nodded, thankful for two such good friends who had done all they could to help him.

"We'll find her," Les said. "I guarantee it."

Wyatt could only hope he was right.

Thirty-One

Every part of Kate's body ached, from her legs, which were covered with stinging nettle, to her forehead where a branch from a lodgepole pine had scraped her in their haste. Worse yet, the blisters on her feet had popped and were oozing a viscous fluid making her socks wet. Even her hands felt sore from clawing at dirt and rocks in their steep ascent toward an unseen trail that she was beginning to believe didn't exist. Finally, she'd had enough and stopped.

"What are you stopping for?" Toby said. "Keep moving."

"I can't keep up this pace," she said, bent over, hands on knees and breathing heavily.

Kate hazarded a look at the man and could see what he must have been like in Afghanistan. He was no longer the crazed madman trying to escape his captors. Instead, he'd taken on a new mantle, that of warrior. Leader. He knew where he was going and it was clearly his job to get them there safely, with no dissenters. Here, he was in his element, an element he would never find at home in civilian life. She'd heard of men who couldn't adjust when they returned home, who only felt "normal" in combat. True to type, he was wearing khakis and his combat boots from the war. Not an ounce of fat clung to his body.

What frightened her most was the fact that at his belt, he now wore a gun that he had pulled from a knapsack, and wore a knife sheathed next to the gun.

"Here," he said, retrieving the canteen he'd filled with water by the river. He held it up for her to drink.

She merely looked at the water, which had come straight from the river. Who knew what bacteria the river held.

As if reading her mind, he said, "Don't worry, I used a chlorine tablet. It's safe."

Reluctantly, she took it and was met with the freshest, best tasting water she had ever had the privilege to drink. Greedily, she swallowed the cool liquid only to have it plucked away from her before she was finished.

"That's enough. Too much, and it will make you sick. Besides," he said as he drank from the metal pie-shaped canteen, "we need to conserve water. You never know when we'll see the river again, so take it easy."

Kate licked her lips, wishing she had been allowed a longer drink. Next, he broke off a piece of the emergency rations he had brought with him in his sack, which was filled with dried meals meant only for one person, not two, and the occasional snack. As a result, they had supplemented their diet with berries of all kinds: blackberries, huckleberries, wild strawberries. Even a few roots.

"Please, can we stop for a while?" she pleaded, the heat of the day and the pace of their travel taking their toll.

"Can't. Search and Rescue will have dogs and they will be on horses. We have to go places the horses can't and leave as little scent as possible."

That explained why he had made her ford for miles through the last stream. At the time she had complained bitterly about being cold and tired. How she would trade that cool water over this unbearable heat, but hindsight was twenty-twenty as the pundits liked to say.

"Look," she said, perching herself on a log that had been brought down by the wind, no doubt. "I need to rest. My feet are nearly bloody. How much further do we have to go?"

"See that point? Up there?"

Way off in the distance stood a lone boulder that overlooked the valley below. It was above the tree line, but just below the snowline. Surely, he didn't intend for her to hike that distance today. It would take them until nightfall. The thought of entering a cave at dusk, with God only knew what kinds of animals... She shuddered, envisioning bears, mountain lions, rattlesnakes, none of which eased her fears.

"You can't be serious," she said.

"Dead serious."

The set of his jaw made it clear he would broach no opposition. She *would* go and she *would* make it to that point by today or else... Or else what, she wondered? Could she merely refuse to go any further? She looked at the gun on Toby's belt. She had made her case for him keeping her alive, but would he change his mind under the right circumstances? She didn't know. All she knew is the one thing she was good at was marketing, and she had to make sure that she marketed herself as a valuable asset, one worthy of keeping until Wyatt or the sheriff could catch up to her.

She thought about Wyatt. She had been so upset to learn that he, like Palmer, had cheated that she hadn't given him a chance to tell his side of the story. And maybe he *had* changed. *Could* a man change? Or any person for that matter.

She hoped so. More than anything in the world she wanted this relationship to work out. Never before had she felt so comfortable with a person. It was as though she had always known Wyatt. And yet, you could think you knew a person for years and never really know them. That, she had learned from Palmer... and the men before him.

Slowly, she rose to her feet and began the long slog up the hill, giving her much time to think. Why *did* she pick men who wouldn't stay? Men with one foot out the door. Maybe it was something about her, something that drove men away like it had with her mom, and yet she had loved her mom. Her mother could be stubborn and thoughtless at times, but she could also be fun. She was wildly creative with boundless energy, but she could just as easily sink into depression when life took sudden twists and turns in directions she wasn't prepared to take. Over time, she had become so depressed that she had gained weight--the light of her eyes had dulled. She had wanted so much more from her life, but back then women weren't given the opportunities they were today, though even that was questionable.

Wyatt, where are you?

Kate prayed silently that he would come, that he truly cared. And that they could overcome the hurdle of infidelity that seemed as substantial as the mountain she had yet to climb.

* * *

For hours, Wyatt scanned every rock, fern, and square inch of earth in his path, searching for signs of Kate and Toby, but he lost them at the riverbed where they had undoubtedly crossed. Fearing he had missed something, he doubled back to the river and scoured the water's edge for clues. He had nearly given up when he spotted what he had missed earlier because he hadn't gone far enough--a muddy footprint. It appeared as though someone had stumbled, the footprint sliding until it met purchase on solid ground. Further down the riverbank, he noticed broken ferns and more footprints, which explained why the dogs had missed the scent. Like him, they had not gone far enough downstream. He had to hand it to Toby, he knew the woods, and he knew how to cover his tracks.

Wyatt gave a whistle to Les who whistled back, their unspoken communication should either one of the men discover something. He waited for Les to catch up.

When Wyatt had first started searching for Kate, he had thought it would be easy to find her, but the longer they were on the trail, the more he realized it would be like searching for a flea on a bear. And yet time was of the essence. Any delay could spell trouble, so he was relieved when Les came trotting toward him, the horse choosing its footing carefully so as not to slip.

"What did you find?" Les pulled back his brown hat to reveal beads of sweat. He was a good man for helping Wyatt, considering he had no skin in the game. He could have been back at the cabin now, relaxing in the cool air conditioning. Instead, he'd chosen to aid Wyatt in what could very well be a quixotic quest that just might end in tragedy. He mentally thanked his good friend.

"Footprints. Look!" Wyatt pointed to what appeared to be a woman's footprint and at the matted bracken close by.

"Do you think we should call the others?" Les said, quieting his roan-colored quarter horse with a tap on the reins and a soft cluck.

"No time. They're so far away that it will take a good half

hour or more to catch up. Let's just keep moving."

"And like they say," Les added, "two eyes are better than one."

For the next hour, they moved ever upward, the forward motion painstakingly slow as they zigzagged up the mountain. Fortunately, Toby and Kate were on foot. Being on horseback gave Wyatt and Les a clear advantage. Still, the pair had a head start, nearly a full day's head start, and either Wyatt and Les found them before nightfall, or they would have to spend the night out in the open and hope that they could recapture the trail by morning.

Wyatt paused briefly for a drink, handing his canteen to Les who took a swig and wiped his mouth. The past few days had been hard on him, and Wyatt could see that he was tired.

"I want you to know how much this means to me--coming out and helping me like this. You didn't have to."

Les tried to protest but Wyatt raised a hand to stop him. "No, you've been a great friend and I appreciate it."

Les merely nodded and then quickly changed the subject. "So, what's our plan, boss?"

"This guy knows the area, right?" Wyatt said.

"He and his father used to hunt up here every winter. They've got a reputation for being pretty good hunters. More than pretty good, really. They know this territory better than just about anyone else in these parts. Why?"

Wyatt took stock of what his friend had said. A person heading into the woods with as much knowledge as Toby was said to possess, surely had a plan of his own. A place to go. Somewhere to overnight, as he would when hunting. Maybe a place to stay for a while until the law stopped tracking them.

"Okay, someone this smart would know where to hide out, yes?" Wyatt asked.

Les shrugged his shoulders, then nodded, his blond hair damp and curling slightly from the steady ride in the afternoon heat.

"You're a hunter. Where would a hunter go, spend the night maybe?"

"There are all sorts of places. We usually build a blind."

"What if he didn't have that, or didn't want to be that exposed."

Les frowned, thinking, then snapped his fingers. "There are caves, but most of them are higher up."

Wyatt felt like they were finally getting somewhere. "Can you show me some?"

"In this direction?"

"Yeah."

"Well, I can only think of two," he said, as the horses bent down and gently nibbled at some grassy stubble.

"Close to here?"

Wyatt's mustang stamped impatiently, an impatience that Wyatt could easily understand because he felt it too, but without a direction they could be searching for days. They needed a strategy of their own if they were to succeed in catching up with Toby and Kate. And they needed to locate any potential hiding places, the sooner the better.

Les bit his lip. "I'd say the first cave's about another half hour from here."

"Then let's go."

* * *

Kate and Toby had arrived at the last clearing before the final ascent toward the cave that reached just below the snowline. The Teton's peaks, jagged and irregular, appeared blue and majestic in the waning light, the white caps glistening in the fading sun. But most of all, they appeared daunting as Kate viewed the final leg of their journey.

"Won't someone see us? We'll be out in the open for a good twenty minutes."

Toby had clearly been worried about the same thing because his lips were pressed in a tight line. He ran a grubby hand through greasy hair, the smell of sweat heavy in the still air. She was sure she smelled just as bad, but that was the least of her worries now.

"By my calculation we should be far enough ahead of anyone tracking us that if we sprint the rest of the way, we should be--" Before he could finish his words he frowned and peered up at the sky. "Get down," he hissed.

Kate had heard it too, the sound of rotors from a helicopter. Just then, Kate ducked as a helicopter appeared overhead. Toby grabbed her and yanked her back into the shadows of the trees. For the next few minutes, he held her tight, his hand over her mouth as his eyes scanned the sky above. Finally, as the sound dissipated, he gradually released her.

"Now what?" she asked, feeling both relieved and frightened.

Toby cupped his hands over his face, then let out a breath. "I need to think. Think! Think!" he said, as though talking to himself.

Suddenly, he stood and began pacing, his hands balled into tight fists as he struggled over how to proceed. As she watched him pace, she calculated her next move. The only thing she had going for her were her ideas. That's what her business had been based on, and it's what her life had been based on, if the truth were to be told. Every time she had suffered a blow, her ideas had pulled her back from despair. She would set her sights on the next horizon in the hope that any new objective would hold the answer to her problems. But they hadn't, she realized. She had unresolved issues, and, until she faced them, history would continue to repeat itself. Only one tool was left in her arsenal.

"I can't go any further," she said. To prove her point, she sat on a fallen log, chin up, daring him to make her move.

He did a quick about face and ran to where she sat, balling her damp shirt in his fist. "You'll go if I say you'll go, do I make myself clear? Do I?" he shouted.

When she didn't answer, he lay a hand on his sheath in warning, his eyes never wavering from hers.

"I'm done," she said, so softly that he had her repeat her words. "We're both going to wind up dead at this rate. We run into that clearing and we're sitting ducks. Sure, the trackers may not see us, but that helicopter sure as heck will. You want out of this alive, right?"

His breathing was labored, but he didn't move. "Go on."

"What if we hug the tree line."

"What good will that do us?"

Even Kate didn't know where she was going with this, but she'd been forced to come up with on-the-spot ads to win over potential clients and had learned to think on the fly. This was no different. She just needed to use her skills in a new way.

She scanned the wide expanse before them. Off in the distance she could see a spot where water was falling from the snow-capped mountains into a winding makeshift brook. If they could make it there, they could walk as far as possible through the water to lose any scent that a hound might follow. And, if they were lucky, there just might be somewhere that they could bivouac for the night.

"I could be mistaken, but where the water falls over that boulder, I believe there's a space behind it. Maybe we can spend the night there, then begin descending the mountain... there!" she said, pointing to a spot that was hidden by much taller trees, possibly Douglas fir.

Toby picked a piece of wild grass and chewed on it. "Then what?"

"Then we double back."

"They'll be watching your SUV. No way can we go back for it."

"Right..."

Suddenly, he snapped his fingers and laughed. "But there is a shack, if the pass is clear. We might face a little snow, and we could lose the path if we're not careful."

The fear in his eyes made it clear that what they were proposing was not to be taken lightly. And she was a novice. What's worse, she was afraid of heights.

Heights and snow.

He seemed to think a minute. Finally, he nodded and said, "On your feet."

Although she tried to stand, the blisters on her feet made it impossible and she quickly sat down again. "My feet," she said, tears filling her eyes.

Toby scanned the area, and seeing no one, bent down and

removed first one shoe, then the next. Huge liquid-filled blisters covered much of the pad of her feet as well as her heels. Several of her toes were bleeding.

Toby dropped his pack to the ground and rifled through the zippered pocket in the front of the bag until he came upon a roll of silver duct tape.

"What are you going to do with that?" Kate demanded, crawling backwards on all fours.

"Sit still. I'm going to tape your feet, but first we need to get rid of some of this liquid."

From his knapsack, he pulled out needle and thread, wiping off the needle with a moistened antibacterial towelette. He then stuck the needle into the blister and warm water spilled out onto the forest carpet below. Quickly, he dabbed at the spot with the towelette and did the same for the remaining blisters. Then he dabbed an antiseptic salve onto the wounds. Using his knife, he cut off a large strip of duct tape and wound it tightly around first one foot, then the next.

"How is this going to help?"

"You're not a survivalist, are you?" he said with a grin.

For the first time since he'd abducted her, he seemed almost human. It was too bad he couldn't use these qualities for good instead of for evil. Not for the first time, she wondered if people were redeemable, if second chances were possible. Or once people were firmly set in a pattern, perhaps it was impossible to stray from that pattern. But then she'd either known or heard of people who had redeemed themselves in one way or another. Drug addicts who had gone clean. People who had escaped prison and lived ordinary, productive lives. A young woman who had made a mistake, had a child out of wedlock, but then went on to raise a healthy, well-adjusted child. But she also knew the person had to *want* to change.

Did Wyatt want to change? Could he? She didn't know, and that's what was eating her up. Some people's lives... and mistakes... were set in stone, as unmovable and unchangeable as the seasons. Well, there was nothing she could do about that now. For the foreseeable future, she just needed to stay alive.

She put her shoes back on and was amazed how much

better her feet felt already. Every muscle in her body ached
from the exertion, but if her feet held out, she could press
forward a while longer.

"Okay, you're the guide. So lead us."

For the second time that day, he laughed. It was as though
the monster were transforming into a human right before her
eyes.

Thirty-Two

"I'm sorry, Wyatt," Les said as they came to the second cave and found it empty. "I really thought Toby would pick one of these two spots."

For the first time since they had begun their ascent up the western slope of the Grand Tetons, Wyatt felt cool from the shade of the musky smelling cavern. Someone had spent time in these caves, but from the look of the objects--an empty can whose expiration dated from the late eighties, a very old fork with bent tines, and a couple of crumpled cigarette wrappers that were yellowed with age--it was long ago.

"Can you think of any other place Toby might have taken her? Any place at all?" Wyatt knew he was grasping at straws, but he needed every straw he could get at this point.

Les merely shook his head, clearly as frustrated as Wyatt at the prospect that they might never find her.

"Wait!" Les shouted suddenly, then tempered his words by adding, "Sorry."

"What?" Wyatt implored.

"There's a cave up above the tree line."

Wyatt rubbed his eyes. "Do you think Toby would risk taking Kate there?"

Les shrugged. "It would be risky. They would be out in the open for quite a distance, but it's all I've got."

Then it was worth a try. Weary from a hard day's drive steadily upward, and feeling sore from being in the saddle for so long, Wyatt nevertheless pressed forward, determined to find Kate. She might never forgive him for the words Charlotte had spoken, but that didn't matter anymore. Kate deserved the truth. Whatever she decided after that, then so be it. If she never wanted to see him again, he would dust off his heart and go on. Still, it wouldn't be easy. Silently, he prayed that she would forgive him. Whatever she chose, at least there would be no more lies between them. They could start off with a fresh slate and move on. What they did with their lives after that would decide their future. And he was determined to make it a good one, to prove to her each and every day that he was honorable and trustworthy. Without that, their relationship had no foundation.

"Wyatt," Les said, his voice low as though he were talking to one of the horses at feeding time.

"Hmm?" Wyatt said, still wrapped up in his thoughts.

"I've known you a long time."

Les had been Wyatt's friend since elementary school. They had ridden the bus together, had played sports together in the field that straddled the two farmhouses. After Iraq, Les had chosen to stay single, said he carried too much baggage to bring to a marriage. Wyatt had hoped he would one day change his mind, but for now, the boys had become Les's family and that seemed to be enough. Oh, he went into town on Saturday night and danced with a few girls, and he had more than his fair share of women fawning over him, but in the end he knew his strengths and weaknesses and he'd chosen to deal with them alone.

"I've never seen you like this with any other woman. It sort of gives me... hope. That there's someone out there... What I'm trying to say is that you could easily screw this up again, you know?"

Wyatt knew only too well.

"Well, don't. Because if you do I'm going to come back and kick your ass."

Wyatt laughed, but he knew his friend was serious. Kate deserved someone faithful, someone true. He didn't want to be the one to mess that up.

"I'll remember that."

"If you can't be faithful, let her go. Let her find someone who will love her."

"Is there anything I should worry about?" Wyatt said, looking at his friend thoughtfully.

Les laughed. "No. It's just that I know a good thing when I see it, and she's a good thing. She may make mistakes; she may do stupid things sometimes. But she loves you. Really loves you. That doesn't happen too often in a lifetime, *comprende?*"

Wyatt had never heard Les talk to him quite like this before. It gave him newfound respect for his friend.

"I promise. I'll be good to her." Then Wyatt kicked his horse into a trot as they wound their way up the mountainside.

* * *

Above them lay the final leg of the journey beneath a spray of waterfall that jutted over a granite cliff. The lip wasn't huge, but Kate felt certain it would provide them protection for at least tonight. And although she knew she should be doing everything she could to escape, she felt she had been placed here for a reason, though what that might be, she couldn't be certain. She just knew she needed to keep putting one foot ahead of the other.

The long hours of climbing had tested her determination and perseverance more than she could have ever imagined. Whereas the fear that had dogged her every step had slowly evaporated and she felt her power returning in small increments. She was *not* a helpless victim. She *could* determine her own fate. And she would *not* be trampled on. More than that, she knew now that she deserved someone worthy of her trust. It had been a hard slog to come to this understanding of herself but worth every minute. She wanted love, loyalty, and respect. She would accept nothing less. She hoped and prayed that she would have it with Wyatt, but if not, she would search until she found that person who felt as she did.

"There it is," Toby said, pointing to the dark spot just below the waterfall. "You're right. I think we have ourselves a cave!"

To her surprise, he reached over and twirled her around, then quickly set her down, his head lowered in penitence. The hard lines etched in his face were gone, replaced by almost a boyish enthusiasm. Had Iraq been the turning point in his life that had turned him into the hardened man he'd become? Or had that seed been planted in him long ago, before the war? She didn't know. She just knew that this new transformation was a positive one and she hoped it would last.

Whatever happened, she first had to make it to the cave, yet every nerve in her body ached for rest. Now, seeing the waterfall close at hand, she willed her feet into action and, like Toby, she was nearly running. For the next half an hour they traversed ever upward, the mountain growing steeper as they mounted the last lap toward their destination. Toby reached out a hand. She hesitated for only a moment, then took it in hers and together they made the final ascent.

When they were seated in a relatively dry spot tucked deep beneath the outer edge of the waterfall, the spray pungent with the smell of ferns and wet soil, they finally relaxed.

Toby reached into his knapsack and pulled out a mixture of rice, dried cranberries, and vegetables, and what appeared to be a soy-based meat of some sort. He took his canteen and poured water into a lightweight, collapsible bowl.

"I used the quick-cooking rice so we don't have to light a fire." He ducked his head in apology. "Safer that way."

At this point she didn't care what the food looked or tasted like. She was so famished she would have eaten it without any water at all, if need be. He handed her a spoon and she tucked into it with relish, never looking up until the last morsel was eaten and her stomach full.

When she had finally finished, she saw that Toby was watching her with a twinkle in his eye. She flushed with embarrassment at the heathen she'd become in a single day. She hadn't even offered him any. What if he had meant for them to share the bowl?

"Get enough?" he asked.

She merely nodded, still licking her lips for any remaining flavor.

"Good. I thought I might have to scrape lichen off the cave floor and feed it to you."

For a moment, she wondered if he was serious--after all, who knew what survivalists ate in a pinch. But then she saw the beginnings of laughter that grew until both of them were laughing so hard their sides ached and they moaned from the pain of an exhausting day spent out in the forest.

When they were finally through laughing, Toby suddenly became more serious and his lips formed a straight line.

"What is it?" she asked.

"I don't know." He spread his hands out to encompass the cave. "This..."

To her questioning look, he said, "I haven't laughed since... since..."

She finished for him. "Before the war?"

He nodded. "It feels good. I had forgotten how to laugh. I've been mad at everything ... everyone. It seems like I put my life on the line for the country I love, for everyone I love, and then you come home and no one gives a crap. 'It was your duty,' they say, 'so get over it.' Go on like nothing happened, but something sure as hell did happen."

The anger in his voice had risen a notch, but instead of pushing him away as most would do, she reached over and cupped his hand in hers.

"It sure as hell did," she agreed.

How many times had she held her brother's hand like this as he'd struggled in a moment of crisis? How many times had she listened to him cry, felt her shirt grow moist with tears... tears that he could never shed with his buddies for fear of being humiliated? Often, these boys never caught a break. And now women in the service must feel exactly the same. Throw in sexual harassment and physical abuse and it was a pain that would never go away, would haunt them their entire lives.

"You can't believe the things I saw, the things that were done to me, to my friends."

She put an arm around his shoulder and held him tight. Only in a cave, far from civilization, could he ever utter the words that would finally help to lance the wound that had been festering inside him since the war. Only in a basement, with his sanity hanging by a thread, could her brother utter the words that had helped him heal. And yet, the wound might never completely heal. If the man or woman was lucky, it would scab over, form a scar that would remain with the service man or woman for the rest of his or her life.

Those who couldn't move forward were the unfortunate

ones... the ones who never learned to cope. These were the disposable vets, who had been used up and left to die on a different battlefield, the one that played out in their minds and in their lives each and every day. These were truly the ones who deserved a medal, but a medal could never replace a life. She hoped that somewhere, someday, the powers that be would learn that compassion trumps duty any day. That human lives have value beyond the duties they perform. That these men and women who had served their countries are worthy of love by virtue of being human.

One day...

*   *   *

Something in Wyatt stirred. It was as if he could feel Kate's presence. The nape of his neck prickled as he scanned the horizon back and forth, back and forth searching for that one needle in the proverbial haystack. What was he missing?

Then he saw it. Just a glint of silver in the horizon as the sun flashed against a small stream. If Kate and Toby were nearby, they would be searching for water. It was the one thing that all veterans knew. You could go a long time without food, but without water, especially in this heat, the game was over. Like Wyatt and Les, Kate and Toby had been on the march all day. They were no doubt tired and in need of rest... and a drink.

"There!" Wyatt pointed the spot out to Les. "Water."

For the first time in many hours, Les's face lit in a wide smile as he doffed his hat and tamped it against his horse's flank to remove the dust from the day before moving on.

"I'd say we've got ourselves a winner," Les said. "Have you been able to contact the sheriff, see where the search party is located before we move in?"

Wyatt shook his head and his Mustang whinnied as if in agreement. "Still no reception. Too high up. I don't think there's a tower close enough, so we're on our own, *amigo*."

"It's not the first time," Les said dryly, to which they both laughed.

The sun was hovering low in the west. In just a little over an hour, official sunset would be upon them and the going would be rough.

"What do you say we take the horses to just below the falls," Wyatt said, "have ourselves something to eat and drink, then we go in under the cover of darkness."

"Lead the way," Les said, the slump of his shoulders revealing the weariness they were both feeling.

For the next hour, they spoke little. It wasn't until they were part way up the trail and were forced to walk their horses because of the narrow path that Wyatt stopped Les and pointed. In a whisper, he said, "Tracks."

Les's eyes traced the groove in the trail. "Two sets. A man and a woman, by the look of it. I think we've hit paydirt."

The air had grown a good fifteen degrees colder in the past mile and a half as they reined their horses ever upward. The snowline was still a good one hundred feet or more above their current location, but already the temperature felt refreshing. When night fell, however, that coolness would become frigid almost instantly. Fortunately, experience had taught both him and Les to carry heavy coats when out scouting or hunting. He even had a pair of long johns, if it came to it, and it might.

"How do you think the two will hold up tonight?" Les asked Wyatt.

"Toby should have no problem," Wyatt said, fingering the reins as they continued their trek to the waterfall. "He's an experienced mountaineer and has had survival training in the military. It's Kate I'm worried about."

Les was even quieter than usual and appeared pensive. "Do you think he planned to take Kate, instead of one of us?"

"You mean as a hostage?"

Les nodded.

"He could have taken anyone. It didn't have to be Kate."

"I know. But what are the odds that it was Kate?"

Wyatt shrugged. The thought had occurred to him as well. After all, Toby would have wanted to get Kate out of the picture, if what Nora and Jack had said was true... that this man was working for Ian.

"It would kill two birds with one stone... to use Kate as his hostage."

The thought was a chilling one. Wyatt was glad he had brought his double-barreled shotgun and that it was safely stowed inside his scabbard. Although he hoped he wouldn't need to use it, he wasn't ruling it out as an option. He would leave with Kate, even if he had to do it by force.

* * *

Funny how life could change on a dime. One minute it could be wonderful, the next minute it could be like seeds scattered to the wind, never knowing which way the winds would blow or where they would take you. Life had always been like that for Kate. Intermittent lulls followed by huge changes that swept in and blew her world apart. It had been like that with every man she had ever known. And here she was with yet another man, a boy, really. Oddly, she wasn't afraid. Nor was she fearful of the future. For some reason, she felt calm, here inside this cave with no outside distractions to confuse her. Here, she was living in the moment. She could be alive tomorrow or dead, but whatever happened, she had made peace with herself.

The world was a powder keg of warring factions, her business merely a mirror of the world beyond, this world that had brought men like Toby to this desolate place, lost to the outside world. Lost to themselves and their values. Alone, except for her.

How many other young men had faced this same inner darkness? How many had come out alive? She didn't know. She just prayed that somehow Toby could let go of the anger and bitterness that had caused him to team up with a very unscrupulous man.

His head lay on her shoulder, her arm around him still. She fingered the wisps of black hair that fell against his pale skin and was again struck by his youth. He was a baby, really. But one who had faced circumstances that no young man should ever have to face. War had forced these boys to grow up almost instantly, only without the positive influences that would help them become good husbands, good fathers, good citizens of their community. It wasn't something that could be mandated. It was something that had to be taught by example. Who would teach them that? Not the Ians of the world, surely. And no one could beat that into a boy. The Tobys of the world had to learn it through modeled behavior, through positive reinforcement, through love and kindness.

Kate caressed Toby's face gently, wondering what her little boy would look like, should she ever have one. Restless, Toby stirred, then moved in closer looking for all the world like a small child who was afraid of society and everything in it. And, as though he *were* a child, she held him tight, wishing she could take away the pain that he had experienced, the hours of wondering when he would be next, or his buddy next to him.

The world was definitely a confusing place. For Kate, *and* for this young man. She couldn't change the world. But she could do what she could for Toby. And for now, that was enough.

Thirty-Three

Nighttime fell as the sun crested the hilltop and finally receded, lending the mountaintops a blue-gray hue before the sun winked out and the stars settled into the night sky. Wyatt tied his horse, while Les followed suit, and then they crept near the waterfall by the remaining daylight, scoping the area out ahead of time. Together, they decided to wait until Kate and Toby were asleep and then creep in quietly. With any luck, Wyatt could get a bead on Toby while Les grabbed Kate. At least that was the plan, but plans were apt to go awry, as Wyatt had learned in the military. No matter how well a leader planned, an unexpected surprise almost always shot the plans all to hell. You could train, and train, and train, but to be really effective, you needed men who could fly by the seat of their pants. Men who could use good judgment. Trustworthy men, and he trusted no man better than Les.

He listened for any noise beyond the sound of falling water, but even the crickets avoided this elevation. The only thing that seemed to thrive at this time of night were the mosquitoes. Wyatt slapped at his neck, cursing softly. Still, mosquitoes were the least of his worries. Everything had to go just right tonight. Kate's life depended on it.

"You ready?" Les whispered, only his eyes and outline visible against the waning moonlight.

"As ready as I'll ever be," Wyatt said, giving his horse one last pat before heading out, shotgun in hand. He prayed he wouldn't have to use it, but he would, if necessary.

For the next twenty minutes, they moved in silence as they advanced up the hillside. As much as Wyatt would have preferred, he couldn't turn on his flashlight. Instead, he counted on the moon, what there was of it, to light their way. Yet as they ascended, the air turned brisk, despite the earlier heat of the day. Wyatt had to rub his hands together in order to keep them from freezing.

Just then, an owl hooted overhead, giving the place an eerie feel that made Wyatt's blood run cold. Always, while in Iraq, Wyatt would imagine tomorrow. If he could just envision the next day, then he knew he could get through this one. In keeping with tradition, he imagined Kate, safe in his arms at home on the ranch. Once he had her securely in his mind's eye, he gave a silent signal to Les who immediately understood and moved to the left of the waterfall. In the meantime, Wyatt eased up next to him against the rock wall.

"You go in," he whispered. "I'll be right behind you to give you cover while you grab Kate and get out."

Les nodded, his face shadowed against the moonlight.

Wyatt's heart slowed as he prepared for what lay ahead. If Toby didn't come willingly... well... Wyatt would do what he had to when the time came.

Saying a silent prayer that all would go according to plan, Wyatt tapped Les's arm three times, then they moved into position beneath the waterfall where they had a clear view of the pair. Wyatt hoped to mask the sound of him pumping his shotgun with the crashing of the water. But despite his best laid plans, the sound woke Toby, who instinctively reached for Kate and pulled her in front of him, his gun to her temple.

"Let her go!" Wyatt yelled, hoping his bluff would work. "Now, or this first shot's going straight through your temple."

"You shoot me, you shoot her, so fire away."

"Stop!" Kate shouted. Then to Toby she said, "Look, you don't want to do this. I won't let them hurt you. I promise you. But you can't keep running. It's time to stop. To own up to what you've done and start a new life. I'll help." Then looking around the dark cavern, she said, "We all will."

Wyatt couldn't believe what he was hearing. This bastard didn't deserve her kindness. He had wheedled and intimidated her and everyone around him. He had been so filled with hate and venom that he couldn't see the aid that had been offered him. And now, Kate, of all people, wanted to help Toby when no one else had been able to get through to him. It was a pipe dream to believe he would ever change. He had been given so many opportunities and had squandered each and every one of them.

"Let... her... go," Wyatt said, his voice so low and menacing that it surprised even him.

"People like you think you're big shots," Toby said. "You can just come in here and screw everyone around. You come home and you've got a house, money... what have I got? My dad and I have lived here our whole lives... hunted, fished. Then I go off to war and my momma gets cancer. There's no one to work the land, to keep up with payments on the property... property my family has owned since the eighteen hundreds. They foreclosed, took everything my family owned. It killed my dad."

"That wasn't Wyatt's fault," Kate implored. "Surely, you see that."

"What I see is the same damn people getting all the luck, while other people get screwed over and over and over. Well, I'm done with that. Now it's your turn to get screwed."

"You don't mean that, Toby," Kate said, still the voice of reason.

"If it's the last thing I do, I'm going to destroy your ranch and everything on it," he said, crying now.

Worried that things were getting out of hand, Wyatt gave Les the signal to move in and watched as he crept forward. Toby had clearly seen the movement too, because he held Kate tighter, his arm now around her throat.

Kate attempted a garbled, "Toby, please," but the words died off as her airway became further constricted.

Slowly, Les scooted within inches of Kate. Toby's eyes grew wild with fear and anger as Wyatt yelled, "Last chance, Toby. Let... her... go!"

Instinctively, Wyatt leaned in for the final shot as Les reached in to grab Kate. Just as Les attempted to pull her away, a shot fired and Kate screamed then dropped to the ground.

What have I done?

Thirty-Four

Kate awoke to discover her ears ringing and the sound of voices that seemed like muffled echoes. There, in a pool of blood, lay Toby, the sweet little boy she had held in her arms only the night before, with a shot to his temple. The young man who had poured his heart out to her. The man, who she had believed would change, given the chance, or at least she had *wanted* to believe it was possible.

"Why?" said Kate as Wyatt dropped the shotgun and ran over next to her, running his hands across her ribs to make sure she wasn't hurt. "You didn't have to kill him. He wouldn't have hurt me."

"I know he wouldn't have meant to," Wyatt said, his voice choked with emotion.

"Then why? Why did you do it?"

Wyatt shook his head. "I didn't."

Kate heard his words as though from under a waterfall, an irony if ever there was one. She frowned at him. "If you didn't... then who?"

She peered up at Les only to see him shaking his head as well.

"I don't understand."

Wyatt looked at her with such loving kindness in his eyes that it made her want to stay with him forever.

"You were right, Kate. He couldn't hurt you." He lifted her carefully into his arms, making her feel more secure than she ever had before.

"What Wyatt's trying to say, Kate," Les inserted, placing a hand on her shoulder, "is that Toby took his own life. He cared too much about you to see you hurt, but he couldn't go back. Some men can't let go of the past, they can't get beyond the pain and bitterness. It festers until it spills over onto everyone around them when it's really themselves they hate. It's a whole lot easier to hate the world than to hate yourself."

Kate blinked back tears. She had wanted so much for him to change, for him to find a corner of the world where he could feel that he belonged. Where he wouldn't have to strike out at others in order to ease his own pain. Maybe, in that last act of grace, he had done just that. He had spared her in order to redeem himself.

"I need to say goodbye to him," she said.

Wyatt and Les exchanged nervous glances, but Wyatt finally nodded. She crawled over to where Toby lay on the cold, lumpy floor of the cavern and took his hand, just as she had the night before. She rubbed it gently with her thumb.

"I wish you could have found another way. I wish you could have turned your life around. I know you were thrown some pretty bad curves. I know that," she said to the lifeless form, his body still warm.

Why, Toby? Why?

But she would never know why, because no one could live in another man's shoes. She just wished she could have found a way to get through to him, to make him stop this mad progression toward oblivion. To make him understand that goodness existed in the world, too, and he could have been part of that goodness if he had only wanted it badly enough.

"Despite everything, I love you... the part of you that remembered how to care, how to feel, how to show compassion," she said. "And Toby... I forgive you."

Grace.

Maybe that's what it took to survive a war, the brutality, the sheer and utter madness of it all. She hoped she would find it in her own life someday, but for now, this was enough. For one last time, she kissed his cheek then she felt herself being lifted into the arms of a man she could only describe as her hero.

Wyatt was taking her home.

* * *

How many times had Wyatt kissed Kate's hand as the horses made the long trek home? How many times had he told her he loved her and that he was sorry? He felt a lump in his throat thinking about how tightly she had held him as the horses stepped gingerly down the mountainside, slipping at times, then correcting their gait. And maybe that was the thing about horses. They knew that a slip didn't mean a fall. Whenever they made a wrong step, they simply righted themselves and moved forward.

For too long, Wyatt had slipped and continued the slide, never thinking about the consequences or the future, only about the pleasure of the moment. He had catered to his own selfish desires because to look too deeply at the things he had done and the people he had hurt would have set him into a freefall. So, instead, he had just kept on the path of least resistance, just kept plowing forward never caring who got thrown because of him.

Emajean was right when she had pulled him out of the bar that day and told him it was time to grow up and become a man. When a man never knew if he was going to live or die, thoughts of others and what they might think no longer mattered. That man lived for himself, for his team. Wives, children, society... they were a distant memory. They didn't count in the grand scheme of things. Only the here and now mattered. No wonder the divorce rate among the military and the police was so high. When a person's life was on the line each and every day, values got skewed. His had. He had forgotten what was important. He had forgotten that there might be a tomorrow and that tomorrow might be difficult to explain. More importantly, he had forgotten how to love... truly love another person enough to think more about that person than himself. And that's what he needed to change, to get right, or he was going to die a very lonely man.

He squeezed Kate's hand, felt the warmth of her against his back. They had a very important talk ahead of them, and they would have it just as soon as they were home and she felt safe again.

He had scarcely got that thought out when he heard voices in the distance. Les appeared hesitant.

"Probably just the sheriff's crew," Wyatt assured him.

Wyatt eyed the tarp draped across the croup of Les's horse. Beneath the tarp were the last vestiges of a man who had struggled to survive the aftermath of war. If Emajean hadn't pulled Wyatt from the bar might this have been him? His fate? He shuddered to think. He didn't want to be like that, didn't want to be angry and turn that anger outward... or inward, as Toby had in the end. He wanted to survive this war. It's time he came home. Truly came home.

He had just ended that thought as they made the clearing and heard helicopters buzzing overhead. Lights around him flashed, blinding him momentarily, and noises crowded in on him as newscasters reached in with microphones. They hammered him with question after question.

Had they found Toby? What was his condition? Had he hurt Kate? How were they feeling after the long ordeal?

His head was swimming as he struggled to answer question after question, while trying as best he could to shield Kate from the press's prying eyes and even more prying questions.

"Give her space, please," he said more than once. At one point the journalists became so aggressive that Les, seeing Wyatt's dilemma, stepped his horse in front of the newsmen and women to enforce the needed distance.

One especially aggressive red-headed female reporter snuck behind Les's horse and shoved a microphone toward Wyatt's mouth. "What will this mean to your veteran's rehab ranch? Will this black stain on your record prevent you from staying open in the future? Where will the vets go if you have to shut your operation down?"

Wyatt had been so caught up in finding Kate and making sure she was safe that he hadn't even thought of what could happen should word get out that one of the vets had threatened someone on the ranch, had vandalized the place, and now had abducted a woman. News of Toby's death would only provide more fodder for the media grist mill. He felt as though he had awakened from a nightmare only to stumble into an even bigger one.

One of the male newscasters had apparently done a little investigating of his own, and had lifted the tarp allowing a hand to fall into the open. An audible gasp from the crowd was followed by a hush that filled the clearing with a palpable tension.

"Is that him?" one of the newscasters asked. The man was in his late twenties at best, his hair slicked back and his shoes so shiny that the early morning sun glinted off them, nearly blinding Wyatt.

It was too late for damage control. How many times had Wyatt been forced to make split decisions in combat? Too many.

"That's him," Wyatt said, unable to hide his complete and utter exhaustion. "Died of a self-inflicted gunshot wound."

He couldn't hear the rest of the questions--just caught little snapshots of words... autopsy... hearing... closure. Behind him, he felt Kate tremble. Then he heard small sobs.

Screw the media, he decided. He turned away from them and tucked Kate's head against his chest, kissing her on the top of her forehead. She had experienced her own private war, her own private hell. What he hoped for her now--what he hoped for them both--is that one day they could put all this behind them, could live a life of love and tranquility. A life without fear. A life spent together, forever.

Thirty-Five

The entire night had felt like a bad dream--the highs, the lows, and everything in between. Kate couldn't decide which was worse, her stubborn belief that things might change without anyone getting hurt, or the fact that they hadn't. She had always wanted to believe in the ultimate good in people, but some people were so steeped in their own misery that they had to inflict that same pain on others. The fact that Toby couldn't envision another life, a life where justice replaced vengeance, where hope replaced despair, where love replaced hate, made his life and his loss the ultimate tragedy.

Kate curled up in the quilt that the sheriff's assistant had provided. Wyatt had been her saving grace, as they had trekked down the mountainside yesterday. However, once the sheriff discovered that Toby was dead, he had insisted that Les, Kate, and Wyatt travel in separate cars for questioning. Wyatt had gone in the sheriff's SUV, whereas Kate had taken one of two unmarked cars, the paparazzi flashing cameras through the open window, which she quickly closed.

"Reminds me of my days in Sarajevo," said the female officer, who introduced herself as Nadiya. She was short but wiry and bore only a slight accent. She had a swarthy complexion and a scar that puckered her right cheek.

"Sarajevo?"

"My family was Bosnian. The Serbian secret police pulled us from our house at night, removed us at gunpoint. But first they made us destroy every document that showed we had ever existed, including all of our family photos. That way if we turned up missing, no one would be the wiser. Ethnic cleansing, they call it. All our memories... gone."

Sadness marked her features as clearly as though she'd worn a scarlet letter to identify her as one of the walking wounded. Even her hair lay limp as though unable to recover from the damage done to her.

"How did you survive?" Kate asked, feeling like a survivor herself.

"Our car was shelled, the driver killed. I don't know what happened to the cars behind ours. Everyone scattered. We had family outside the city who were able to help us escape. We were the fortunate ones. Many weren't so fortunate."

"That's not quite what I was asking."

"You mean how did I survive emotionally?" The woman turned to inspect Kate, as though really seeing her for the first time.

Kate nodded, tears pricking her eyes and making them sting. Ian had detested tears, felt they were a sign of weakness. One poor office girl had made the mistake of crying after his verbal abuse. He had made sure her life was miserable after that, whereupon she soon quit.

As if understanding her emotions, Nadiya said, "Don't be afraid to cry. *Ever.* No matter what people say, they're the body's way of releasing pain. It's like a wound that is allowed to fester. Without tears, to cleanse the wound, you can never heal properly, so never let anyone tell you you can't cry."

Kate thanked her for her words. It was exactly what she needed to hear.

"And in answer to your earlier question, it was my family, the people who loved and cared for me, who helped me survive. Don't be afraid to ask for help if you need it." Nadiya placed a hand on Kate's shoulder. "We all need each other now and then, right?"

Every joint, every bone, in Kate's body ached from yesterday's strenuous hike. Her feet were blistered and sore, the duct tape bandages still wrapped around her feet to remind her this hadn't been some awful dream from which she would soon awaken. She had read an article once about *everyone* having a tragedy happen in their life that changed them forever... a car accident, cancer, the loss of a loved one. She could honestly say that this was the event that divided her life between before and after. It was as if she'd been an entirely different person, a naive person who believed that all things could be fixed. That everyone was truly good. But now she knew that some things happened to people that could change them forever, for good or bad, and that sometimes there was no coming back when a person had their thoughts set only on destruction.

As though reading her mind, Nadiya reached over and patted Kate's arm. "It will get better... over time. I promise you. It can take weeks, months, and often years, but it *will* get better. Never look ahead, only at the day, sometimes even the moment. Memories will creep up on you at night, when you least expect it. Get up, read. Do anything you can to take your mind off of your pain. You get through a minute at a time, and then that minute becomes an hour. And someday... *some way*, you find that you've made it through an entire day without thinking about it."

She smiled that same sad smile as before. But Kate saw something she hadn't seen in Nadiya before, and that was hope. Hope for the here and now. More importantly, hope for the future. That's what Kate needed to focus on... the future. She prayed that her future would be with Wyatt.

* * *

Wyatt realized he hadn't heard a word the sheriff had said as he sat opposite him in his office, his eyes focused on the plaques on the wall behind the officer. Words kept filtering in and out as Wyatt grew more impatient to find Kate and go home. He wanted nothing more than to forget this awful night. He'd been so focused on first finding Kate, then rescuing her, that he hadn't yet processed that a man's life had been taken all because he couldn't imagine a life without anger and bitterness.

Wyatt had given Toby every opportunity to change, to give up his vendetta for what he perceived as his victimization. And the truth of it was, he *had* been victimized. So many of these boys had been, in one way or another. The very fact that they'd had to give up their youth, to risk their lives often never understanding why, even before they'd had a chance to become men or to make a life for themselves--that was in and of itself a form of victimization. Then they'd been bullied and frightened in order to teach them to fight. No wonder they had come back so messed up. They often had no idea why they were fighting.

That was the difference, he supposed, between the men from World War II and now. In World War II, the outside threat had rallied the men around the same flag. They understood the cause, believed in it. Now everything was so much more murky. Or maybe it had always been that way and he was just being naive to think that it had ever been different.

He'd been so caught up in his thoughts that he hadn't realized the questioning was over until the sheriff stood and held out a hand. "Stay close, in case we have any questions. There will be an investigation, but as long as all the pieces fall in place like you say, it shouldn't take long."

Wyatt thanked the sheriff and donned his hat. "Can I see Kate now?"

"Let's go see if she's finished up."

They walked down the long corridor to the small cubicle in back. When Wyatt first saw Kate, he once again thought how small and fragile she seemed. And yet he knew she had a strength of heart that she probably didn't even know existed. He would help her find it. He planned to make that his mission.

Kate and the female officer stood and hugged.

"Thanks for everything," Kate said, then turned to leave.

When the pair reached the door, Wyatt put out a hand to steady Kate. "We'd better go find Les," he said.

"One of our officers drove him to the ranch," Nadiya said. "He told us to tell you he would meet you there."

Wyatt thanked her, then wrapped an arm around Kate and prepared to leave. But as they did, Kate turned back and said, "Nadiya?"

"Hmm?"

"Would you come to the ranch, talk to the vets? Tell them your story?"

Nadiya paused as though considering it. "Of course. I would love that."

As they turned to leave, Wyatt whispered, "What was all that about?"

Kate merely said, "Just wait. You'll see." There was a glimmer in her eye, and as long as she still had that glimmer, he knew there was hope.

<h1 style="text-align:center">Thirty-Six</h1>

As Wyatt and Kate rode in the back seat of the sheriff's sport utility, Wyatt couldn't keep Kate close enough to him. He circled her with his arms wanting to protect her from the world, from the outside. Still tired from the ordeal, she lay her head on his shoulder and he squeezed her. There was so much to say, so many words left unspoken. It felt like an eternity since he'd first learned the news that Kate had been abducted instead of just over twenty-four hours ago. Any words would have to wait until they were home alone.

The SUV drove from the back parking lot past a blanket of photographers and newsmen who realized they'd been had and attempted to trail the vehicle. Wyatt wondered how long they would keep up the vigil. He prayed that this mess would blow over soon and the press would move on to some more spectacular news. Until then, he would try to protect Kate as best he could from their prying eyes.

Wyatt held Kate the entire way home. Another vigil of reporters had been set up at the gate that headed his driveway. He shielded Kate's face with his head. The photographers surely had enough photos for their tabloids.

When he and Kate arrived at the ranch, Emajean ran down to greet them, having sent Emily home until things calmed down. She threw her arms around them both, then swept Kate up in her arms and led her off ahead of him. After everything that had happened, Wyatt had to laugh. Leave it to Emajean. She knew just what to do.

By the time he had entered the living room, Kate was already seated at the kitchen table with a cup of hot herbal tea and a muffin with sliced peaches next to it. Apparently, Wyatt was going to have to fend for himself. Again, he felt a small chuckle welling up inside him and was grateful for Emajean. Kate needed solace and food, and he needed laughter. His father had been one lucky man when he'd found Jeanie. She was a jewel.

The phone rang and Wyatt turned to get it when Emajean threw out an arm and said, "No! Leave it! The press has been hounding me day and night since you've been gone. And people love to get on the bandwagon, so we've had our share of crank calls."

Just then there was a knock on the door. Wyatt turned to see Les standing there looking damned near as tired as Wyatt felt. He quickly opened the screen door and ushered Les in.

"Some of the paparazzi have broken past the fence in the back forty trying to get a closer look at the cabin."

Wyatt started to swear, then seeing Emajean's glare amended his words. "Can't cut a break," he muttered. "You watch over Kate. I'll be back as soon as I can."

He walked over and kissed the top of Kate's head, then raced for the door.

"Wait!" Kate said, standing for the first time since her arrival at the kitchen table. "This has gone far enough. They're going to get what they want no matter what you or I say."

"So?" Wyatt said, confused.

"So, why not give them what they want?"

He shook his head, still not understanding her point.

"Show them the cabin. Tell them about all the work you and the men have put into it. Tell them what you do with the men to help make them feel whole again. Have them interview the success cases. Why not Ryan? He's made a remarkable turnaround."

Even tired and sweaty, Kate still looked beautiful to him. "Always the marketer, eh?"

"It's in my blood."

For the first time since he'd found her, she actually laughed. That was a start.

"Okay. I'll market the hell out of the place." He grabbed a muffin and an apple from the bowl and plate Emajean had set on the table, then doffed his hat.

To Kate, he said, "We'll talk when I get back."

She gave him a watery smile, then he and Les left. As he walked past the barn and saw the remnants of the fire where the pine had gone up in a blaze, he had a feeling that smile would have to hold him for a very long time. Because he felt certain that the earlier blaze was just one of many he would have to put out before day's end.

And before the day's end, he realized he'd been right.

* * *

"Let's take our lunch out on the porch," Emajean said after Kate had been given a chance to clean up and look presentable again.

Kate was still about eight hours short on sleep, and way many more hours short on rest. The warm water had soothed her, but now that the warmth from the shower had worn off, every muscle in her body ached with fatigue. When she had removed the duct tape from her feet she'd been left with tape residue and bloody blisters that made each step she took feel like she was walking on glass. Still, she persevered.

"Do you mind if I sit in the sun?" Kate said. "I could use the warmth."

"Sure, honey. You go right ahead."

Emajean seemed to prefer the shade of the umbrella and sat opposite Kate, who took in the wide vista of open grasslands that led to fields further on, obscured only by the weeping willow. From where she sat, she could see the ravages of the previous day's fire. They were lucky it hadn't set the adjoining forest on fire as well.

This ranch, this homestead, was the balm to Kate's soul. It's what she had needed. No wonder the men loved it here. She thought of the vet hospitals and the rehab clinics filled with corridors smelling of disinfectant, of puke and body fluids. How could a man or woman ever recover in a place like that? She knew that there was a need for those places, but there was an even greater need for accommodations like this, places where former warriors could forget about their infirmities, could forget about obligation and duty. Where they could simply heal, both physically and emotionally. Where they could remember what it was like to feel at peace, to simply have fun.

Now everything that Wyatt had built to help these men was in question. He could lose it all, because one man hadn't made it, hadn't survived the war that was going on in his head. But look how many others *had* survived it, *were* surviving it, because of a place like this.

For the first time in years, she prayed. Prayed that these men could find peace. Prayed that there might someday be a better way, both to hold a war and to care for the men and women who returned from those wars.

"Did I ever tell you I am a Lakota, Sioux?" Emajean asked quietly.

Kate had never really thought about it before, but now, looking at her... at her long straight black hair that had grayed in places, and at her dark brown eyes, she saw it. The older woman had just the remnants of a click to her words as though they had been spoken a bit too crisply, precisely.

"No."

"In my culture, there is no word for 'I.' There is only 'we.' *We* help each other. We look after one another when we've suffered loss. Or at least we *used to*... before we were pulled from our native lands and placed on a reservation. The government took everything from us. They gave us blankets filled with smallpox germs. They removed us from our families, made us live in white schools, cut our hair and made us wear white man's clothing. Then they stole our history, sold it on the open market. We had nothing."

"I'm sorry," Kate said.

"Don't be. It's not your fault."

For all that had happened to Emajean's culture, she seemed tranquil as she sipped on her coffee and looked out over this beautiful spread of land.

"We have a proverb. It says, 'true peace between nations will only happen when there is true peace within people's souls'."

Kate looked out over the wide vista, at the trees and hills, and at the Sawtooths that flanked it, snow-capped mountains still visible despite the summer heat. She could see why Emajean loved it here. Why Wyatt loved it here. Kate felt exactly the same about the land and what it represented.

"And that's what this place offers... peace."

Emajean smiled and took another sip of her coffee. "Yes... yes it does."

241

Wyatt loaded the last bale of hay onto his neighbor's truck, sweat pouring down his forehead. He mopped his brow with his handkerchief, then stuffed it in his pocket. Despite all the hard work, he wouldn't trade it for anything. This place had been his refuge, his salvation, and now he was about to lose it. There would be no going back. He sighed, determined to plow forward until the bitter end.

Two weeks had passed since he and Les had brought Toby's body down from the mountain... two weeks of pure torture. It was as if everything had conspired at once to bring down Wyatt's dreams of keeping the vet's rehab center alive. There had been an investigation. Fortunately, he was cleared of all wrongdoing. Toby's death was determined to be a suicide. That hadn't stopped the feds from stepping in to do an investigation, which had set alarm bells off for the bank. They had called in their note. Wyatt had one week to come up with two-hundred-and-twenty-thousand dollars. He might as well be shooting for the moon for all the good that would do him. Where would he ever find that kind of money?

"You're good to go!" he called to his neighbor who had just purchased a load of hay for nearly fourteen hundred dollars, a drop in the bucket compared to what he would need to save the ranch.

He had been working nonstop, selling anything and everything he could, but he was still nowhere near what he needed to save the ranch.

"Good luck," his neighbor said, then waved out the window as he drove away.

Wyatt turned and spotted Kate at the farmhouse window looking wistfully out at him. He tipped his cap to her. Moments later, she stepped outside and walked over to him.

"I have to go into town and check on the company, see how Gladys and Stanford are faring."

"Do you want me to go with you?"

Fortunately, the bulk of the media had glommed onto other stories, but a few diehards remained, and those seemed relentless in discovering that extra nugget of sleaze to fill their tabloids. All the responsible journalists had moved on, only occasionally checking in to see if there were any new news.

"No, I think I'll be alright." And yet she didn't move. He could see that she was dancing around something, but he wasn't sure what.

"Okay, you want to say something, spit it out," he said, teasing her in hopes that it would garner a smile. They came much more rarely these days.

"I wanted you to have this," she said, handing him a check for six-thousand dollars.

He chewed on his lip as he glanced down at it. "What's that for?"

"I've been here three months. That's rent."

He started to protest but she stopped him by saying, "Part of it's from me, but most of it is reimbursement from the company for my work here. Nora and Jack threw in an extra thousand to help out."

"I can't accept this, Kate." He backed away, feeling embarrassed and more defeated than he'd ever felt. He had never accepted charity. Never. And he wasn't going to start now.

"Look, Wyatt. I know what you're thinking, but we all need help sometimes. You helped me. You saved my life. And you've been more than gracious to me and my company. You took us in, fed us, and have housed me for over three months. But most of all, you came to my rescue after a very tough time in my life, and I appreciate that."

She scuffed the dirt with the boots he'd bought her. For some reason, that endeared her to him more than anything else she could have done. It was as though she was saying she accepted his way of life, embraced it. Accepted him.

"You are too much. Come here," he said, wrapping her up in his arms. "Did I ever tell you I loved you?"

"No," she said, grinning. He noticed small freckles on her

nose that hadn't been there when she'd first arrived. His grandmother used to say that a person had freckles because he or she had been kissed by the sun. Gently, he kissed the freckles on her nose, then he wrapped her in an even tighter embrace and kissed her passionately. One day soon, he hoped that they could spend every day of their lives doing just that. But first, he had to find them a new home.

* * *

When Kate was finally able to come up for air from the passionate kiss that Wyatt had bestowed upon her, she smelled the odor of fresh-cut hay, of the horses in the pasture, of the remaining roses that filled one of the side beds along with delphinium and phlox, with a mixture of pink and yellow glads thrown in that swayed in the afternoon breeze. It was as though a picture postcard had come to life and she was the lucky person who got to live here... for now. But that would soon come to an end. No matter how hard Wyatt scrambled to gather enough money, it would never be enough. She knew her drop in the bucket would be futile in the end, but like Wyatt, she was determined not to give up. If they failed, they failed together. But it wouldn't be because they hadn't tried. She had promised herself that, and she knew Wyatt had too.

She was just about to give Wyatt one last kiss then head into town, when she saw a long procession in the distance.

"What the hell is that?" Wyatt said, taking off his felt hat.

"I don't know. Do you think the paparazzi is back? Has something happened?"

Indeed, she recognized many of the former press members who had been there earlier. A queasiness settled in the pit of Kate's stomach as the procession made its way up the driveway.

Wyatt pulled Kate tighter into an embrace as if to physically protect her from the onslaught. The media parked to the side and immediately set up camp, despite Wyatt's protests.

"Look, bud," one reporter said, "we got permission from your ranch hand, Les."

"*Les?*" Wyatt and Kate turned to see Les and the boys approaching them from behind, huge smiles alighting their faces.

"What's going on?" Wyatt demanded. "Do you know what's happening?" he asked Kate.

"No," she said, just as mystified as Wyatt.

Then it was as if the seas parted. Behind the reporters, who had appeared in the first wave, came Gladys and Stanford, Nora and Jack, and with them, the mayor and the sheriff, along with just about every other neighbor in town. Car after car piled in, then parked up and down the driveway that stretched nearly half a mile.

A thrumming of motors followed, accompanied by a huge cloud of dust.

"What is that?" Kate asked Wyatt, feeling the thrumming in her chest.

"I think they're motorcycles," Wyatt said, appearing just as confused as Kate.

And true to his word, motorcycles began riding up in a wave of Harleys that rivaled the Sturgis rally, their deep-throated engines revving and roaring up the driveway, spooking the horses.

"We'll take care of the horses, you stay put," Les told Wyatt as he turned to go steady them. "We have a little surprise for you."

A laugh burbled up from Kate's throat. For the first time in a long time, she was able to laugh. She knew she must look like a crazy woman, but she felt certain that whatever was about to occur would be positive.

Finally, the sea of people parted for one big burly man on the most beautiful blue Harley Kate had ever seen, and on the back of it was a large American flag. The man wore a black leather vest with patches he had earned as a Vietnam vet. On the brim of his leather cap was another insignia identifying him as Army.

He reached into his leather pouch and pulled out an outsized check. On it were written the words "e pluribus unum, *in honor of our fallen soldiers*." It was written for one million dollars, but Kate could barely see it through the tears that were streaming down her face. Wyatt, who she'd never seen cry, had moisture in his eyes, clearly just as touched as she, if not more.

"We want to thank you for what you're doing for our servicemen," the vet said. "God bless."

Emajean, who could feed an army if need be, had finally met her match. She simply threw up her arms. The motorcyclists had prepared for the crowd and had brought barbeques that they set up on the lawn, while a truck delivered food. For the next two days, they set up camp with food, drinks, even an ice cream truck that sold desserts to the kids and adults alike.

Throughout the hubbub, Kate could have sworn she'd caught glimpses of the old lady she'd met in the coffee shop before she'd ever set out on this journey, the woman at the ice cream shop who had offered advice. Even the gypsy woman who'd warned her not to go to work that fateful day. Before she could pursue them further, she'd been called away and never saw them again, but they were with her in spirit, she felt certain.

When the phalanx of people were finally gone and nightfall had settled over the trampled earth from so many visitors, Kate and Wyatt stood out under the oak, looking up at the night sky.

"There!" Wyatt said, pointing to one especially bright star that twinkled in the inky void. "That one is for you. I'm naming it Kate."

Kate rolled the word around on her tongue as though hearing it for the first time. "I like it," she said.

"Then it's yours." Like a king bestowing a title, he touched her shoulder with his pretend sword.

Afterward, they hugged in silence, except for the crickets that sang a tune on their "fiddles," as her grandpa used to call them.

"When I was little," Kate said softly, "my grandmother used to say that there were a thousand bits of wonderful in the night sky, and that the reason we're put on earth is to find that special one that is ours."

She turned to him. "I've found mine," she said, meaning it.

"And I've found mine."

Then he entwined his hands with hers and she laid her head on his shoulder as they watched the stars until the moon rode high in the sky. Finally, they were home.

247

Epilogue

Kate stood on the porch beside Wyatt and welcomed Nora and Jack with open arms. It was amazing what changes could take place in a year, Kate realized as she embraced Nora who was now wearing jeans and cowboy boots, a first for her no doubt. Jack was... well, still Jack. Same shorts, same Hawaiian shirt, and looking as relaxed as ever with that jowly face of his that always reminded her of a very contented bulldog.

Bringing up the rear were Gladys and Stanford. Stanford had done something spiky with his hair and had added a peculiar dash of white that reminded her of a skunk, but who was she to judge? He had done his job admirably. Between the pair, they had pulled the organization up by its bootstraps so that J & R Marketing was now the third major marketing firm in the business.

Kate took hold of Gladys's hands and turned her around. "Look at you, girl! You look amazing."

And it was true. She had lost nearly seventy-five pounds and had gone from a chubby, middle-aged woman to a svelte young thing who looked as if she was in her early thirties, not her forties.

She giggled. "It's those darn quinoa salads of Stanford's."

"I make her run, too," he said. "We put on our jogging shorts at lunchtime and do a couple laps."

No way could Kate imagine long-legged, image-conscious Stanford in jogging shorts and tennis shoes, but if someone had told her a year and a half ago she would be helping run a dude ranch for vets with PTSD she would have laughed.

"I was sad to hear you wanted to sell your share in the business," Jack said to Kate, "but we understand. You've got your work here. Still, you'll be pleased to know that you will be a very rich woman."

Money was only important in the fact that she would use it

for the ranch and the vets. With that money she and Wyatt would be able to help improve the lives of these men and women, give them a skill that they could take into the outside world, one that would rebuild their pride in themselves and in the world at large. They had lost so much. It was time that someone gave back to them, taught them the true meaning of life--that love *does* conquer all.

"And we've decided to buy your share," Stanford said, nudging Gladys who had dimples lining her cheeks. "Haven't we, Gladys?"

"Sure have."

A twitter of nervous excitement seemed to trail in on the warm, pear-scented breeze as Kate realized this was a time of change for everyone. Change for the better.

"I heard you've started a foundry," Nora said, clearly impressed. "And got some pretty high level artists out here to train these guys."

"Sure did," Kate said, proud that her idea had taken off. "Wanna scc it?"

"Do I want to see it? Lead the way."

They had built the foundry between the cabin and the house, a stone structure that fit into the landscape beautifully. Next to it, they had built a wood carving studio. More people had heard about the ranch and poured money into it. So far, with these two new enterprises, the young vets had designed and worked on several major structures, including massive wooden doors with egrets and other waterfowl carved into it for a lodge in Washington state. And they had done several large bronzes for a museum opening in DC. Kate couldn't have felt prouder of the young men and their successes.

"We're building another log cabin," Kate said, feeling pride in their accomplishments. "This time for women vets, and we're going to teach them the same skills, only we now offer classes for entrepreneurs so that they can start their own businesses. We've even got some banks involved and angel investors to help fund these men and women once they have a solid plan."

At that moment, a strapping young man appeared in an

apron from the foundry and yelled, "Hey, sis!"

The changes in her brother since he'd arrived nearly eight months ago had been profound. He was no longer sullen and pale. Now he had a deep tan, and the lines that seemed to mark his face had morphed into smile lines that told a different story than the one before.

He gave her the thumbs up, then quickly returned to the job at hand, calling out, "Good to see you all!"

His head tilted, Jack said, "Is that the same young man you were always worried sick about?

Kate nodded and Wyatt placed an arm around her, giving her a gentle hug.

"What does this mean?" Nora asked, reading the plaque beneath the bronze statue out front of the foundry.

The bronze had been dedicated to her and Wyatt, a wedding gift from the men. It was of a man and a woman reaching for a single star. They had named it "A Thousand Bits of Wonderful."

And that's what these men... and women... were to her. A thousand bits of wonderful.

Acknowledgments

Special thanks go to Darrin Brenner, my book designer extraordinaire! And to Sara Rolat for her excellent copywriting skills. To my two partners in crime, Laine and Elaine, my writing critique partners who have urged me on for countless years. To Laine Stambaugh, retired University of Oregon acquisitions librarian, who has sent me home with stacks of articles on every aspect of writing known to mankind. She is my teacher, mentor, and guru. To Elaine Stek who can turn a phrase like no one's business, who has had me wilting in my seat when called upon after she has read an excerpt from her writing. To my amazing daughter, Sara Baker, who has read every book I have ever written and given me her honest feedback. Also, to my granddaughter, Kaylee Baker, who has managed to extricate her tech challenged grandmother from many a snafu with modern technology. Many blessings! And lastly, to my ever patient husband who has put up with my writing all these years and has helped me describe different widgets and whatnots. I appreciate all of you more than I can say. Lastly, to James Kirk, who allowed me to use his design as my logo.

And, as always, to those in the past who have helped to make me a better writer and editor, many thanks.

www.ingramcontent.com/pod-product-compliance
Lightning Source LLC
Chambersburg PA
CBHW021118110726
47900CB00007B/2239